Shawnee Trail

Other novels by Alfred Dennis

Chiricahua
Lone Eagle
Elkhorn Divide
Brant's Fort
Catamount
The Mustangers
Yuma
Rover
Yellowstone Brigade
Sandigras Canyon
Fort Reno

Shawnee Trail

Alfred Dennis

Walnut Creek Publishing
Tuskahoma, Oklahoma

SHAWNEE TRAIL

This novel is a work of fiction. Names, characters, places, and incidents are either the product of the author's imagination or are used fictitiously. Any resemblance to actual events , locales, organizations, or persons, living or dead, is entirely coincidental and beyond the intent of either the author or the publisher.

ISBN: 978-0-9893241-5-1
Second Edition, Paperback
Published 2014 by Walnut Creek Publishing
Cover painting "Indian Rescue" by Asher Brown Durand.
Design and editing by KD Galbraith
10 9 8 7 6 5 4 3 2
1. Action/Adventure 2. Native American Fiction 3. Historical Fiction

Books may be purchased in quantity and/or special sales by contacting the publisher;
Walnut Creek Publishing
PO Box 820
Talihina, OK 74571
www.wc-books.com

This book is dedicated to my son Carl Dennis and
my daughter-in-law Gala Christine. Over the years
we've worked many a bronc together.

Introduction

The year 1749, the wild but beautiful Allegheny Mountains of western Pennsylvania, tower over the fertile valleys and cold clear rivers that lay nestled beneath their lofty heights. Acres and acres of rich fertile land blessed with the untouched tall forest, rich grass and sweet smelling flowers of every kind, kindles the blood of every white settler gazing upon it.

Once, with the abundance of wildlife, the mountain ranges and the valleys traversing their lengths were the sole domain of the great tribes of the North Country. Nevertheless, with the coming of the long hunters of the whites, followed by the white invaders with their hordes of children and the evil plow that the Indian hate, the land is now also the habitat of the English speaking white settlers.

The land hungry farmers encroach farther and farther into the hunting grounds of the warlike red men. Bacon's Crossing, Frasier's Settlement, and several other small stockades are in almost every valley where the land is suitable for tilling and planting. Small farms with their sturdy log cabins dot the beautiful landscape surrounding the strong stockades that protect the scattered settlers and their families from the raiding warriors.

The families of Ham Hawkins and Oscar Trent went west looking for fertile virgin land, free to cultivate, and a place to raise their children. Both settling on land farther west from Bacon's Crossing than any other settler. Both Ham Hawkins and Oscar Trent know settling so far from the protection of the stockade at Bacons is dangerous. The hostile bands of Shawnee can strike at any time. Other settlers warn both men of the dangers of settling so far from the safety of the stockade at Bacons but the land allures them. Many a long hunter, friends of Ham Hawkins who at one time was a long hunter too, hints at the danger without offending Hawkins.

The summer of seventeen forty nine passes and the beginning of fall changes the leaves in the forest. The Shawnee led by the War Chief Black Panther, with the aid of the Frenchman St Georges and his men, lead his warriors to the southwest towards Bacon's Crossing. This time only a few warriors follow the great Chief. Not enough to attack the stockade walls of

Bacons itself but enough to raid the smaller outlying farms like the ones of Hawkins and Trent.

The Shawnee fell on both farms with a vengeance; killing, plundering, and taking captives. Little did they realize their barbaric attacks on the two small farms will set in motion a series of events resulting in the deaths of so many, both red and white.

A long hunter of the whites, only a young man at the time of the raids, is destined to become the deadliest and bloodiest of all the white long hunters. Lance Hawkins, the one the Mohawk call the Lonamourchee, is destined to become the scourge of the tribes and the avenging angel of death. He kills many red warriors and Frenchmen in his quest for vengeance for his dead family. Some of the ferocious and warlike warriors tremble at his name. Many thought he was touched by evil spirits. Some believe he is a spirit that mortal man cannot kill. All who hear the name, Lonamourchee, glance nervously over their shoulder, looking into the darkness of the forest, in fear of the evil one. They call him, "the devil who walks at night".

As the Shawnee and St Georges retreat to the north and east with their captives, little did they realize close behind them one follows with hate and death on his smooth face. Many warriors from all tribes and many French will perish beneath the long blade of this bloodthirsty long hunter before the long trail of destruction and death finally ends.

St Georges the Frenchman, Black Panther the Shawnee, and Tenkiller of the Abenaki, all want to possess the beautiful young woman Tracy Trent, the lifelong love of Lance Hawkins. Her beauty and courage in the face of hardships and death make her desirable to them. She is also the reason Lance Hawkins follows their trail relentlessly in his quest to deliver her safely from their grasp.

However, to obtain her, they first have to kill the evil one that stalks their every step across the vast Allegheny Mountains. Lance Hawkins, the young son of Ham Hawkins, is close behind them, following them, even into their villages. Only death can stop him from rescuing and delivering Tracy Trent and his sisters, Iona and May Lynn, from the bloodstained hands of the savage warriors of the Shawnee. They raid and burn their homes and murder their parents. They have to kill Lonamourchee to erase the scourge of the Shawnee and French. To them, he is a spirit that can disappear before their very eyes like a wisp of smoke. Who among the red warriors has the courage to face this great warrior of the whites?

Chapter 1

Only the angry scolding of a grey squirrel, watching from a lofty oak tree, breaks the silence as two trespassers pass through the little animal's wilderness domain. The soft deerskin moccasins of two men pad silently as they trot along the sandy game trail. The squirrel barks again and scampers to another limb for a better vantage point from which to spy on the two intruders.

Turning, one of the interlopers points his finger at the fat grey noisemaker and pretends to shoot. "Ah, my fine fat little friend, you're the lucky one today. If I had the time, you'd be in my stewpot come suppertime."

An angry hiss from the other traveler causes the straggler to quicken his pace and catch up. "We've no time for your tom foolery today, Lance Hawkins."

"I'm coming brother Lucas. I'm right behind you."

The shorter but heavier of the two whispers low. "Keep yourself close behind me and stay alert."

"What's all the whispering about big brother?" The younger of the two boys gives a good-natured smile. "You done gone and got scary on me or what?"

"If you'd been listening you dang fool, instead of playing patty-cakes with that squirrel, you'd know." Lucas shakes his head at his fun loving younger brother.

Instantly alert from his brother's tone, the younger of the two listens as he studies the small trail. "You're right Lucas, ain't nary a sound out there; nothing."

"Yea, I don't figure that squirrel was chattering at just us alone." The one called Lucas whispers again. "I'm a thinking we've got company somewhere about us."

Quickly quitting the trail, the two youngsters slip silently through the knee-high ferns and late summer flowers that grow abundantly through the forest of the Allegheny Mountains of western Pennsylvania. They make sure to leave no trace of their passing. Many times during their young lives, the Hawkins boys were in this situation. They were both taught the art of surviving in the forest. They know to be always on alert and each one knows the art of evading the hostile warriors that roam the wilderness. Most who fail to pay attention to any of these teachings do not survive long out here on the frontier.

The younger Hawkins glances repeatedly over his shoulder, covering their retreat from the trail while his older brother scours the dense forest that lay ahead of them. Lucas Hawkins surveys the forest floor, anxiously looking for a place to hide. Finally, he finds exactly what he needs. A huge hollowed out log lay dead and rotten among the brush and grown up foliage.

Motioning towards the down tree Lucas watches as his younger brother disappears into its hollowed out belly. Scanning their back trail, he makes sure there are no signs of their passing. He then slips quickly into the opening, feet first, behind his brother.

"What do you think Lucas?" Lance whispers from deep within the bowels of the hollow log. "I don't like being trapped in here like a bug."

"Don't know, ain't seen or heard nary a thing out there." The dark eyes of the older youth stare unblinking through the grass and ferns that grow about the dead log partially hiding it. "We'll watch a spell and see what comes along. You know what Pa always says, patience is a virtue."

"Something else he said." Lance laughs lightly. "In case you don't remember older brother."

"What is that younger brother?"

"I believe he said for us to come straight home after delivering Mister Stanton his rifle." Lance studies the forest through one of the woodpecker's holes that perforated the dead log. "Don't remember him saying nothing about us visiting Miss Mary Ada McKay. Do you brother?"

"We were hunting." Lucas frowns, annoyed with his brother. "He wouldn't expect us to travel these mountains after dark, would he?"

"We've done it many a time coming home from Peter Moore's barn dances and shindigs."

"We were hunting, Lance Hawkins and that's final." Lucas growls lightly but forcefully. "Now shut up and be quiet."

"Yep but what were we hunting?" Lance smiles. "These woods are plumb full of game and we ain't got a thing to show for being out all night."

"You're a fixing to get something to show if'n you keep running off at the mouth."

"Ssh, we got company." Lance instantly becomes serious. "Injun company. I can see them from this side."

"Where are they? I can't see a thing from here." Lucas whispers over his shoulder.

From his peephole, Lance makes out a line of Shawnee warriors as they pass in single file along the very game trail they just abandoned. "On the upper trail, they've stopped."

"Tell me brother if'n it's time for us to run. I still can't see them from where I am."

"They're studying the trail right where we turned off." Lance watches the dark warriors examine the sandy ground motioning excitedly towards the forest. "They're on to us alright. If I say run brother, shuck out of this hole like your pants are on fire."

In spite of the cool fall weather, sweat trickles down the face of the younger Hawkins as he waits anxiously to see which way the Shawnee are going. Finally, after a short argument, the file of warriors continue east ignoring the tracks and visible bent over grass left by the passing of the two brothers.

Slipping quickly from the log, the youngsters kneel alongside it studying the surrounding forest. Could it be a trap to lure them from their hiding place? The Shawnee could be waiting and watching for them from somewhere up on the trail. Only minutes pass before the little creatures of the woods resume their chattering and calls.

"Breathe easy brother." Lucas nods as the noise of the forest resumes. "They're gone."

"Why didn't they come after us?" Lance cannot believe the warriors are not planning to come screaming at them from the brush.

"Don't know. Only thing I can figure is they've got much bigger fish to fry than just the two of us."

"You mean the settlement?"

"That may be or it could be our place and the Trents."

"You're right." Lance frowns, worrying as the danger to his family dawns on him. "What'll we do Lucas?"

"How many did you count?"

"Twenty, maybe twenty five, no more." Lance shakes his head. "I think I seen some white men with them Lucas."

"I figure with that few warriors it's a raiding party out to do what mischief they can and spy out the settlements too." Lucas looks over at his younger brother, worrying. "They're too few to attack the settlement so it's probably our place or the Trents they're after, maybe both."

"What'll we do?" Lance repeats, scared for his folks. "What can we do?"

"The settlement is ten miles due north of here. Our place is back to the west five miles." Lucas starts towards the trail. "You cut out over Bear Spring Mountain and come into Bacons from the southeast. I'll head cross country for our place to give the alarm."

"Shouldn't we stay together?" Lance does not want to leave his brother.

"I wish we could Lance but we've got to sound the alarm about them red buggers." Looking about the woods, he hefts his rifle and looks at his brother. "You up to a good run brother?"

"I don't like splitting up one bit. I think we should stay together." Lance shakes his head. "The folks may need us both."

"Maybe, but we can't gamble with the lives of the people in the settlement." Lucas looks at his younger brother. "Lance, we've got to warn them. It's our duty. Sides, it only takes one to give the alarm."

"You take care of yourself, Lucas." Lance still doesn't like it, but Lucas is the oldest and he always gives the orders.

"Bring help on the run, if you don't run into trouble out there yourself."

"I'll do my best."

"I know that, little brother." Lucas touches his brother's shoulder. "Stay alert and keep your powder dry. You know how sneaky them red devils can be."

Cutting over the top of Bear Spring Mountain, the settlement is about what Lucas estimates; ten miles. However, it is a rough ten miles across the steepest part of the mountains. The Shawnee war party will know this. They know this part of the country like the back of their hands. They know exactly how to cross Bear Spring but they are taking the longer way around the steep mountain, coming into the settlements from the east. They know crossing the high places will take too much energy. Energy they will need if and when they attack. No, if they are going to attack Bacon's Crossing, they will follow the easier trail to the settlement. There is no reason for them to cross the steep mountain ridge. It is late fall, a time for hunting, drying and laying in of food for the oncoming winter. No, they didn't figure anyone in the English settlements would be expecting them to be out raiding, so there is no hurry.

Lance knows Lucas is right; he has to warn the settlement. He worries as he looks off to the west towards home, knowing they will need him badly if the Shawnee veer off towards their farm instead of attacking Bacons. He needs to defend his mother, sisters, and little brother. He knows it will be impossible to run to the settlement and give the alarm, then race home before the Shawnee reach the farm and launch an attack. He does not have time to do both.

Sweat starts to bead on his forehead as he trots slowly up the steep mountain. His thoughts are of his father who was a long hunter before he married and settled down to the life of a farmer. The older Hawkins was always warning Lance and Lucas to go slow on a hard run. He remembers his father's words well. "Always pace yourself for the long haul boys, you're no help to anyone if you fall out." Still worrying about what is taking place at his home, he has to fight the urge to run full out for as long as he can. Lance knows that at such a speed, he would be winded before he gets halfway up the steep mountain. No, he must pace himself.

With a final lunge, his lungs almost bursting, sucking in all the air he could like the bellows that sat in the blacksmith shop, Lance pulls in the pure sweet air of the mountain in great gulps. His legs burning as if fire is shooting up through them as he takes the final step to the peak of Bear Spring Mountain. Shaking weakly, his side hurting from the long run, Lance bends over as he gasps in ragged breaths. Finally, he straightens and looks down on the peaceful settlement far below him. If the Shawnee have Bacons on their mind for a target, they will be along any time, providing they aren't waiting and hiding in the heavy underbrush already.

Switching the Kentucky Long Rifle into his other hand, Lance draws in a long breath and sprints off down the side of the mountain. So far, there is no sign of the Shawnee. They have farther to travel, but their route is flatter and much easier to navigate. The young hunter knows he is probably wasting his time, but he gave his word and he would do as Lucas ordered. He will warn the people below in the settlement and then hurry on back towards his father's farm. The peaceful and serene look of the stockade gives Lance a forlorn feeling. Clutching at his chest, now he knows the Shawnee veered off to the Hawkins' small farm.

Throwing caution to the wind, his legs carrying him with the speed of desperation down the side of the mountain. If he is wrong and the Shawnee are there waiting, they will not be watching for him to come off the steep mountain in a dead run. Even if he is spotted, he will be in range of the settlement before they can pursue him.

Lance is a young, nineteen year old, in prime physical condition. Many years of hard work behind a plow and on the working end of a double bladed axe or a crosscut saw, made him physically strong for his age. Running the forest since birth, behind his older brother Lucas, gave him the lungs and wind to outrun any man or boy in the settlements. He is a strong runner. He was never outrun in the footraces that were held at every celebration in the settlements. Lance doubts, in a flat-out footrace, there is a Shawnee alive who could catch him.

Both him and Lucas are the pride of Bacon's Crossing every holiday when foot racing, wrestling and target shooting are the events every man wants to win. From a distance, the brothers look full-grown, both already over six feet in height with broad shoulders. Up close, they look younger. They both have the smooth baby face skin and the twinkling eyes of youth.

Nearing the shorter timber and burned stumps that surround the settlement, Lance slacks his speed and surveys the woods closely. Seeing no impending danger, he fires off a warning shot knowing it would warn the people and have them alert when he reaches Bacons. Sprinting from the timber, he races with the speed and agility of a big-eyed frightened deer towards the stockade and log homes.

"Shawnee, ya'll need to fort up." Lance gasps as he enters the heavy gates. His long legs tremble weakly from the long run up, over and down Bear Spring.

"Lance Hawkins." A lanky man, homespun of a farmer, looks at the disheveled youth up and down curiously. "You look like you've run a far piece lad and in a hurry."

"Where did you see them Lance?" A man of somber face pushes his way to the front of the crowd and asks the lad. "How many?"

"Over at Bear Spring, Mister Wilson." Lance is still breathing hard making it difficult to speak loud as he looks over at the man who asked. "Maybe twenty or so."

"How long ago?" Another settler questions.

"Maybe two hours. Can't say for sure."

The lanky man looks up at the tall mountain and shakes his head. "You crossed Bear Spring Mountain and ran all the way here in just two hours?"

"Yes sir, now I've got to be headed home for I fear they may be headed that way instead of coming here like Lucas thought." Lance turns to leave.

"Your brother with you?" Wilson takes Lance by the arm, stopping him.

"He was, we parted company near Pine Branch cut off. Lucas went home while I came on here to sound the alarm."

"We're a thanking you, Lance Hawkins. We'll never forget this day." Wilson looks about at the gathering people. "Jedidiah Long, go sound the bell and call the people into the stockade."

A young blond headed girl, almost Lance's age, hands him a dipper of cool water and some corn pone. "Eat this Lance, you're done in."

"Thank you, Miss Piffle." Lance takes the offered food from the pretty girl. "I am."

"You can't go out there alone Lance." The girl steps closer as he wolfs down the pone. "It's too dangerous."

"I've got to go now, Piffle. The folks may need me." Lance finishes the pone and washes it down with water. "If those red devils attack, they'll need me for sure."

"You're run out boy and it's nigh on eight miles back to your Pa's place." Wilson turns to where Lance spoke with the girl. "Rest here a spell lad, then head out."

Quickly reloading his rifle, Lance nods his head as he looks around the settlement. "Thanks again, Miss Piffle."

Tears roll down her cheeks as he trots off to the west in the long shuffling trot of a long hunter. "He never even asked for help."

"No lass he didn't and he wouldn't, he's proud like his old Pa." Wilson watches as the youth disappears around a bend. "He knows we need all our men here to protect our womenfolk and young'uns. Young he may be but already he's got the makings of a real man."

"But, he came here to warn us instead of going to help his own folks."

"Yes he did and that took great strength." Wilson hugs her to him. "Well, now he's on his way to help them."

"It ain't fair Pa, it ain't fair. We should go help him."

Wilson shakes his shaggy head. "No, it ain't fair daughter but out here we've got to look out for the majority or we may all be killed."

"It ain't right, he's all alone."

"Come girl, we have to fort up and get ready in case those heathens pay us a visit." Wilson looks towards the forest. "I'm feared he'll be too late to help his folks. I figure he's already too late."

Piffle Wilson walks several paces forward, where she last saw Lance, until her father takes her arm and turns her around. "Come Lass, we've got to fort up. When help arrives from Fort Stanton we'll go to their aid."

"When help comes Pa, it may be too late to help them."

"Pray child, pray hard."

Chapter 2

The corn pone and water renews his energy, taking the weakness from his youthful body. Now as Lance trots to the west, he takes in a second wind and picks up his speed. Mile after mile seem to pass effortlessly beneath his flying feet as he notes the familiar landmarks revealing he is nearing the farm. Skirting away from the rough Wilderness Road, he approaches the small farm like a ghost, slipping silently through the heavy timber that closes up around the cleared fields lying close to the log cabin.

As he draws near, only the smell of burning wood, the crackling of the hot embers and a strange silence greet him from the log house. The only home he has ever known. For fifteen years, since his Father moved them to this remote and wild part of the frontier, he and Lucas hunted and trapped in the woods and have been happy in this cabin. Fighting the urge to rush forward, he kneels in the underbrush and studies the smoldering ruins of the cabin. He was taught from an early age, by the Elder Hawkins, to be cautious, use patience, and to not rush forward carelessly into a waiting enemy. He knows from the deathly silence he arrived too late to help. A yellow patch lay prone, unmoving near the front door. Lance knows at a glance it is their collie dog Lad, riddled with arrows. One more reason for the silence, if the dog were alive, he would be sounding the alarm, as the smell of an Indian always sends him into a frenzy.

Cautiously he studies the yard that was strewn with articles the Shawnee discarded in their eagerness to kill and destroy. Finally, after surveying the carnage, he rises from his place of concealment and walks boldly into the yard, dreading to find what he knows is waiting. He saw the work of the Shawnee many times over the years. Seldom were there any survivors. Only dead and mutilated bodies were left in their wake. Any survivors of value march north as slaves or for ransom and anyone resisting or showing weakness in route are killed instantly.

Fire and smoke belches from the doors and windows of the small log house as Lance crosses the yard. The heat reaches out its hot fingers searing anything within reach, but Lance is too intent on the carnage to feel the flames. His stomach squeezes tightly, knotting up hard like a ball, knowing what lies inside. Quickly kicking in the half-burned door, Lance can see his father and younger brother lying face down on the dirt floor.

The Shawnee were indeed in a hurry, he can see both are scalped but neither body was mutilated, as was their custom. The fire forces him back from the burning porch, as the roof caves in. Lance clinches his fist, knowing there is no way he can pull their bodies from the roaring flames. Driven back by the heat, he circles the house where he finds the lifeless and mutilated body of his mother lying near the corncrib. He moves in a trance as he covers his beloved mother as best as he can, he looks around for a blanket or anything to wrap her nakedness.

Searching about the cluttered farmyard, behind the barn and smokehouse, he can find no evidence of his two younger sisters, Iona or May Lynn. Lance knows the girls are the right age, as they are old enough to make the difficult journey to Canada. There the captors will sell the girls for ransom or marry them off.

He looks back to where his mother lay, covered with an old quilt he found. He should have been here to protect her and his siblings. His heart aching as he looks at the pitiful bundle of the woman he loves so much and then over at the flames that are turning his father and little brother into ashes. Where is Lucas, did they take him captive? Lance knows the fighting spirit of his brother, he doubts Lucas will give up unless he is badly wounded or dead.

"I'm here Lance." The weak rasping voice came to him like an answer to his question.

Wheeling, his rifle cocked and ready, Lance is shocked at the bloody figure that stands before him.

"Lucas." Lance races to where his brother sways, reaching him just as he collapses. There are several wounds with blood covering his entire chest.

"The folks?" Lucas' eyes turn towards the burning building. "I couldn't save them. The Shawnee were already setting fire to the house when I got here."

"You tried Lucas."

"Mama, I seen them devils drag her from the house." Lucas cries out burying his face in Lance's arm. "I was hurt too bad to help her. I couldn't save her. Oh dear God, Mama!"

"She's dead now Lucas, they can't hurt her anymore." Lance holds his brother closely as the sobs shake the bloody body.

"Papa."

"Pa's gone, so is Tommy." Lance does not say anything about them remaining inside the burning cabin.

"The girls, are they?"

Lance shakes his head. "They're not here, they must have been taken."

Only a groan comes from the bloody lips as the thought of his sisters struck Lucas. "You promised me Lance; you'll get them back if they're alive. Kill every red son you can that is responsible for this. Promise me brother. You won't quit killing until they're all dead. Kill'em all Lance!"

"I promise Lucas. You have my word. I'll go after the girls and kill all who are responsible, soon as I take care of you."

Lucas shoves at Lance's hands feebly. "Go now. I'm dead already brother, they're alive, go now."

"You're not dead yet, Lucas Hawkins. You stay alive and help me get them back. I need you brother."

"Look Lance, look." Lucas points a bloody finger towards the west over the trees. "It's the Trent place; those red devils are burning them out."

"Tracy Trent." The name slips from Lance's mouth as he thinks of the beautiful girl he is sweet on since their first meeting when her family moved on the homestead next to them, almost seven years past. Many a Christmas shindig or birthday was celebrated at the Trent's place. Even a stolen kiss under the mistletoe hanging from the rafters was allowed by the young lady.

"Go Brother, go help them."

"No, it's too late." Lance shakes his head as he examines Lucas. "I'll clean these wounds and get you back to Bacons. Then I'll go after them."

"You can't Lance. I'm finished already and you know it." Lucas pushes at his brother roughly. "Go! Maybe there's a chance you can help them. Go brother, go quick. The girls need you now."

Lance looks down into the pale face and then nods slowly before picking up his long rifle. "Alright Lucas, I'll be back as quick as I can."

"If only I'd come in last night, like Pa said."

Lance touches the bloody cheek. "Don't blame yourself. It weren't your fault Lucas. The two of us wouldn't have made much difference."

"We should have been here anyway." Lucas shakes his head in despair. "I should have died with them."

"There's no use second guessing or crying over spilt milk."

"Go, save them if you can. Go!" Lucas watches as Lance slowly retreats out of his view. "God speed brother and don't leave one of them heathens alive, promise me you'll kill them all."

Lance kneels beside a huge tree and studies the burning Trent farm, which lies only two miles farther west of their farm. It is the same as their place, only this time the raiders remain. They were running about the yard, fighting over articles of clothing and arguing over the prisoners that were standing, huddled in a group, in front of the burning cabin.

A huge warrior painted for war, his arms bloody up to the elbows, pulls Tracy Trent from the family group bodily, laughing as he rips at her homespun calico dress. Amos Trent pushes the warrior backwards and pulls Tracy behind him. Blood spatters across her face as the warrior buries his war axe into her father's head.

Lance clinches his rifle hard in rage as he listens to Tracy's frantic screams. Sighting in on the huge warrior Lance tightens his finger on the trigger then slowly relaxes. He cannot fire. As much as he wants to fire, he knows if he kills the warrior, he will sign a death warrant for all of the Trent family and his sisters. There are far too many warriors for him to fight alone. He knows to save them he has to bide his time and wait.

The lone white in the group steps forward and speaks to the big warrior. Lance cusses under his breath as he recognizes the renegade Frenchman, one of the cruelest of the English settler's enemies. Even the Shawnee listen with respect when these white demons speak. Partly because of the rifles and powder, the French provide, but mainly because the red men need the French. The tribes are instinctively warlike but their wars are small raids against other tribes. They need the French to unite all the tribes and lead them in a combined confederacy against the British and the encroaching white settlements, where the captives and plunder is plentiful.

Before the French and English Wars, the Indian tribes fought the new settlers moving into the frontier, raiding and stealing. The tribes cause havoc all along the frontier but not with the confidence or success they now enjoyed with the French as their allies and advisors. The Shawnee Chiefs are the undisputed leaders of their warriors but they still listen to the advice of the French.

Lance knows the French fighters are unlike other whites. These men assimilate into the tribes, join in their rough and tumble games, and with the exception of their lighter skin color, almost becoming a red man. Marrying the native women, they live with and bond with the warlike tribes. Few can match their knowledge of the warlike tribes, few can speak their language, and very few whites of the English settlements can match their stamina or cruelty in battle. Only the few long hunters of the English are as capable as the French on the war trail. Most of the settlers are peaceful farmers from the east, not familiar to the cruelty and bloodshed the tribes inflict on the settlements.

Lance can tell the Frenchman is arguing with the big warrior, probably over the white captives. Dead settlers are of little use to the raiders as they bring no ransom and they cannot sell them as slaves in the far north. The warrior drops his arm and slips the bloody war axe back into his belt. Finally, their blood lust cools. The Shawnee raiders finish their raid and then pack up and turn back north as no other farms exist past the Trent's farm. The French with the Shawnee are too few in numbers to attack the settlement at Bacons. Now they have to retreat to the north before the stockade can muster a force to send in pursuit of the raiding party.

The leaders of the settlement warned Amos Trent that his family would be alone and unprotected because the Trent farm is too far west and north of the settlement and stockade than any other homestead. Shaking his head the big Irishman argues. All he can think about is the dark rich farmland and the timber bordering the farm. Lance remembers the argument well. Now Amos Trent lay with his life's blood spilling onto the dark land that he desired so much.

Lance watches with the feeling of helplessness as his sisters Iona and May Lynn and the other captives are jerked roughly to their feet and pointed north away from the homestead. All he can do is hide, watch, and follow. There are just too many Shawnee for him to contend with. Tears and frustration rack his body as he watches a huge warrior shove Tracy Trent roughly from behind. The warrior is apparently her captor and new master. Forced north on the long march to Canada with winter coming on, the captives will face numerous hardships, such as cold and hunger, before they reach the villages of their captors. However, at least he knows they will not subject them to other humiliations until they reach the Shawnee Villages.

Rising slowly from his hiding place, Lance is so intent on watching the captives disappear in the heavy foliage. He does not see the surprised look on the Shawnee when he suddenly appears less than thirty feet from the warrior. Shocked at the white's sudden appearance, the warrior quickly recovers. Yelling his war cry, he lunges forward intent on killing Lance and earning the respect of his people by capturing the fine long rifle the young white carries.

Whirling with the sound of the yell, Lance ducks sideways away from the charging warrior. He knows he must end the fight quickly, as he does not know how many more Shawnee are scattered about the woods or if any leaving the yard heard the challenging cry of this warrior. The young Shawnee screams his war cry again as he lunges at Lance, his war axe and long knife poised to kill. The warrior is young. He was always told by his elders the whites are a cowardly weak race, unwilling to stand and fight. Contempt showing on the dark face as the warrior charges recklessly towards Lance. The Shawnee is careless, thinking only a mere boy stands before him. He is also intent on the glory he will receive by killing this white. Yes, Lance is young, but he is hardened by the many years of warfare with the tribes. The fight is short as Lance avoids the thrust of the warrior's knife and slips with blinding speed under the man's blade sinking his own knife deep into the vitals of the charging warrior. Lance kneels over the warrior after studying the woods around him.

"You should have stayed in your village," he said to the dying warrior and then scalps the Shawnee throwing the bloody hair into the warrior's face. "You're the first buster, the first to pay for my folks but you sure won't be the last."

Despite the extreme pain, the coal black eyes show no fear, only disbelief as the white speaks to him in his own language. "You speak the Shawnee tongue?"

"Tell me Shawnee, who is the Frenchman with your raiding party?"

"St Georges. He will kill you if you follow him."

"Well then, he's gonna get his chance for sure." Lance watches as the warrior takes a ragged breath. "Cause I'm sure fixing to follow him."

Repeating his words, the warrior shakes his head again. "You speak our tongue; few white men do this, only the French."

Lance watches the warrior as he bleeds out and makes a final shudder.

Then the dark eyes went blank and unseeing. "Helps to know what your enemy is saying."

Slipping silently away through the deep foliage, Lance follows quietly along behind the line of captives. He is careful that no other warrior will surprise him again as the last one did. He waits, hiding in the tall grass until the last of the captives walks out of his sight and then he creeps forward with the stealth of a wild animal. There is little use to look for survivors among the ruins, as there will be none.

For two days, he follows the Shawnee. Keeping close enough in the dark, he can almost touch the exhausted and sleeping captives. He watches as they are kicked roughly to their feet then they start towards the north once again. He could try to release one or two, but can he flee fast enough with the exhausted girls before the Shawnee find their prisoners gone and take up the pursuit? No, he will wait. The Shawnee will become careless the farther they travel and the closer they come to their hunting grounds. Then if they make a mistake, he will be waiting. The third day starts with the killing of four year old Abner Trent. Too exhausted to continue the march, the young boy is unable to regain his feet. The big Shawnee is enraged when Tracy Trent pulls the boy into her arms as she tries to shield him. Grabbing the crying child from her, the warrior splits the boy's head with his war axe.

The brutal killing enrages the Frenchman who advances towards the big Shawnee warrior as he is pushing the women before him. Heated words follow as the two men argue over the captives. Finally, in a rage, the Shawnee along with six of his followers brake off from the main body and head further north towards the far borders of the Shawnee Hunting Grounds.

Lance lies hiding in the tall grass watching as the men argue. The Shawnee forces Tracy Trent and his sisters, Iona and May Lynn, to their feet. Pushing and motioning at the girls, he forces them to follow him away from the Frenchman and the other captives.

"It is good Black Panther leaves us." Another Shawnee warrior stood beside the Frenchman. "His hate is strong for any white, even you."

"No Tashita, we should stay together, at least until we reach the river." The stocky Frenchman shakes his head and scans the forest. "We may have been followed, there's safety in numbers."

Lance can almost feel the brown eyes of the Frenchman touching him as he lie hiding almost within earshot. He knows this Frenchman. He saw him at Bacons once long ago before the border wars with the Indians started escalating. The man brought furs in to trade for supplies but now Lance knows his true reason was to scout out the small post and ascertain its strength.

The raiding force is too small to attack Bacons this time but come spring Lance knows the Frenchman will probably return to lead many more Shawnee Warriors in a surprise attack on the settlement. Lance swears as he studies the cruel face that this Frenchman will die, not only for the raid on his folks and their murders but also for what he is planning to do.

Watching as the Frenchman and the remaining warriors gather their captives and supplies, he waits concealed until the last of the stragglers disappear through the forest. Rising slowly to his feet, Lance follows the trail of the warrior, called the Black Panther, who has Tracy Trent and his sisters. Six of the Shawnee stay with the Panther. One Shawnee has another woman captive but Lance does not recognize her. He saw her face plainly the day before but could not recognize her. She is probably a captive from a previous raid on another settlement or farm, one he is not familiar with.

For five days, Lance follows the trail of the Panther, careful to stay far enough to their rear to remain undetected. He knows he has to free the captives before they get any closer to the hunting grounds of the northern tribes. If the Shawnee make it to the villages of the hostile tribes with their prisoners, it will be almost impossible for Lance to get them all back.

He realizes his worst fears as the Panther makes an early camp. At sundown, the small party of raiders join up with another party of warriors. The warriors are different and Lance does not recognize the tribe. He figures they are from the Iroquois Federation as each party makes a great commotion at their meeting. Lance wonders is it his unlucky day that the two groups met up or was it planned days before.

Watching from his place of concealment, Lance grips his rifle hard as three of the four women parade in front of the newcomers. The Panther struts before his guests as he brags on the beauty and good health of the white women. Tracy Trent is of particular interest to the strangers as she is the oldest of the women. His sisters Iona and May Lynn are still young and immature but Lance knows they can sell any of them, splitting them up again, making it impossible for him to follow both parties. The warrior that waits with the smaller woman does not let her parade around as Tracy and his sisters did. Lance knows he needs to do something and whatever it is; he needs to do it soon.

Looking up at the darkening skies, he can feel the change in the air. A storm could be brewing over the mountains. His sharp eyes went back to the girls as he watches the warriors argue, probably haggling over the price. A slender warrior, his hair cut into a thin strip down the middle, keeps pointing at the girl Lance does not recognize. The way they are acting, they appear to be afraid of the small girl. Lance is not sure but his guess is the new arrivals are of the Seneca tribe.

Retreating further into the underbrush away from the camp, two Shawnee Warriors leave the others. Lance follows quietly behind them at a safe distance. He has to cut the odds; the two will be the first. As the warriors disappear from the view of the camp, they split off from each other, each going their separate ways.

Chapter 3

He locates both of the men before he starts to stalk the first one. Lance does not know but the way the men are scouting the woods, they appear to be out on a hunt. If this is the case, neither man will be missed soon because hunting and stalking deer takes time.

The warrior is standing fifteen feet away with his back to Lance. His attention is on three small deer as the knife hisses quietly through the air and penetrates deep into his dark back. In deep shock and without making a sound the warrior instinctively tries to grab for the hilt of the knife before he collapses to the leaf covered forest floor.

Retrieving his knife, Lance turns his attention to the second warrior. Now he is in no hurry, it is one against one. He can take his time, stalk the remaining warrior and then kill him quietly.

Lance watches the second warrior quartering around, keeping the wind into his face. Even in the heavy foliage and dead leaves, the hunter makes no sound as he passes quietly along the trail. Silently Lance stalks the warrior taking a course through the timber that will intersect with his quarry. If he must, he will kill this enemy from behind. He has no qualms about how he kills the red raiders; the ones who mutilated and burned his people.

They are no different; they would kill him without hesitation if given the chance. They are bloody Shawnee warriors. By attacking their farm and killing his people, they made the young long hunter as bloodthirsty as they are. Only this white is different from the Indian. He does not kill for plunder or captives, he kills to avenge. He kills with desire to taste the blood of his enemies, the Shawnee.

The warrior shrinks back too late as the unknown shadow launches itself from its place of concealment behind the huge oak, driving the axe down powerfully, splitting his skull almost in half. Lance smears his face with the man's warm sticky blood, smelling it and tasting it, as he looks down at the dead body. The Shawnee was young, too young to die but he helped kill his people and took the girls captive. Slicing the ears from the dead man, he stuffs them into the warrior's mouth. He should have stayed in his village; at least he would still be alive.

Lance swears, he will become as cruel or crueler than the Shawnee. He will hate and this will make him stronger than his enemies. He will kill and use any means he can to free the women from a fate worse than death. He will avenge his dead mother.

There is no use in trying to hide the bodies. He does not want to. Hopefully, the Shawnee will send out more warriors to look for the two hunters. It was his only chance; he has to lure them out alone so he can kill the warriors, one at a time. After cutting off the ears of the other dead warrior, Lance gathers up his rifle and cautiously retraces his steps back to the camp of the Shawnee. He remembers his Father saying, Indians are superstitious and will spook at anything they cannot understand. Maybe by mutilating the dead warriors he will put a little fear into the heathens. Lance smiles, the act gives him grim satisfaction and it sure can't hurt anything.

The clouds thicken as the snow clouds gather. Lance can smell the oncoming storm. Pushing aside the foliage, he scans the small fire that was built. The women all sit in one group, huddling together fearfully. He knows they are exhausted but none sleep, they are too scared. His eyes narrow as he focuses on the campfire. A jug of trade whiskey passes among the circle of warriors, as laughter and words of banter passes between the red men. Lance smiles, in the short time it took to kill the two Shawnee, the others start on the road to getting drunk. The whiskey makes it dangerous for the women but it will make the Shawnee and their new friends careless, maybe even drunk enough to pass out.

Several times the warriors look over at the women and say something which makes all of them laugh loudly. With the whiskey holding their attention they do not notice the fine flakes of snow starting to blow and swirl around the camp. An hour passes, another earthen jug of whiskey appears and they pass it around the fire.

Lance watches and waits. The raiders probably took the whiskey from one of the farms. Lance knows how powerful the homemade corn liquor is. He and Lucas tasted it at a barn raising. Already several of the new arrivals swallowed the pungent brew in great gulps, causing them to either pass out or fall asleep. Lance watches as the Panther stands and sways drunkenly then advances towards the women. Grinning broadly, he jerks Tracy roughly to her feet, ripping at her dress, as he drags the fighting girl towards the fire. Standing straddle legged before the fire, the huge warrior runs his hands up and down the frightened girl, laughing as she slaps at his hand.

Suddenly the peace of the camp breaks as the long rifle belches smoke and lead as Lance pulls the trigger. Laying the smoking rifle aside, he charges the campfire screaming like a demon with only his war axe and skinning knife. Only three of the warriors can get drunkenly to their feet as he hits among them like a devil, his weapons slashing at the warriors, finding their mark.

Blood covers his face and arms as he turns to where the girls are starring in shock, their faces white as death. Walking to the body of Black Panther he looks down at the dead man then kneels and scalps the warrior.

"Lance." May Lynn finally recognizes the tall bloody figure that rushed the campfire. "It's you, brother!"

"You've killed them all." Iona steps towards the fire and looks down at the dead bodies. "I'm glad."

"No, some are just passed out drunk." Lance looks over where Tracy sank down on the ground shaking. "Are you alright, Tracy?"

Nodding, she rises to her feet as he holds out his strong arm. "I'm alright, just in a state of shock at seeing you. How did you get here?"

"I've been following behind you all along. I'm sorry I took so long to free you." Lance looks over at the other girl. "I don't know this girl."

"Her name's Sadie." Tracy pulls the frightened girl to her. "She can't talk or won't."

"Where you from Sadie?"

"She won't speak a word." May Lynn looks down at the girl. "At least we've not heard her say anything."

"Maybe she don't understand our language?" Lance studies the dark haired girl by the glow of the fire. "She looks Indian to me."

"No, she is white. I think that is why the warrior that captured her was in awe of her. He wouldn't trade or sell her to the Shawnee Chief." Tracy points at the dead Black Panther. "The warrior wants to protect her. No one was allowed to speak to her or even touch her. It's funny, all of them except that big one seem scared of her."

"She's dressed like a Mohawk squaw." Lance takes in the deerskin dress, moccasins, and the headband that decorate her head. He knows it shows her to be an Indian woman but he is not familiar enough with the Mohawk to know for sure. "She's awfully fair skinned."

"She's white brother, almost as pale as Tracy is." Iona laughs. "I never knew of an Indian girl being named Sadie."

"Did she tell you her name?"

"No, the warrior that had her when they raided our farm spoke her name and then he made her stay with us." Iona nods at a dead warrior. "That one. He was different than the other Shawnee."

Lance studies the subdued girl. "She's Mohawk or I miss my guess."

Iona looks up at him. "Mama and Papa, are they… ?"

"Yes they are. I'm sorry, I got there too late to help and here too late to save some of you."

"You're here now, brother." Iona hugs him trying to change the subject. "All of us are free and we're thankful."

Lance looks around at the camp then back at the girls. "I know you're tired but we must leave this place now."

"We're ready. I for one want to go home." Tracy takes Sadie by the arm. "Sooner the better."

"Grab anything warm you can wrap up in. I think there's a storm coming, you'll need covering." Lance looks down at the passed out warriors touching the hilt of his knife then changing his mind he takes the moccasins and leather shirts they wear. "Let's go."

Looking up at the dark clouds, he passes along the same trail he took when he followed the Black Panther and his raiders into this vast timbered valley. He knows it is fixing to get cold. Studying each girl he shakes his head, they are thin and fatigued from days on the trail without proper clothing, food or rest.

It is almost midnight when Lance halts and hides the girls in a thick stand of elm and cedar trees. The trees will protect them from the wind. Looking into the eyes of each girl, he nods. "I'll be back in a few minutes."

"Where are you going?" Iona grabs his wrist. "Don't leave us alone, please."

"You rest, Sis. I'll be right back." Lance pushes her back to the ground. "It'll be alright. You're safe now. I'll bring you back something to eat."

Tracy follows him a few yards down the trail. "You can't do it. It'll be cold blooded murder."

"I have to Tracy. When they sober up, they'll come after you girls." "Especially Sadie, for some reason they hold her in awe." He frowns. How did she know what he was planning to do?

"They're passed out drunk." Tracy argues, "and why would they want her so bad?"

"I don't know, I've just got an uneasy feeling about her is all." Lance shakes his head. "They seem to have deep respect for her. They didn't want to touch her back there and the way she sits so quiet and dignified."

Tracy shakes her head. "She's just scared half out of her wits is all."

"Maybe."

"You can't do it, Lance Hawkins, you're not that cold hearted."

"Tracy, we're over a hundred miles from the settlements, probably more, and I'm not familiar with this country. There's a storm brewing, the girls are given out and poorly clothed." Lance takes her by the shoulders. "Those warriors back there are trackers and killers. Soon as they get sober and on their feet, they'll be on our trail and they know this country like the back of their hands. Do you want the girls back in their clutches?"

Dropping her eyes, Tracy shakes her head. "No, you know better than that, no I don't."

"Then go back and wait. I'll be back as quick as I can."

Searching the camp, where the Shawnee and Seneca's are passed out, for any movement, Lance steps from his place of concealment and draws his long skinning knife from its sheath. A week ago, he was just a youth. Now with the death of his folks and the kidnapping of his sisters, he becomes a man overnight. Now circumstances make him a heartless killer, a stalker of men, no different from the Black Panther lying dead in his own blood. A cold hard look comes over his face as he steps towards the dying fire and passed out warriors.

Tracy notices the heavy splattering of blood on his sleeves as Lance steps behind the cedars where the girls are sleeping. She could not look into his eyes. The young boy she knew only a few days ago no longer exists. Now a man replaces him but what kind of man is he?

"There's a storm coming, we've got to find shelter." He looks over at her. "Wake the girls."

The cave is concealed behind a grove of cottonwoods. It is almost a day's walk from where the dead bodies lay about the campsite of Black Panther. The cave is small, barely large enough to accommodate the sleeping girls and him. Lance knows it will have to do for the night, it is cold outside and they need rest. The wind picks up into heavy gusts and the first early snow of autumn arrives. There will be no need now to erase their tracks into this hideaway. The light snow will cover them quickly. Nevertheless, come morning with the snow covering the ground, their tracks will betray them as they travel to the southwest.

A small fire is all they need to heat the cave and roast the four rabbits that lay skinned and ready for the fire. The heavy sheltered woods, full of large cedar trees, were loaded with cottontail rabbits, squirrels, and other small game hiding beneath their ample branches. Their small runs are easy to locate and just perfect for Lance's rabbit snares. It takes Lance very little time to set snares and catch enough meat for their supper. His sleeves are still wet from the sand scrubbing and water he used trying to erase the bloodstains from them. Lance notices Tracy looking at them. He also notices the way she averts her eyes when he looks across the fire at her. What he had to do, he did not enjoy but it had to be done. Even rested and well fed, the women cannot outrun or stay ahead of the Shawnee and Seneca Warriors. If left alive, he knows they will gather others and track them down before this day or the next.

The warriors of the great northern woods are great hunters and trackers, none are better. No, he has no qualms against killing the drunken warriors. He has to protect the girls, what had to be done was finished. Maybe Tracy will understand and forget what he did when she is safe back at Bacons. Lance looks over to where she is chewing slowly on the rabbit and wonders, will she? Right now, it really does not matter. It is their lives or the heathens that killed his folks.

The dark haired girl called Sadie nibbles slowly on a hind leg, her eyes never leaving the small blaze. He watches her closely; a light bronze face and coal black hair encases her dark eyes, eyes that are thoughtful, deep and untouchable. Lance wonders what did she go through with the Mohawk. If that is indeed her tribe, did she lose her mind completely? He never saw it but he heard of people losing their senses because of things they witnessed and were subject too. Perhaps Sadie is one of those. Still, he studies her face curiously. There is something about her that makes her different. When she did look across to where he sat, she seems frightened of him. Still, he can almost sense the girl reading his mind while he is trying to puzzle her out.

The storm is of short duration. The snow stops just at daylight but it did its damage. A half-blind man could follow their tracks now through the light powdery snowfall. Moccasins lined with rabbit fur, taken from the dead warriors, are snugly secured on the girl's feet with strips of leather. The moccasins will keep their feet dry and warm for a short while anyway.

"We'll stay in single file as we walk." Lance looks at the tired girls, hating the ordeal they are fixing to undergo. "Try your best to step in each other's tracks as we walk so if we are tracked they won't know how many we are."

"Why?" Iona questions, "Does it really matter?"

"Like I said Sis, just in case we're followed or a stray warrior should stumble across our tracks."

"I'm hungry again." May Lynn speaks up, "The rabbits sure didn't go far."

"I know, Sis." Lance looks over at the freckled-faced thirteen year old. "We'll get something along the trail but now we've got to travel fast. We've got no time to hunt."

"I'm not ungrateful." May Lynn touches his arm. "I know you haven't had time to hunt."

"I know, Sis." Lance repeats himself knowing she is hungry. He can feel hunger pains himself. "I'll get us something before dark."

May Lynn smiles, "Pa always said you were the best hunter in the family. He always bragged on you but only when you couldn't hear him."

"He did?" He looks back at the girl in shock. He never heard the elder Hawkins say a kind word about either him or Lucas. He knows his father was a strong man and for him to show softness in any way would make him weak in his own eyes. He was not a cruel or mean father. The boys all loved and respected him. He was just gruff, it was just his way, they all understood. Until he married their mother, he was always alone with only the wild animals that inhabit the woods for company. He drummed it into the boys that to survive alone in the wilderness a man has to become tough and strong.

Now, since the raid on their farm, Lance is having that lesson driven home well.

"I heard him say it too." Iona speaks up. "He was really proud of you and Lucas."

Embarrassed, Lance takes the lead following a flat path across the valley. The trail leads them due south towards a stand of high cottonwood and oak trees. Pushing the girls as fast as he dares until late afternoon, he starts looking for a safe place for them to camp for the night.

It is late afternoon with the sun resting on top of the tallest trees. Dark is near and only a short time away as Lance sights down the barrel of the long rifle at a huge buck. He slowly tightens his finger.

"Someone might hear the shot." Tracy standing close behind him, "Should you fire?"

"No, probably not but they've got to eat, if not they'll weaken and won't be able to travel. We don't have time to wait on the snares."

With what seems like an hour is actually just a few seconds. The last echo and smoke of the rifle evaporates into the late evening sky. Now the girls will have meat to fill their stomachs. Food will give them strength and energy for another long walk. Lance hopes no one heard the shot so they will have time to cook the meat. Reloading the rifle, he hefts the buck effortlessly over his shoulder and starts back towards the girls.

The blue haze hangs silently, floating atop the tall peaks of the unexplored mountains. The light snow from the night before covered the limbs and downed timber, glistening in the early morning sunlight. To the untrained eyes, the mountains are empty, nothing stirring, and no animals are out roaming the vast land. However, they are there plus the little forest creatures hiding under the long branches of the big cedar and spruce. There are birds sitting in the tall oaks and the raven black crow is waiting for a squirrel to show their hidden acorn cache under the soft dirt. The sharp-eyed hawk perches, waiting for a rabbit, squirrel or field mouse to show themselves.

A good hunter knows food is here and where to find it. No one, the experienced hunter or hunted, went hungry in these ample mountains. After cooking some of the deer meat and feeding the hungry girls, Lance wraps the rest of the meat in the deer hide then leads them south and west back towards the far-off settlements. Sometimes he sends the girls on ahead while he falls back to watch their back trail, looking for anyone following their trail. Other times, he leaves them behind to rest in the warm sunlight while he scouts ahead, trying to find the easiest paths up and over the high ridges.

Patience and caution was driven into his father's lessons, over and over until it was always utmost on his mind, as they travel the well-beaten forest path. He is trying his best to hide the tracks of the girls. However, the forest's lingering snow and muddy ground make it virtually impossible to keep their tracks hid from warriors that can read signs almost in the dark.

Chapter 4

The big warrior looks about the campsite shaking his head in disgust at the bodies that lay dead, strewn about the cold campfire. He can read the signs that lay plainly before him; the empty whiskey jugs, the unseeing eyes staring blankly seeing nothing, the weapons not drawn or used. The signs are plain. These fools were killed in their drunken stupor unaware that an enemy was upon them. Their throats were cut as they lay passed out. They never woke up from where they lay in their own blood.

The Mohawk scalplock shakes slowly. "Fools!"

The dark eyes study the ground searching out any sign the lone killer left. Not to follow to avenge the killings of the dead ones: they are not from his village. No, the warriors, both Seneca and Shawnee, caused their own death. Getting drunk far away from their village here in enemy country was suicide. The youngest of warriors in the Mohawk society knows better than these older warriors. The topknot of his shaven head bobbed up and down as he seem to sniff out the killer, following him around the bloody campsite, and then off to the south. No, he must follow this enemy and kill him not only for interloping into the hunting grounds of the tribes but he is also a dangerous killer. No red man will be safe while he lives. The big warrior can sense the trail is of a crazy one, a white man that kills for the love of killing. All are scalped but not for the scalps. Their hair was flung back in their faces and their noses were cut off. This the big warrior understands all too well.

"He was a white long hunter. No one else would have done this thing."

Another warrior speaks as he appears from the surrounding woods. "There is no honor in killing a helpless enemy. Now he travels fast towards the south."

"True, Blue Elk my son, but anyone could have killed these drunken fools, anyone."

"Perhaps Ravenhair is right, but we must pursue this one." Blue Elk studies his father's face. "You are the leader of our village. We must kill this one before he kills more, maybe even our people."

"And the women he has with him?" Ravenhair kneels beside the trail. "I think they were the ones captured near the white settlement called Bacons."

"You think this white hunter has come this far into our lands to free the women from so many warriors?" The younger warrior looks across at the dead ones. "How do you know these were the captured women of Bacons?"

"It is on the winds, our brothers the Seneca says the Frenchman St Georges brags of the raid." Ravenhair shakes his head. "We have heard of no other raids to the south, they have to be the ones."

"Perhaps you are right. The Seneca we met said the Black Panther went his own way with three women a few days before we talked with him."

"I have seen the track of a fourth woman." Ravenhair looks with worry over at Blue Elk. "Have you not recognized the track?"

"No, my father. Tell me, what have you seen here in this place?"

"I worry. I think I have seen the track of our Medicine Woman here."

"Satia here?" Blue Elk in shock. "It cannot be."

"I hope not, but Satia has a crippled foot, the same as this track shows." Ravenhair shrugs. "She goes south with this hunter and the other women."

"This lone hunter must be a brave man to come so far alone into enemy territory to rescue squaws." Blue Elk studies his father's face. "Will my father follow and kill this one?" The tall warrior rises slowly to his feet, his long coal black hair spread across his muscled chest and shoulders. "I think this one must be killed. Now we will follow."

"Shall I go get others to help us?"

"Why, he is only one man with helpless women to protect." Ravenhair shrugs. "Should we be less brave than he is?"

Shamed in front of his father the young warrior drops his eyes. "You are right, my father. We will follow this one alone."

"Maybe he killed because he had to protect the women." Ravenhair looks off towards the south. "He had no choice if they were to escape. I would have done the same, was I him."

"Yes, I would have done the same; kill your enemy so they could not follow." The younger Mohawk shook his head. "Squaws are too weak on the trail to outrun warriors, this white may be bloody, but he is smart."

"Any warrior would have done the same but they were still our brothers, Blue Elk." Ravenhair looks off to the south. "He probably didn't know it, but by killing these warriors he was also protecting our Medicine Woman if it is her tracks we see."

"How could she get this far alone and why would she come here?" Blue Elk kneels and traces a woman's small footprint.

Ravenhair looks over at his son. "Perhaps you could tell me, your father?"

Blue Elk turns his face from his father to avoid the question. "If it is our Medicine Woman and this white has touched her, he will die."

"And if he has saved her from the Seneca?" Ravenhair looks curiously at Blue Elk. "Perhaps it is not the white man who is at fault for getting our Medicine Woman captured?"

"That is simple my Chief; then he will not die."

Lance works with the hide from the dead deer fashioning it into coverings for the girl's feet while Tracy cooks the deer steaks over a small flame. With the aroma from the cooking meat, Sadie appears to come alive. Her eyes watching closely as the meat sizzles and drops grease into the flames.

"You girls eat as much as you can. This is the last I will cook of this meat." Tracy turns the cooking meat slowly.

"Why Tracy? It looks and smells okay." Iona studies the half-cooked meat.

"The weather is not cold enough to preserve it. We can't take a chance of getting sick and having to wait for someone to recover from the bellyache."

Sadie shrinks back as Lance tries to put the new leggings on her feet. "I won't hurt you girl."

"Let me do it Lance." Iona takes the homemade shoes from her brother. "She doesn't seem to trust a man touching her."

Lance watches as Iona laces the footwear on Sadie then starts another pair for May Lynn. He was curious, the girl looks okay, but she retreated when he came near her. Why did she fear him so?

"She'll be okay in time." Tracy hands him a piece of steaming deer meat wrapped in green oak leaves. "It's just these last few days she's been scared half out of her wits."

"I don't know about that Tracy, she don't seem that scared to me." Lance studies the girl.

"If she ain't scared, then what is it?"

Lance shrugs. "Don't know, but I reckon when she gets ready she'll tell us."

Finishing with the last of the leatherwork and eating his fill of the meat, Lance takes up his long rifle and crawls out of the small cave entrance.

Looking back over his shoulder, he glances at the curious faces of the girls. "Rest now, when I return we will travel hard towards home."

"What home, brother? I saw what they did to Pa and Mama." May Lynn starts crying softly.

"We'll have another home, Sis." Lance touches her damp face then turns towards the dark. "You'll see, now get some rest."

"Is Lucas dead too?" May Lynn looks closely at her brother before he walks from her sight. "He is, isn't he? Or he would be here with you."

"I don't know" he half smiles. "I truly don't little sister. He was hurt bad when I saw him last, but he wasn't dead."

Three hours of steady traveling brought Lance in a complete circle of the cave where the girls lay hiding. Nothing stirring in the forest, only the breaking of a dead limb heavily covered in snow, the occasional hoot of an owl, or the call of a wolf breaks the silence. Lance found nothing to arouse his suspicions or cause him alarm. No camp smoke or light came to him across the silence of the vast and dense forest. The sun is barely beginning to show itself in the east when he slips quietly into the cave. All the girls, except for Tracy, are in a deep exhausted sleep.

"They slept well." Tracy smiles down at the peaceful girls. "They're good girls."

He agrees, "Good, I hate to wake them but we must leave now."

"Couldn't we let them rest one day?"

"No, we can't waste one day. To do so could put us in danger if anyone follows." Lance shakes his head. "While they sleep an enemy could be closing in on us, wake them."

"You're a hard man, Lance Hawkins."

"You've seen what them warriors are capable of Tracy, to wait here for them is suicide." He touches Iona's shoulder lightly. "We must hurry."

"Apparently from the blood all over you, the warriors are all dead."

"There are many more warriors out there." Lance frowns. "These woods are full of game and full of hunters looking for game."

"That should make you real happy. There's more for you to kill."

"It does." He looks at her strangely. She has no idea of the danger they are in.

Two hours later and several miles from the cave, Lance stops at a small stream and allows the girls to rest. He is pushing them hard, much harder than he should but they have to make up for the long night's rest. Something nags at him. The back of his neck tingles, a second sense he always feels when he is hunting and game is near. His father always advised him and Lucas to take heed of anything strange they feel while on the trail.

Quickly rising as the feeling becomes stronger, he leaves the girls to rest as he melts into the surrounding forest. For an hour his dark blue eyes studies their back trail but to no avail. The path is vacant of any living thing. Returning at a trot to the stream, he looks down upon the tired girls.

"Pull off your moccasins and tie up your dresses." Lance quickly removes his own worn moccasins.

Tracy glances up at him curiously but does not speak.

Iona is the one to speak out. "Why brother? The ground is cold."

"I know Sis, but we've got to hide our tracks as best we can."

"In the water?"

"Yes May Lynn, we'll wade awhile."

"We'll freeze, brother." His younger sister objects, "It's too cold."

"Get them off." Lance's face turns hard. "If we are to escape these woods we must be prepared to suffer many things. The cold is one of them things or do you want to be a captive of them Indians again?"

"No, I don't." Iona jerks at her moccasins.

The water rushing down from the tall mountains is cold and with the nights turning colder, it almost freezes. Not another word of complaint comes from any of the girls as they wade in the ankle deep water. Holding hands, helping one another across the smooth slick rocks, they forget the cold, laughing lightly when they slip or splash water.

Finally, almost two miles farther downstream, Lance holds up his hand and motions them up a rocky outcropping where they quickly dry their feet and replace their moccasins. Giving them no time to rest, he quickly starts them across the timbered valley to the west.

Tracy picks up her pace and speaks to him. "You've made us walk in water for hours. Now we've changed direction away from Bacons. What's wrong Lance?"

Looking back at the straggling girls, making sure they are out of hearing, he pulls Tracy close. "I think we're being followed."

Coldly shrugging out of his grasp, she stares around at the woods. "You killed all of those warriors back at their camp."

"This is the hunting grounds of many tribes, all hostile to the English and us settlers." Lance looks to where the others walked. "Any of these warriors could have come across our trail."

"Have you seen them? How can you be sure?"

"No Tracy, I'm not sure. I've just got a feeling." He looks down at the girl. "It could be a hunting party that's found the campsite and followed us out of curiosity."

Tracy looks at the tired girls as they trudge tiredly along. "What can we do?"

"First, we've got to find a safe hiding place, then I've got to hunt us something to eat while they rest."

"I won't fight you anymore. Just let me know what you're doing from now on."

"Fair enough, I'm proud of the way you knew we had changed direction."

"I may be a girl, Lance Hawkins, but I'm not a complete stranger to the outdoors."

"Sorry." Lance looks away. "And I know you're a girl."

"My brothers took me coon hunting all the time." Tracy seems to tear up. "And with them, you better know how to get home by yourself."

Lance shakes his head. The picture of the dead Trent brothers flashes vividly across his mind. Tracy knows they are dead and how they died. She saw their bodies herself as she was led from the farm. He cannot understand her reaction to his killing the warriors back at the campfire. To him, killing the warriors responsible for the attack dend massacre at the Trent Farm is exactly what they deserve.

She looks into his eyes, almost reading his mind she exclaims, "They were human beings. They didn't deserve to die as they did, even if they were Indians."

"Perhaps Tracy they didn't, but they're dead now and they won't kill any of our people again."

"Some of those warriors didn't kill my people." Her face hardens, "They came later."

"You're a fool, woman." His look hardens, "Those were Seneca warriors. The scalplock's they wear so proudly can only be worn by bloodied warriors. The only way you become a blooded warrior, Tracy Trent, is to kill your enemies and that includes killing innocent white settlers, men, women, and babies."

Tracy shudders. She knows that in her heart it is not right to kill a man, even an enemy while they are asleep. She looks hard at the boy she knew just a few days earlier. He became a man right in front of her eyes. She still cannot believe he is capable of such hard, ruthless actions. Tracy was raised on the frontier. She saw hardships as they all did but the cold ruthlessness of Lance almost makes her fear him. No, he wasn't the boy she once knew. He has changed. He became hard and deadly. Now all she sees before her is a predator, a man hard as steel, a stalker and killer of men, a devil.

The cave Lance discovers lies above the trail they are following. It is hiding behind a thick stand of Cedar and underbrush that is almost impregnable. Only luck let him discover the cave entrance as he was looking for a rabbit run to set his snares. Pulling the brush back, the girls climb the steep narrow path to the hidden entrance.

Lance explores the inside of the cave then nods in satisfaction. The trail is steep, easy to defend if they are discovered. In addition, the brush below is full of rabbits. Firewood is plentiful. Here the girls will be safe and they can rest while he hunts for food.

"We'll gather firewood while you hunt." Tracy knows he will be out hunting. She also knows he will hunt more than just food.

"You ladies get all the rest you can." Lance ducks back through the cave entrance. "I'll return soon with food."

Chapter 5

Ravenhair and Blue Elk study the game trail leading down to the crossing of the small rocky stream. The two Mohawk Warriors track Lance and the girls through the day, following them to the exact spot where they entered the water.

"This white is smart. He makes the women hide their tracks in the water." Ravenhair looks down at the cold mountain stream. "It covers their trail well."

"It only slows him down. We know which way he must travel." Blue Elk argues. "He is white, not Indian. He must travel south to the white settlements and safety."

"But, we don't know where he will leave the water." Ravenhair starts across the small stream. "You follow this side and look hard my son. This hunter is tricky and we know he will kill. Do not underestimate this white one. Whoever he is, we know he is a smart and dangerous enemy."

Blue Elk frowns, "He is not Mohawk, my father. He is no match for us."

"Be alert my son, and listen to me. I tell you again this one is very dangerous." The two Mohawk Warriors explore every trail and rock that leads away from the creek, overlooking nothing. The going is slow but Ravenhair did not care. He does not want to miss any clue where the women left the water. Somewhere along one of the banks, he knows some sign will betray their trail. A misstep by one of the women, the least print, an overturned rock, one bent or broken twig, is all they need to put them on their track. Several times, he calls softly for Blue Elk to watch close. He knows his son is young and impatient on the trail.

Ravenhair does not know who this white with the women is but he is probably one of the ones the whites call "long hunters". They are tough and courageous men. He fought them on many occasions since his youth and he has great respect for their fighting ability. He does not want to run into this white without warning. Their long rifles send death with every shot. His sharp eyes study the dense forest cautiously before moving forward.

"The white women will not stay in the water this far." Blue Elk calls out across the water. "They are a weak race and this water is cold."

"We will look further." Ravenhair is slowly becoming annoyed with his son. He taught him better than to be impatient on a trail. "Be patient my son, patient like the stalking cougar."

"You show this white too much respect."

Ravenhair looks across at Blue Elk exasperated. "I hope Blue Elk grows older before he meets one of these Long Hunters in combat."

"Bah." The young Mohawk growls.

A mile farther down the stream Ravenhair stops as he studies the ground then waves his hand, signaling to Blue Elk. "Here is where they came out."

"Are you sure, my father?"

"There."

Blue Elk looks to where his father points and nods his head in awe. "Your eyes are sharp like the red tailed hawk this day."

Nothing shows where Lance and the girls exit the stream, only the slight tipping of a rock. A moss-covered rock is now under the water, moss does not grow under water. The rock was stepped on and pushed down slightly. Only the sharp eyes of a great tracker and hunter would see the rock. Following the game trail away from the stream, Ravenhair finally begins to pick up clues of the girls. There was no way Lance could erase all signs of their passing. The recent melting snow makes the ground soft, their tracks become harder and harder to conceal and very easy for a tracker to spot.

"How far ahead are they?" Blue Elk traces the soft print of a moccasin with his finger.

"What does Blue Elk think?"

"One sleep, maybe a little more." The young Mohawk studies the track closely. "Their tracks weave and are unsteady, they are very tired."

"This is what I think, we go." Ravenhair nods. "The Medicine Woman is with them, I have seen her track, it is her."

Blue Elk nods solemnly. "I too have seen her track. For this the white will die at the hands of our women."

"Perhaps he helps her." Ravenhair looks towards the South. "She does not try to escape."

"He is a white."

"A brave white, my son. He comes alone into our hunting grounds to rescue the white women."

"I think he is a fool."

Lance shoots another deer almost at dusk. Earlier he gathered the few berries and wild onions that still hung on late in the fall. Looking down his back trail, he could not rid himself of the bad feeling he has as he walks back towards the cave. He can almost feel it, something or someone stalking him. To make sure he leaves no tracks as he nears the cave, Lance slips softly across the pine needles and dead leaves.

Slicing the backstrap from the deer, he hangs the remainder of the deer by its horns high enough off the ground to keep the varmints away from it. Only a bear, perhaps a leaping cougar or bobcat can reach it where it hung but Lance does not figure they will come near the smell of humans. He knows the winter is not severe enough yet to make them desperate for something to eat.

The girls sit huddled around the fire, each deep in their thoughts as he eases through the opening. For the first time he could hear the voice of Satia as she croons some kind of spiritual song. He waits curiously; the voice is soft but deep. If he did not know who was speaking, he would have thought it was a much older woman. Suddenly the voice becomes quiet. Lance knows that somehow she senses he is listening.

"You should all be asleep." The hunter enters the cave and hands Iona the deer meat and his skinning knife.

"Satia was singing for us." May Lynn smacks her lips in anticipation of eating the meat. "I can taste it now."

"You better let it cook first." Iona speaks up. "You'll get worms."

"That's just an old wives tale of nonsense." May Lynn laughs as Iona cuts the meat in pieces and runs green cedar sticks through them. Spitting the meat over the fire, she looks to where Lance is relaxing with his back against the wall of the cave.

"You must be tired, brother." She looks at his closed eyes. "You haven't slept but a few minutes in days."

"Just let me rest a little while." Lance looks over to where Satia sits watching him. "She isn't white; she's some kind of Medicine Woman. I've heard Pa speak of them."

"Why do you say that?" Iona holds the knife in midair. "She's the same as us."

"No Sis, she sensed I was outside listening before I came in. She is different."

"That's silly." May Lynn laughs. "She probably heard you, is all."

"You didn't." He yawns and closes his eyes.

Tracey watches the rise and fall of his chest like a child deep in slumber. Peacefully at sleep, he looks again to her like the young man of only a few days ago before the attack on their farms. She knows hardships and stress can age a person, especially one as young as Lance and one with so many dangerous responsibilities. However, aging is one thing, turning into a cold-blooded killer is quite another. Still, she respects him for coming after them, into the strange mountains alone, against great odds.

"We will let him sleep through the night." Tracy takes the long rifle from his hands and leans it against the cave wall.

"Is that wise?" May Lynn speaks up. "Should we wait here much longer?"

"Maybe not wise May Lynn, but smart." Tracy stares at the sleeping Lance. "He needs rest, without him we wouldn't get far."

"He's sure gonna be mad."

"He must rest." Tracy looks over her shoulder as she leaves the cave. She always knew Lance had a fondness for her and at one time, she felt the same but now she wonders. Could she bear his bloody hands to ever touch her?

Startled, Lance rolls to his side with his eyes wide open and alert. Sitting upright, he looks around the cave at the sleeping girls. Only Iona is awake, sitting near the fire, busily smoking the venison.

"Where's Tracy?" Lance misses her immediately.

"Outside, keeping watch." Iona turns the meat. "We've been taking turns. Tracy's idea."

"How long have I slept?"

"All-night brother, it's almost dawn."

"Wrap the meat, then wake up the girls and get them ready." He reaches for his rifle. "We're leaving, now."

"You needed the rest brother." Iona shrugs her shoulders. "We agreed to let you sleep."

"I told you to wake me."

"Here." Iona hands him a large chunk of the cooked deer meat. "At least eat brother, that won't take long."

Outside Tracy looks up at the sound of his approach through the heavy limbs. Locating her slight frame in the dark Lance eases down beside her.

"You shouldn't have let me sleep so long." Lance admonishes her. "We should have been gone from this place long ago."

"You were exhausted and we're a long way from home." Tracy watches him bite into the steaming meat. "I didn't do it for you, Lance Hawkins, but for the girls. We need you rested and alert."

"Maybe I was a little tired but we should have been a long way from here."

"You still think we're being followed don't you?"

"I believe so, I can almost feel them. Yes, someone is following our trail." He shrugs. "Maybe I am wrong. I hope so."

Tracy can see he is serious and shudders. "I'll bring the girls."

"Thanks for letting me sleep, Tracy."

"Like I said, I didn't do it for you alone. We've got the girls to think of."

The sun is breaking as Lance leads the girls farther to the west for several miles then turning back to the south and home. Several times throughout the day, he back tracks only to find nothing but an empty forest. Maybe he is just jumping at shadows.

They travel all day and it is late evening. The girls are holding up well, even at this fast pace. Lance smiles; maybe they are getting in shape. That is good, the way he has to circle to elude anyone on their trail. They still have close to a hundred miles and several mountain ranges to cross. Only Sadie seems to hold back. On two occasions, Lance had to restrain her physically from turning around. Finally calling a halt, he watches guiltily as the girls collapse tiredly.

Looking at Tracy, he shakes his head as he sits down. "She don't act like she's scared of Indians to me."

"Something is different about her alright." Tracy agrees, "She acts like she knows someone is following us."

"You girls eat and rest." Lance rises and takes up his rifle. "I'll take me a look back there while I can still see. Rest all you can."

"You should rest." Iona scolds him. "You order us to rest but you're the important one."

"No I'm not Iona, you girls are." Lance nods over to where Satia sat. "Rest, we will travel throughout the night. Watch her while I'm gone."

The valley floor before him lay flat and clear in the late evening sun as Lance surveys it from his vantage point further up on the mountain. Suddenly the hairs seem to rise on his neck as he discovers the lone warrior casting back and forth trying to sort out their trail. There is no doubt, the warrior is exactly on the same trail they covered only two hours earlier and he is looking for their trail.

"You're a good tracker." Lance touches the trigger of his rifle and replies, "Too good."

His finger itches as he touches the trigger with the half-naked warrior dead in his sights but still too far out of rifle range. The warrior senses someone is watching him, first searching the bottoms then looking up the mountain right where the white hunter is waiting. Several minutes pass as he stands there, then the warrior retreats down the valley until he disappears from Lance's sight.

Only Tracy notices Lance's heaving chest and the perspiration on his face as he returns to the place where he left them. Quickly gathering the women and their meager clothing, he starts them up the mountain as fast as they can travel.

"What's wrong?" Tracy can sense the nervousness in him.

"We've got company behind us."

"Then you were right about someone following us." Tracy looks back down the trail. "How many?"

"I don't know, all I saw was one." Lance turns his back to the girls. "He is probably just a scout, there's bound to be more."

"What are we going to do?" She suddenly understands the danger. "The girls can't out distance men."

"We're going to try our best." He looks behind him trying to figure out what his father would do. "You keep the girls heading over the mountains."

Lance picks out a tall heavily limbed oak and starts climbing. From his perch forty feet in the branches, he can see the length of the wide valley clearly. There is nothing stirring in the bottoms, making him curious. Where are the warriors or was he mistaken and just saw one lone hunter out hunting.

Scrambling back down the tree, he reaches the ground and starts back towards the girls. There is little time to waste. Looking behind him one last time, he runs back down the trail. Hopefully, luck is on our side today; maybe the warrior is alone and not following.

For two days, he pushes the girls hard, letting them rest only briefly at night, then starting them on the trail again. They are getting close to the hunting grounds his father described to him and Lucas so many times, as they sat in the small cabin roasting peanuts beside their fireplace. The tall mountain with the twin peaks marks the beginnings of no man's land, the place that belongs to no one, white or red. Now they are at their most perilous stage of their flight. Hostile red men, renegade whites and the French, always the French. All of them are dangerous, any of them would not hesitate to take the girls back north to Canada if they were re-captured. Each one of the girls would demand a high ransom or perhaps a high bride price.

Exhausted, the girls lie on the cold ground resting near the peak of a tall pass, trying to catch their breath. They ran their race and did their best. Lance knows they need to rest. Stopping for food and rest will be dangerous but he has no choice. The girls, after expending so much of their precious strength in the last two days, are now completely done in.

"They must rest, Lance. They can't go on anymore." Tracy catches him by the arm turning him around to face her. "Lance, look!"

Two warriors cross the lower flats in plain view of them. Then they enter the timber following the valley floor where they traversed less than an hour earlier.

"They look like Mohawk Warriors from here." He spit the words out. "Get the girls moving."

Fear gives strength to the girl's legs enabling them to retreat down the mountain trail at a fast pace. Lance watches the pitiful sight of the exhausted girls making their descent down the rough mountain trail. The place where he is waiting is a perfect place to make his stand. He can guard it giving the girls time to flee. It is the only pass over this range of mountains, at least the only one he can see. Unfamiliar with these mountains and forest, he hopes he is right about the trail.

Before moving out of his sight, Tracy looks back once and waves. She herds the girls down the mountain, looking for a good hiding place. In her mind, she is arguing with Lance wanting them all to try to outrun the following warriors, all the while knowing it is impossible. She knows for him to stay behind alone, could be the death of him but it is their only chance. She cusses him for being hard and cruel. Her heart aches to look back and see him standing alone, placing himself between them and danger. She knows he might be thirsting for revenge against the killers of his folks but it does not matter. Today there is no doubt; she knows he is a brave man. The warriors will have to kill him before they get past him.

Checking the priming of his rifle, Lance places his powder horn and shot within easy reach. There is no sign of the warriors but he knows they are coming. Touching the war axe and his skinning knife, he waits. He knows he is as ready as he will ever be. The girls are exhausted and there is no way they can outrun the pursuing warriors. He also knows headlong flight through this no man's land could be disastrous if they accidentally run into more hostile warriors. No, his only choice to keep the girls safe is to stop the Mohawks here. He knows his shots may be heard if any other warriors are near but it cannot be helped. Now the rifle is their only chance.

Blue Elk is beside himself, he wants to race forward. The Medicine Woman is within his grasp, he can feel it. Ravenhair holds him back counseling caution, fearing a trap. Earlier he sensed someone was watching them from up high on the mountain. He was right. The track of the white hunter shows plainly on the ground as they reach the place the white hunter once stood watching the trail. If Ravenhair did not turn back when he did, the long rifle of the white would have spoken his name.

"We will catch them in the next valley."

"We could have caught them two sleeps ago." Blue Elk is agitated and out of patience, not understanding his father's slow advance. "Why do we hold back?"

"We will have them soon." Ravenhair shakes his head. "Do not be impatient, my son."

From their back trail, the call of a meadowlark breaks the silence. Ravenhair listens for several minutes until the call comes across the valley again.

"It is loud for such a small bird." Blue Elk looks at his father. "You know who follows us?"

"Perhaps we should answer our strange friend."

Blue Elk cups his hands and returns the call with the sound of a bobwhite quail. Easing behind a stand of Cottonwood Trees, the two warriors wait and watch. Several minutes pass until a file of four warriors come trotting down the trail.

Raising his hand Ravenhair greets the newcomers. "We did not expect to find our brothers so far from our village."

"We come looking for Bobcat and Tohito."

Ravenhair nods, "Did you find them?"

"Many days ago. They are both dead." The older warrior frowns. "The Seneca dogs killed them."

"Do you follow the ones that killed them?"

"They were, as we suspected of the Seneca Nation. Now they are dead. They lay with Black Panther of the Shawnee." The warrior speaks again. "We followed their trail to his camp."

"Why are you here, my brother?" Ravenhair looks at the older warrior.

"Our medicine woman Satia was with Tohito and Bobcat. They were her escort on the trail to our village. The Seneca dogs killed our warriors and took her captive." The warrior looks about. "I see her tracks many times but I do not see her here with you, my Chief. Where is she?"

Ravenhair stiffens, he has no knowledge of the Medicine Woman being taken to another village or captured. He did not find her at the Black Panther's camp but he saw tracks that look like hers along with the other women. He could only guess, maybe the white long hunter mistakes her for a captive or did he? Perhaps he knows who the Mohawk Medicine Woman is and hopes to use her to escape with the other white women.

"We see her tracks but she is not with us. She is with the ones we follow." Ravenhair nods off to the south. "Why did she leave our village where she is safe?"

"Our great Sachem Pontila is ill. He asks for her to come to his village." The warrior shakes his head. "We could not refuse his request."

"Why were not more guards sent with her?"

"Why more? She was in our hunting grounds and the village of Pontila was only a day's walk."

"My Chief, do the whites you follow have her prisoner?" The one called Wolf Runner looks at Ravenhair. "If she is we must rescue her now."

"We do not get close enough to the white man to see the women." Ravenhair can see the apprehension in Wolf Runner's face. "This white one is a Long Hunter. He is very dangerous and clever. We cannot count the tracks to know how many are with him."

Blue Elk nods. "He is clever like the fox and he makes the women walk in each other's tracks."

"She is our medicine totem. If they find this out she will be killed." Another warrior named Otter steps forward. "We must attack now!"

"Come, we will hurry after this long hunter and see if Satia is with them." Wolf Runner starts forward.

"No. I am your Chief and I give the orders here." Ravenhair touches the handle of his knife. "We will get her back but I do not think she is in danger from this white hunter."

To the Mohawk people, their Medicine Woman is great magic, greater than their older chiefs and greater than their Medicine Men. To lose her would be disastrous to the Mohawk Nation. They worship her and their tribe's prosperity depends on her blessings and good health. Their future depends on her well-being. The Medicine Woman, called Satia, brought good luck and prosperity to the Mohawk Nation since her birth.

Lance blinks as he counts the line of warriors. Instead of two Mohawks to contend with, now he has six. The long rifle lines up on the chest of the foremost warrior as the man trots easily up the trail right into its sights. The rifle roars as Lance watches the lead warrior collapse and fall. The other warriors melt from his view into the shrubs and tall grass that line the trail.

Reloading his rifle, Lance lines his sights on the down warrior as he tries to crawl from the open trail. Watching as a large warrior waves a piece of deerskin above his head and walks into plain sight, Lance lowers his rifle and waits. He can't believe his eyes. He has never heard of a hostile tribe waving what appears to be a flag of truce. His eyes cannot betray him, as the warrior is less than a good rifle shot away.

Standing up cautiously, he waves the man forward, waiting in plain sight as the warrior advances up the trail to where he is standing. Lance studies the man as he nears. He is a magnificent specimen of the red race; tall, straight shoulders, heavy muscles through the torso. He has a broad forehead with wide intelligent oval eyes set off by a huge hooked nose. The man emits power and courage as he stops within a few yards of where Lance is waiting.

The warrior's hands motion, making the sign for a council used by all the tribes. Lance is thankful his father spent night after night teaching him and Lucas the universal hand talk of the tribes. Again the hands speak.

"I speak a little of your white tongue." Ravenhair speaks as Lance shakes his head when asked if he understands the Mohawk language.

"I speak a little Mohawk, not much," he acknowledges. "What do you want?"

Ravenhair is surprised at the white's youth. "You are young, white man."

Lance frowns. "I'm getting older every day."

"There were six of us, five now."

Lance holds up the long rifle. "My weapon makes me equal to six."

"This is true; you wound another of my people," Ravenhair admits. "You kill many great warriors, white man."

"And you killed my entire family."

"Not the Mohawk. We were in our village and hunting grounds." Ravenhair denies the words. "We have not made war on the whites this year."

"You lie; I myself watched as Mohawk warriors share their camp with the Shawnee Black Panther."

"No. You are mistaken, white man." Ravenhair takes a step forward and then stops as the rifle comes up. "The ones you saw there are Seneca. My warriors have not been on the war trail this year."

"I have four women with me who were taken captive, you know this." Lance looks across at the man. "You followed us for many days."

"We know you have women with you but they are not what we seek."

"Then what do you want?"

"We believe you have taken our Medicine Woman, Satia, captive at the campsite of the Black Panther. We read the signs; you killed him and his warriors as they sleep." Ravenhair watches his face. "My people wish for her return."

"Satia?" Lance is shocked. "Sadie!" Tracy and the girls mistakenly thought the warriors at the camp were calling the dark haired girl Sadie.

"Do you have this one?"

"And if I do?"

"We will trade for her." Ravenhair nods with relief.

"What, what will you trade?"

"Your freedom and the women with you."

Lance looks back down the trail where the other Mohawk are apparently treating the one he just shot. "My freedom? You're the one under my rifle."

"I am Ravenhair, Chief of my village and the Mohawk Turtle Clan." The big warrior looks hard at Lance. "You have my word. If you return the girl to us now; you may leave this place in peace."

"After I killed the ones at the camp?"

"I would have done the same were I you." Ravenhair studies the young white man. "They were fools, to drink the white man's firewater in enemy land."

"That is hard to believe." Lance shakes his head. "I don't think so."

"They were Seneca; they killed Mohawk Warriors and took our beloved Medicine Woman." Ravenhair shakes his head. "If they still live our women would make them scream, wishing for death."

"And if I don't let you have her?"

"You can hold this pass white man but in a day my warriors can circle behind you and catch the women."

"Then why do you trade?"

"My people need their Medicine Woman, we know you kill. We cannot take a chance of her being harmed or even captured by another tribe while we fight with you."

"Sounds reasonable."

"Will you trade?"

Lance studies the tall warrior then nods. "What guarantees will you give?"

Ravenhair looks behind him down the narrow passage. "I give my word, which is all I have."

"No. You and your men will see us safely back to the white settlements."

"My warriors will not allow our Medicine Woman to go farther into the hostile lands." Ravenhair spread his hands. "My people are afraid without her, much sickness could come upon them."

Lance studies the older man. He feels that somehow he can trust the man. "Then you Ravenhair, will be my hostage."

"You will release me as soon as we reach your people?"

"You have my word."

"But you white man, would not take my word."

"No. I have no reason to trust you." Lance shrugs. "I have been taught well to distrust the French and the Indian."

Ravenhair nods solemnly. "I will call my son Blue Elk to this place. He will accompany the girl back to our lands while I go with you to the south."

Chapter 6

Tracy watches from her hiding place as Lance, followed by two warriors, trot easily down the trail. As he still carries his rifle, she knows he is not a captive. She knows Lance; he would not lead a hostile warrior after them even with the threat of death.

Stepping from behind the tree, she waits calmly as the small group approaches. In shock, Tracy blinks as Satia races from behind her into the outstretched arms of the younger warrior. Looking curiously at Lance, she shakes her head.

"Ladies, it seems we've been mistaken. Sadie is really a Mohawk, held in high regard by her people as some kind of Medicine Woman charm or something." Lance explains trying to quiet the women. "Her real name is Satia and these warriors came to take her home and help us get home."

Tracy cannot believe it, how could they be so wrong in mistaking her for white. "We thought her name was Sadie."

"She had me fooled too," Iona steps forward. "She is as white as I am under that deer hide."

Blue Elk steps in front of Lance, a dark scowl on his face. "You white man, have shamed my father. He is a great warrior; now he must be your prisoner."

"He gave his word to go with us. He is not a prisoner, only my safe passage out of this country."

"I, Blue Elk will go with you in his place." The warrior studies each of the women. "I will see them safely to their lodges."

Lance looks into the hostile face. "And I'm supposed to trust you?"

Blue Elk looks back at his father. "I will give my word to my father Ravenhair. I do not lie to him in anything."

For some reason Lance believes the warrior. Perhaps the young Blue Elk will be a better hostage than his father. Left behind, Ravenhair can keep the other warriors from following and ambushing them along the trail. Nodding, Lance turns away from the warriors and rejoins the girls.

"Do you trust them?" Tracy cannot understand Lance's thinking. "They're so fierce looking."

"Fierce doesn't mean they can't be trusted. We don't have a choice Tracy. I have to get ya'll back to the settlements any way I can," Lance said. "From here on to Bacons or Frasier could be the most dangerous part of the trail. I need help."

Not a word passes between Ravenhair and Blue Elk as the Mohawk and the woman turn back to the north. Satia tries once to turn back and follow Blue Elk, but Ravenhair takes her by the hand and leads the girl away. Lance has to admit she was a thing of rare beauty and carriage as she walked away. She carries herself proud, shoulders straight, her head upright, her walk strong, but elegant. The slightly bent left foot is her only fault. Not a word is spoken between her and the girls as she walks away, only a wave of her hand.

Blue Elk turns and faces Lance. "When your people are safe white man, then my father's word to you is honored."

"It is."

"Then we will settle what is between us."

Lance stood there watching as Blue Elk turns away, leading them silently to the south. The young warrior is proud; too proud. Somehow, the young Mohawk thinks his father was dishonored. Lance knows when the women are home safe the warrior will demand they fight to regain his honor. He has no love for any Indian and none at all for this warrior. If Blue Elk wants to fight, he will kill him. It is as simple as that to the young Long Hunter. He is young and he does not know the Indian mind as his father did. Youth does not forgive as easily as age so this outburst from Blue Elk astounds him. However, if the warrior helps get the women home safe, then he will honor Blue Elk's wishes.

Two days pass as the small group travels slowly to the south. Blue Elk alternates between leading the women and scouting far ahead letting Lance cover their retreat. The deep timber of the valleys and grassy meadows they pass through are teeming with game. In this paradise, with deer and small animals in abundance, hunting parties will be out. This is a no man's land. The brush is dense and enemies can be lurking anywhere. So far, they are lucky, no signs of hostile warriors or the hated French.

The silent bow and arrows of Blue Elk are welcome as each night their supper consists of deer meat or rabbit roasting over hot coals. Several times, they saw the young Mohawk let loose an arrow and each time they are astounded with the accuracy of his shot.

Lance nods with admiration. In enemy territory, a hunting weapon such as the bow is a valuable asset, allowing you to kill game silently without worrying about the discharge of a rifle. He smiles; perhaps he will learn to use one. It will probably be a futile attempt as an Indian boy is taught the use of the bow since childhood, perfecting the use of the weapon for years. He knows that to master the use of the weapon will be difficult. It will take a lot of practice but perhaps, if he is aiming to keep traveling the forest this way, it is worth a try.

A yearling buck collapses slowly to the ground as the sharp arrowhead finds its mark. Blue Elk mumbles a few words over the dead animal then starts to skin it out. Lance waits for the warrior to finish, then lifts the back legs over his shoulder and starts back to where the women are.

Looking over as the Mohawk cleans his hands, Lance nods. "Maybe Blue Elk will give me a few lessons with the bow?"

"Why, you have the long gun." Blue Elk looks at the rifle Lance cradles in his arm. "It kills from afar."

"It makes much noise." Nodding, the warrior turns back to where the girls built a small fire and are waiting. "We will see, perhaps we will trade and you can teach me to shoot the rifle."

"Blue Elk kills again; we thank him for the deer meat." Iona smiles as she takes the backstrap from the warrior. "I will fix you a fine steak."

"Amongst our people when a young unmarried girl prepares food for a warrior it means she wishes to marry him." Blue Elk speaks as he hands her the meat.

Iona laughs lightly as Lance translates his words. "And among our people Sir, it means the girl is hungry."

Blue Elk grins then rubs his flat stomach. "It is the same with the Mohawk."

In the days that follow, Blue Elk starts to relax as he trains the girls. With the slightest movement of his hand, they melt silently into the tall foliage and ferns that line the trail. If one is slow to react or does not pay attention, she receives a fierce rebuke from the Mohawk, maybe even a pretend kick with his moccasin foot.

As they cross another smaller valley, Lance stiffens as the warrior gives the warning signal and the girls vanish before his eyes. Slipping silently out of sight beside the trail, Lance scans their back trail and the tall dead foliage that lines the game trail they are following.

For three days, they travel far to the south, letting the women rest only at brief intervals. Blue Elk, in a hurry to return to his village, pushes them relentlessly with very little rest. Lance thinks he knows the reason, but it is only a guess on his part. It is late afternoon as the sun dips low, now almost hiding behind the trees and branches that grow tall and wide in the fertile soil of the Allegheny Mountains.

Suddenly the sharp call of a whippoorwill comes from behind them and another repeats the call off to their side. Lance watches as Blue Elk cups his hand and sounds the call of a bobwhite quail. Ravenhair and another Mohawk rise from their place of concealment and walk quickly to where Blue Elk appears.

"My Father, why are you here at this place?" Blue Elk is shocked to see them. "How did you find us?"

Ravenhair ignores the questions as his dark eye's look around at the women, then look to where Lance stood. "Satia, she is not here with you?"

"Satia is here?" Blue Elk shakes his head. "Why would she be here? She was with you. I thought she was safe back at the village by now."

"Two days ago, she slipped away in the night as we slept." Ravenhair shakes his head. "We followed her tracks and yours for two days, then we lost hers."

"Why would she leave and come here?" Blue Elk is truly astounded. "I do not understand."

Ravenhair shakes his head. "I believe she longed to be with you, my son. I think she came to find you."

Lance stands off to the side with the girls listening to the conversation as best he can, watching the reaction of Blue Elk closely. His suspicions are right, the girl has feelings for the warrior and he for her.

"Where could she be, my Father?"

"We lost her trail only one day ago, she can't be far."

"We must go now, she must be found quickly." Blue Elk looks over where Lance is waiting. "This is dangerous ground; many tribes hunt here, not all friendly to the Mohawk."

Ravenhair studies his son's face. "Do we look for our Medicine Woman, my son, or your woman?"

"Does it matter?" Blue Elk answers agitated. "She must be found quickly."

"It matters; she is the tribe's totem and not just another squaw. She belongs to the Mohawk people so she can never belong to one man."

"We will discuss this after she is found."

"What of these whites?" the other warrior called the Otter asks.

"They are on their own now. We must hurry."

Lance looks across the clearing at the Mohawks. "This is the way the great Ravenhair keeps his word?"

"Satia must be found, white man." Blue Elk glares across at Lance. "Maybe we should kill you before we leave this place."

Lance raises the rifle lazily, pointing it at the warrior's midsection. "Blue Elk can try."

"Enough of this talk." Ravenhair steps in front of his son. "I have given my word and you keep yours, white man. Otter will lead you to the settlements. Blue Elk will go with me to look for Satia."

"My name is Hawkins."

"Hawkins." Ravenhair repeats the name then nods. "We go."

Lance wants to tell them all to go and leave them but he knows they need a guide to get them across the mountains the fastest way. He was raised in the woods. He knows them, he can find his own way by heading south but it will take longer. He could also stumble, head first, into another raiding party. Alone he cannot safeguard the women as well, but with the Mohawk leading the way he can guard the women from behind, watching for any enemy following their trail.

Looking over at Iona, Blue Elk speaks softly. "Otter will keep you safe, we must go find Satia."

"Find her safe, Blue Elk." Iona raises her hand and waves as the warriors turn away.

Lance can feel the dislike Blue Elk feels for him, probably for any white man. However, for some reason, he cannot figure out why the Mohawk seems to like Iona.

Satia travels towards the south keeping the eastern sun over her left shoulder. Blue Elk and the whites could not be far ahead. She did not see their tracks, but she knows no Mohawk would leave his track for an enemy to find easily.

At first she travels as fast as she can, knowing Blue Elk will be following this trail to the south. Now as darkness starts to fall for the second time, she knows she is lost. She should have stayed with Ravenhair and waited on Blue Elk to return to the village. Her feelings for the young warrior are strong, but she knows she is the Medicine Woman of the Mohawk. She is not permitted to marry in her lifetime. No man can have her for a wife; her life belongs to the tribe.

Still, her love is so strong, she could not bear to stay with Ravenhair and let Blue Elk go to the south where the land is dangerous for a Mohawk. Her strong medicine calls to her, warning her Blue Elk is in grave danger, as she fears for his life. Satia is young; she must stay away from the men of her village. She knows nothing of love. She does not know if it is truly her medicine speaking to her or just the feelings of a woman for her man.

Awakening in the early morning cold dampness, she shivers as her eyes took in the surrounding timber. Suddenly dark shapes seem to materialize out of the fog right before her eyes. Drawing back in fright, she watches as a white man and four Shawnee warriors surround her. "Well now." The buckskin clad Frenchman smiles as he takes in the beautiful girl. "What have we here?"

"I know this one." One of the Shawnee steps forward. "She is big medicine for the Mohawk. She is their Medicine Woman. I saw her once at a gathering of the tribes."

"What is she doing here all alone?" The Frenchman asks.

The Shawnee warrior looks nervously around him. "She will not be alone, the Spirits and the Mohawk guard her at all times. She is very big medicine to them."

"Bah," the Frenchman laughs as he stands over Satia. "She is just a woman and a white woman if I don't miss my guess."

"Let us leave this place quickly." The big Shawnee warrior backs away from Satia. "Leave her here! She is big medicine and perhaps bad medicine for us."

The Frenchman, St Georges laughs. "Maybe she does possess big medicine; she already put a spell on me."

As the Shawnee Claw Killer steps back, he watches in fright as St Georges pulls the woman forcibly to her feet and shoves her ahead of him down the trail, tearing an amulet from her neck as he roughly grabs her. Picking up the charm, Claw Killer brushes it off with a trembling hand. He is afraid. Since childhood, he was taught that it is forbidden for any man to touch a Medicine person. He knows touching her could bring bad luck to the white man and anyone else who accompanies him. No good comes of laying hands on a medicine person of any tribe. The Great Spirit will be very angry as this woman is to be protected by all. She is touched by the great ones.

Claw Killer took the war trail many times, taking countless prisoners both red and white. His training since boyhood is so strong. To touch a Medicine person or a person that had been touched by the Great Spirit is forbidden by Shawnee law. Tribal custom speaks strongly of such a thing. The custom spoke strong words that only bad luck and doom will come of such a thing.

"Come Claw Killer. We must cross the mountains to the white settlement and then return to your village quickly."

"Leave the woman, my friend," the warrior demands. "She will bring us bad luck."

"No; I have use for her." The Frenchman motions the warrior forward. "We must return and get warriors to raid the white settlement again before the big snows come."

"Tell me, why do we go back to the place we just raided?" Claw Killer asks.

"We didn't raid Bacon's Settlement, only a few outlying farms."

"They will be waiting this time for our return."

"I don't think so, not this soon," St Georges replies. "We will first spy on the settlement, then go back to your village for the warriors."

"What about the Medicine Woman?"

"Maybe, Claw Killer, if we bring the woman back to the Mohawk safe, they will join us against the settlement."

"And maybe they will kill us." Claw Killer felt ill embodiments as he follows the Frenchman and the girl. "She will tell her people we touched her, we are all doomed for this. The spirit people already saw you touch her."

"We go." St Georges turns to the south dragging Satia by the wrist. The spiritual belief of these heathens sometimes irritates him. He lives with them and married into the Shawnee Nation, but for the life of him, he still could not understand some of their beliefs.

"No! We will leave the woman or I will turn back." Claw Killer did not move, refusing to follow.

St Georges turns as a wicked frown spreads across his face. "Then turn back, I think you are a coward. Leave me."

Claw Killer growls and pulls out his war axe. "No man calls a Shawnee a coward."

St Georges stiffens, as he knows he misspoke. "You are not a coward, my friend. Go back to the village and I will be along in four days. Have the warriors ready."

Claw Killer relaxes and whirls back down the trail with one warrior following him. St Georges shakes his head and turns back to the south. He will not release the beautiful woman. She will help him get the Mohawk to join him, providing she is safe.

For four days, after watching Blue Elk and Ravenhair disappear back to the North, the Otter doggedly leads Lance and the girls to the South, meandering around heavily timbered lands and crossing flat valleys. Several times, he stops and backtracks his own trail and then he turns in a completely new direction. Lance knows that by changing directions the warrior is trying his best to hide their trail. Although with the girls, it is almost impossible to hide their passing from any experienced eyes that happen to cross their path.

Lance can speak Shawnee fluently but only very little of the Mohawk language. The Otter speaks no English at all so any interchange taking place between the two is accomplished by both voice and hand signs. Lance surmises after a series of hand signals and sparse words that they are near the white settlement. He thought he recognizes the country they now travel. He has only been this far hunting with Lucas one time and these lands all look much the same with heavy timber and tall grass, so he cannot be certain.

Dark was almost on them as Otter holds his hand up. He appears to taste the air with his nose and ears. Sensing something is wrong he motions for the women to hide. Suddenly the warrior cries out and fell back in pain as an arrow penetrates his upper leg. Movement of the underbrush to their front discloses the attacker's location. Otter looks down at the feathered shaft sticking from his leg where blood quickly flows downwards into his moccasins. Slipping quietly up beside the warrior, Lance pulls him into the dense foliage and kneels beside him.

No other arrows or sound come from the thickets ahead as Lance tries to locate the hiding attackers. Examining the Mohawk, he can see the wound is painful, but it is not fatal. The arrow completely penetrates the fatty part of the warrior's leg. Only the gritting of the warrior's teeth grinding together come from Otter as Lance breaks off the feathered shaft and pulls the bloody arrow through the wound. Iona and Tracy crawl up beside the men and start ripping pieces from their dresses to bind up the wound, trying to stem the flow of blood.

"What's he saying?" Iona looks at her brother as Otter mumbles then motions something with his hands.

"He said we're to go and leave him."

"We can't do that."

Lance nods as Otter motions again. "He says one of the settlements is just a few miles the other side of this mountain."

"One of the settlements?" Tracy looks at the warrior. "Not Bacons?"

"Stay here, be quiet and stay alert." Lance hands Tracy his rifle then slips quietly off into the darkening light. Otter watches the young white hunter disappear, then grabs Tracy's arm as he tries to rise. Pulling himself slowly to his feet with the girls help, he pushes them father off into the darkening woods away from the trail. Collapsing against a huge oak the warrior motions the three girls down next to him.

Silence deafens their senses in its eerie way with only the strange quiet of the darkness coming forth from the tall trees. Otter and the girls listen intently, straining their ears, expecting some kind of noise from out of the dark, but not knowing exactly what. Lance is out there somewhere in the dark with an unknown enemy or maybe several enemies. There is no way of knowing and only the deathly stillness of the night surrounds them.

"Where can he be?" Iona whispers to May Lynn and Tracy. "I'm scared."

Only the warning hiss of Otter's compressed lips came to them as they shiver in fear and anticipation. The girls are young but several times in their young lives, they laid inside their log cabin, waiting for the war cries and screams of the attacking warriors to come out of the night, just as they are waiting now.

The long night lingers on. Still no sound comes from the darkness, nothing, not a sound, not even the sounds of the forest animals who prowl the woods at night. The girls wait anxiously as the night drags on slowly. The hours creep by and still Lance does not return.

The night is passing agonizingly slow for the women and the wounded warrior. Finally, the first rays of the morning sun begin to break slowly through the limbs of the tall trees that populate the woods. Otter and the girls sit close together, their eyes and ears straining for some sign of Lance. The girls are afraid, not knowing where Lance is or even if he is alive. The Mohawk is gritting his teeth against the agony of his wound. They fear the worst as the girls wait for the war cry of the attackers that could rush forward out of the morning fog for the kill.

"Lance." Tracy gasps looking in shock at the amount of bloodstains that cover his hunting shirt as he appears from the timber and fog barely twenty feet in front of them. "Are you hurt?"

Helping Otter to his feet Lance takes his rifle from Tracy and half-supporting half-dragging Otter, he starts off to the south. "No, I'm not hurt, but we must hurry."

"The ones that shot Otter?" Iona follows behind Lance. "Where are they?"

"There were only two of them, they're dead." He looks behind at Tracy. "The bigger one had these on him."

"What is it?" Iona looks at the knife and amulet Lance shows her.

Lance holds it up a little higher. "I believe it is the medallion that Satia had around her neck and the skinning knife belonged to our father."

"It is the necklace she wore." Tracy touches the amulet. "I am positive."

Lance points out the initials burned into the leather scabbard. "And this knife is Pa's; these are his initials H.H., for Ham Hawkins."

Exclaiming loudly, Otter points at the ornament and speaks something. "He must know it is hers too." Tracy nods at the warrior.

"Shawnee?" Otter speaks and makes the cutting motion with his hand, then speaks to them in Mohawk while he signs with his hands. "They have our Medicine Woman."

Lance nods absently as he helps Otter to his feet. "One of them said something interesting as he died."

"What?" Iona takes the warrior's other arm.

"From what I could make out, something about it being a bad omen to touch a Medicine Woman." Lance shrugs. "Then he whispered something about the Great Spirit."

"Medicine Woman?" Tracy steps closer. "He was talking about Satia. He had to be."

"Perhaps, but we don't know for sure."

Otter looks at the Amulet again, then at Lance. "If Shawnee hurt Medicine Woman, there will be big trouble between Mohawk and Shawnee, many die, much killing."

"Sounds good to me." Lance mutters under his breath.

Chapter 7

It is almost a month since the raid on the far settlements but already Frazier's Settlement settles back into its normal routine. The gates stand wide open with no guards, inviting the risk of another attack.

The Frenchman, St Georges, stands back in the dense timber and smiles as he studies the stockade and its fortifications. No guards on the walls, nor are there any posted at the gates. Either these English settlers are complete fools and stupid, or it is some kind of a trick they are playing, trying to lure the Shawnee into attacking. He studies the movements about the settlement. It is so peaceful around the stockade.

St Georges scrutinizes every palisade of the settlement as its inhabitants go about their daily work. He does not believe it is a trap. No, the English settlers on the frontier never learn, repeatedly failing to respect the fighting ability of the red man. They rely too much on their long rifles, something they will be sorry for one day. A movement to his right quickly averts his attention from the gates. Lance and the girls start across the cleared area that surrounds the settlement. Turning, he looks at the warrior beside him speaking in fluent Shawnee as he recognizes Tracy. "Those are the captives Black Panther had when he left from us."

"Then the great Panther must be dead." The warrior looks out across the open space. "He wanted that tall white girl for his woman. He would never trade her or let her escape."

"Perhaps it is so." St Georges could not fathom a great warrior like the Panther killed because of a woman. "Could the bloody long hunter following the women have killed the Black Panther and rescued the women?"

"The white hunter has a Mohawk Warrior with him." The Shawnee nods in surprise, pointing at the bloody bandage on the warrior's leg. "He has been wounded."

"Perhaps they tracked us to this place." The third warrior speaks up.

"No, remember Black Panther captured these women farther to the west at another settlement, they only come here for safety."

"The Mohawk is not a captive. He still carries his bow and he has his knife and war axe too."

St Georges already takes in the weapons, but why would a Mohawk, the enemy of the English, be with these whites? The Mohawk are of the Iroquois Confederation, not longtime allies of the Shawnee as the Seneca or Ottawa, but they join with them on occasions to attack the settlements.

The Frenchman watches as the Mohawk Woman turns her attention on the wounded Otter by staring at him. Stopping, the Mohawk pulls from Lance's grasp and stares hard towards where the Frenchman and the girl are hiding deep in the woods. Slowly the Mohawk turns his head back and forth trying to penetrate the forest and foliage.

"He knows we are here." The taller Shawnee looks towards the girl in awe. "She carries much power, the Medicine Woman warns him."

"Hogwash," St Georges scoffs. "Superstitious nonsense. Is the Turtle scared of a small girl?"

"This one is not a girl, she is a Spirit Person."

St Georges pulls his skinning knife and pulls Satia to him. "We will see Turtle, a spirit does not bleed."

Both Shawnee Warriors jump back in fright. "Do not do this thing Frenchman; it will be the death of all of us."

St Georges cusses and releases Satia putting away his knife. "Superstitious heathens. Come we go." He finishes in Shawnee.

The settlement at Frazier's became a beehive of activity as Lance helps the limping warrior as he follows the girls through the gates. The people do not know Lance or the girls but they do know about the raid on Bacons. They know all about the killings and the girls that were captured. Otter becomes the center of attraction as the people recognize what tribe he is from and push closer threateningly.

"He is with us. He helped us find your stockade," Lance says as he takes his rifle from Tracy. "You people stand back!"

"He's Mohawk!" A big red head exclaims. "No friend of ours."

"He's wounded and needs a doctor." Tracy steps in front of the man. "He is a friend of ours."

The red head pushes closer pulling out his skinning knife. "He won't need a doctor for long."

Only the impact of the rifle stock alongside a man's head is heard as the big man falls at Lance's feet. "I won't tell you people again! He's with us and I will protect him."

"Why would you protect a red killer?" another settler asks. "Them Mohawk have raided us almost every spring since we been here."

"He helped us get here." Iona steps up beside Otter. "We owe him."

"Take him to the Tavern, the Doctor is over there," an elderly man orders. "You won't be bothered there."

"Thank you." Lance nods to the man.

"I'm Benjamin McDowell. I'm kinda the leader of this settlement."

With the help of McDowell, Lance helps Otter through the door of the tavern. "I'm Lance Hawkins, these are my sisters, Iona and May Lynn, and this is Tracy Trent, our neighbor."

McDowell helps settle Otter onto one of the rough tables. "They were the women taken at Bacon's Crossing a month back, aren't they?"

"They are. Have you heard anything from Bacons?" Lance asks.

"No, a long hunter passing through here last week told us the farms around Bacons were raided and several folks were massacred. He said a young man went after them all alone." McDowell looks curiously across the table at Lance. "This store is the best I can do for your Indian; the folks here about had a pretty bad year. They've been harassed all summer by the Shawnee and others, that's why they acted like they did towards this red man. If we try to put him up in a bed, we're all liable to be killed."

"It'll do fine." Lance looks about the inn. "We're a thanking you, Mister McDowell."

"Just call me Benjamin," the older man looks at the blood covering Lance's hunting shirt. "You're not hurt are you?"

"No sir, the blood that stains my shirt belongs to the other feller." Lance looks over to where the girls are sitting. "I need a favor Benjamin."

"Tell me, Lance Hawkins, what can I do for you?"

"I've got to go back out. I need a place for the girls to stay, where they'll be safe while I'm gone."

"Alone, you're going out alone?" Benjamin looks hard at the young man. "Must be important!"

Staring down at the amulet in his hand and the knife strapped to his broad belt Lance nods. "It is; maybe for all of us."

"How old are you lad?"

"Coming twenty."

"For one so young it appears to me you've already done a man's work bringing back the girls. Now you're going out again?"

"The warrior is Mohawk. His name is Otter." Lance ignores the remark and motions over to where Otter lay watching them. "It's important to me he stay safe and taken care of along with the girls."

"You have my word young man." McDowell points to the large storeroom. "Take any supplies you will need, plus some clean clothes."

"I can't pay for them."

McDowell smiles, "you already have lad."

"Thank you Sir." Lance starts for the room that holds the stores supplies. "One thing Mister McDowell; it's important that Otter be well taken care of. If anything should happen to him, we'll have the whole Mohawk Nation down on us."

"I understand," McDowell nods his head. "You have my word; no harm will come to him."

Lance speaks briefly with the girls then returns to where the doctor is busy working over Otter. Motioning with his hands, Lance signals to the warrior with a flat hand and then quickly departs from the Tavern. Tracy follows closely behind him as he exits the building. "You're going after Sadie?"

"And the warriors that have her," Lance nods, "I believe they are the ones that killed our people."

"Stay with us. You're needed here."

"You'll all be okay and well taken care of. I have Mister McDowell's word on it."

"I wasn't worried about us," her eyes pleading with him. "Please stay here."

"I'll be back."

"He looks handsome in those new buckskins, doesn't he Tracy?" Iona smiles over at the taller girl.

Frowning, Tracy nods as she watches the retreating back of the tall youth. "Well, at least he ain't still all bloody; at least not yet."

As the small settlement watches, Lance turns from the girl and trots back out the open gates of the post. Where he is going, to find the girl or Ravenhair, he does not know. He can only follow their back trail and hope for the best. He has to try. If he can find Satia, perhaps the Frenchman and the Shawnee will be with her. Looking back one last time at the settlement gate, where the girls are standing, he starts back to the north at a ground-breaking pace. There is no doubt; whoever has the girl is involved in the killing of his folks. The knife and the amulet he found on the dead Shawnee ties them to the raid on their farm.

The tall warrior that shot Otter carried his father's skinning knife along with Satia's amulet. Somehow, there is a link; perhaps the Frenchman led the attack. Lance wants the Frenchman he saw with the raiders. If he can find and rescue the girl, perhaps she could be the key to the whole affair but he has to find her.

He will travel to the north. If he finds the Frenchman's tracks he will follow them, if not he will continue on to the Shawnee Villages and their hunting grounds. The Shawnee are the tribe that raided their farms but mostly Lance wants the Frenchman he saw with the Shawnee the morning he and Lucas were hiding in the log. He will never forget that face; the face of the man that is the cause of his people's death. Their blood calls out to him. No matter how far or how long the Frenchman travels, Lance will someday find him. Thinking of Lucas he felt ashamed, he never even asked at the settlement if they know anything about his brother. McDowell probably does not know anything, but it shamed Lance that he did not think to ask. It is no excuse, but since finding his father's knife and killing the Shawnee warrior that carried it, the white man consumes his mind. The Frenchman is near; Lance can sense it. One day he will die by his hand.

St Georges with his two Shawnee Warriors sprint to the North Country unaware that Claw Killer is dead and his killer is only a day behind them. Pampered all her life by her people and unused to traveling long distances because of her crippled foot, Satia tires quickly, slowing them down. St Georges and the Shawnee are traveling on their way back to their village and by pure luck Lance winds up on the same trail.

The Shawnee are great warriors and hunters; to leave a track for an enemy to find only happens if the ground is too muddy to hide their tracks. As night falls, the cold rains come suddenly from the west. St Georges cusses their luck, only days from the Shawnee hunting grounds and the village; he knows the heavy rains will slow them down even more. The girl is completely exhausted and now needs support on the slippery trail. With the unrelenting rains that made the trails run with water, and the low places almost unpassable, he knows he has to find shelter until the storm passes. He cusses his luck again as the heavens burst wide open. Planning to launch a major attack on the settlements before the heavy snows and cold weather of winter can slow their movements; he knows this storm will hamper his plans.

"The Medicine Woman is in no shape to continue. If she dies, the Mohawk and other tribes of their confederation will make war on the Shawnee," Small Turtle states looking over at St Georges daring him to refuse. "If something happens to her, we will be cursed by the Spirits forever."

Normally the French are very influential among the warlike tribes, never challenged because of the supplies, weapons and trinkets they supply the northern tribes. They are all bribes to encourage the warlike red warriors to carry out raids against the settlements and British. However, the roots of superstition run deep in the Indian culture. It is instilled in them since childhood and to the Shawnee, the Mohawk Medicine Woman is untouchable. St Georges can see the scowl on the Shawnee's face. The Frenchman knows in this he will have to let the Indian mind win out. "I will do as Small Turtle asks; we will find shelter and let her rest."

"This is good," the Shawnee answers as he steps back.

Lance follows the game trail that leads north into Shawnee hunting grounds for three days. No tracks are on the trail but he knows the Indian. Almost all Indians are trained since childhood, never step where they will leave a track. The rains come suddenly, without warning from the west, wetting the ground with torrents of water, turning the trail into a quagmire, softening the ground. With his eyes scanning the trail and the surrounding forest, Lance runs on wearily to the north in his endless pursuit.

Suddenly there it is; the slight footprint of a small person, perhaps a woman, perhaps Satia's footprint intermixed with larger tracks of men. With the ground saturated, the warriors ahead of him, whoever they are, now find it difficult to hide their tracks. Over the years with his father's teachings, Lance is now a fine tracker, maybe as good as most Indians. He practiced for years tracking deer and other game as he hunted. The tracks left on the ground now are easy for him to read and follow.

Uneducated and illiterate from the white man's standard and unable to read the small books that many settlers brought west with them, Lance nevertheless is like a hunting dog on the trail. His eyes are sharp as a hawk, making him able to sort out the worst of tracks. All tracks differ; animals or man, male or female, white man or red man, size or weight. Lance can read a lot in any track, providing the tracks are plain to see. Now with the heavy rain, the tracks in the wet ground are visible, as easy to read as those books.

The signs are plain; three men and one woman are ahead on the trail. The turned in toes tells Lance two are Indian. One track belongs to a white man from the slightly turning out feet. The last track is a woman with a crippled foot. The track is that of Satia, he remembers it well from when she traveled with him and the girls. The track of the woman's crippled foot and the tracks he remembers of Satia are one and the same. If indeed it is Satia, then they are carrying and dragging her between two warriors. Lance smiles grimly. With the exhausted woman to slow them, he might catch them before they can reach the safety of the Shawnee Village.

Raising the leather wrapping that protects his powder in the firing pan, Lance frowns and dumps the damp powder onto the ground. Raising his powder horn, he drops it back to his side. With the rain coming down in torrents, there was no use in repriming the rifle. The elder Hawkins always taught his sons to keep their powder dry and their knives razor sharp but in this weather, it is impossible.

The muddy tracks of the Shawnee Warriors and woman started to show more plainly on the wet trail; they were slowing. No longer did the warriors attempt to conceal their tracks. In the muddy ground, it was useless.

Lance stops suddenly and steps quickly from the trail. The tracks are too plain and easy for anyone to see. The warriors were walking down the very center of the trail. Lance studies the tracks; he knows the warriors ahead could be laying a trail for him to follow into their ambush. If this is true, the raiders could possibly leave a warrior lagging behind to keep watch over their back trail.

The Medicine Woman of the Mohawk is a liability to them and the Shawnee know this. For some reason, Lance cannot understand why they still carry her with them. Lance knows that in most Indian cultures a squaw or captive white woman is left behind if they slow down the raiding party.

Ravenhair and Blue Elk cast back and forth across the wide valleys. Luckily, they cross the tracks of St Georges and his Shawnee. They also find the track of the young white as he follows the Frenchman.

Blue Elk kneels and traces the footprints in the muddy trail. Looking up at Ravenhair, he shakes water from his face and nod. "The white hunter Hawkins follows the track of Satia and the Shawnee. I know his track."

"Are you sure they are Shawnee?"

"They are Shawnee, my father." Blue Elk traces the prints again. "The curl of their moccasins and the design of the laces are only made by Shawnee women."

Ravenhair nods, his facial expression shows pride in the tracking abilities of his son. "Who else is with them?"

Blue Elk studies the muddy prints for several minutes walking back and forth beside the tracks. "Our Medicine Woman and one white man are with them."

"The Frenchman, St Georges." Ravenhair studies the tracks. "It is his track; I have seen it before."

"Why does this white man follow them and where is the Otter?"

"This I do not know, perhaps he stays behind to protect the white women."

"No." Blue Elk shakes his hand. "The white hunter's hate for the Indian is too strong. He would not leave them alone with the Otter."

"Perhaps you are right, my son," Ravenhair agrees. "Your question has no clear answer now; perhaps soon. We will follow quickly, they are not far ahead."

"With the rain muddying their tracks, it is impossible to tell."

Ravenhair's dark eyes stare hard along the trail leading to the north. "They are near; come we must hurry."

Lance's instincts are right again, St Georges left a warrior behind to watch their back trail. A tall Shawnee Warrior is waiting quietly under a heavy branched Oak Tree. Even sheltered under the foliage of the tree, the water dripped from his broad face and rivulets of water ran down his dark torso. The dark eyes watches the trail solemnly, unblinking, despite the cold rain that beat against him.

The rain settles down from a cold blowing rain to a steady drizzle. The smaller animals and bird life take shelter, leaving the forest quiet with the exception of raindrops dripping from the soaked trees or a fallen branch falling noisily somewhere out in the woods. As always, the storm changes the forest, leaving the air pure and clean. The drenched, damp bark of the trees and down limbs emits a refreshing smell on the wind. Small brooks run knee-deep with cold water, cascading down the mountains then flowing out along the meadows and across the rocks making a gurgling noise when passing over the rocks.

Lance eases quietly through the wet forest, staying far off to the side of the trail as best he can. He moves closer to the trail to be sure the Shawnee are still following it. Several times, he kneels concealing himself behind a cedar or oak tree, watching quietly, surveying the forest and foliage for danger before moving cautiously forward. He wants very much to catch up to the Frenchman but walking into an ambush will not get the Medicine Woman free. It is worse if he dies, then the hated St Georges would live.

St Georges does as Lance suspects he would. He left a warrior behind to watch for anyone following their trail.

The second Shawnee warrior, Mad Wolf, waits patiently, watching the forest off to the south and east. The dark eyes blink away the water running down his forehead as he focuses on the trail. Suddenly the sharp eyes of the Shawnee narrow as he focuses on a lone figure that stalks warily along their trail, stopping at intervals to study the surrounding woods.

Mad Wolf looks down at his bow then quietly set it beside the tree. The foliage along the trail is too dense for him to get a clear shot with the weapon. Something he did not think of in his haste to find a good place to conceal himself. Pulling out his long skinning knife, the warrior slips silently from his place of concealment.

Lance is intent on studying the wet forest drenched with soaked trees and limbs. Moving forward cautiously, he knows an enemy can be lurking behind any of the huge trees that cover this valley and line the trail. His eyes and ears are straining to their breaking point as he follows the trail. In the maze that closes in on the trail, he knows an enemy can be concealed anywhere.

Mad Wolf follows slowly, stalking his unsuspecting prey, his leather moccasins silenced by the soaked leaves, only squishing slightly as he walks. Ever so slowly, he inches closer and closer to the white hunter. Peering around the base of a huge oak, the warrior opens his eyes in surprise then smiles slightly. This white is just a boy. The familiar beard that most whites grow on their faces has not yet begun to grow. The warrior smiles contemptuously, the youngster will be an easy kill.

Lance stops in his tracks, watching closely as the tall figure materializes from out of the drizzle. There is no doubt; he knows the warrior sees him. What puzzles him is the Shawnee does not try to conceal himself but steps quietly, like a ghost, into full view on the trail.

The knife and war axe the warrior holds in his hands show plainly, making his intentions very clear to Lance. The warrior knows the rifle the white carries is wet, useless. He watches as Lance leans it against a tree and pulls his own knife and axe. Nodding in respect, he steps towards the white, at least this young hunter is no coward. To kill a coward brings no glory, nothing worth bragging about. This one is brave, to follow them alone and now stand and meet his enemy armed only with a knife; this will be something to brag about around the winter fires of his village.

The two men retreat to where the trail broadens into a small clearing and then start to circle each other cautiously. Mad Wolf knows this is a youngster before him but even in a child's hand, a knife can still kill if a warrior is careless. Both men parries at each other several times before closing together and grasping the other's wrists.

The Shawnee's eyes widen as he feels the immense power of the young white. He would never guess the tall slender figure could possess such strength as he felt. Breaking his hold on Lance, the Shawnee steps back, still flicking his knife out like a serpent's tongue. He is now fighting in earnest, serious. He knows this white, even though a youth, is very powerful and dangerous.

As they forget about the cold rain, the men fight back and forth across the clearing. Lance can tell already, he is not nearly the knife fighter this Shawnee is. He must stay calm and bide his time, hoping the warrior will make a misstep or a mistake. His father talked of defense when fighting and he listened to the lessons well. Now he is trying his best to parry the thrusts of the warrior. Not a word or sound comes from either fighter as they circle the clearing.

Mad Wolf grows angry with himself. Here is a mere boy, a white, keeping the mighty warrior at bay, making a fool of him. Both fighters are bleeding lightly from several small cuts to their arms and chests. Lunging powerfully forward, the warrior starts to bring his knife into the vitals of the white when the wet grass of the clearing betrays him. Losing his footing, he falls backwards, off balance, onto the wet ground. He feels the blade of Lance's knife slice across his stomach and chest. Rolling sideways away from the white, he lunges savagely to his feet his own knife slicing the empty space in front of him.

Mad Wolf misjudged this one. Maybe he is the killer of the Black Panther or maybe the medicine of the Mohawk Woman is helping him. Suddenly, the easy kill he anticipated seems to fade away. Lance can sense the hesitancy now in the warrior's movements. Now is the time, his father spoke of, the time to push the fight to his adversary. Again and again, he parries and thrusts at the warrior. Several times, he feels the Shawnee's blade bite into his arm or hand; still he pushes forward, bringing the fight to the red man. His father's razor sharp knife bites deeply into the warrior's arm, laying a wide gash in his stomach. A mere inch or two more and the fight would have finished.

Mad Wolf knows he is tiring. He lost too much blood. Scowling deeply, he lets out his death song and lunges forward into the white. Slapping the warrior's knife hand away, Lance plunges his steel blade deep into the stomach of the warrior and then he twists the knife and disembowels the Shawnee. Jerking the knife blade from the man, Lance pushes the man away from him and watches as the gasping warrior falls to his knees. With a final shudder, he stiffens and settles onto the wet ground. Only the dark eyes of the man move as they watch Lance, then glaze over as the air bubbles from his mouth in death.

The small cave that St Georges finds to rest the woman, is not far from where Mad Wolf is waiting, guarding the trail against any intruder. He hears the loud death yell of the Shawnee from within the cave. The Frenchman rushes outside into the cold rain, just in time to see Mad Wolf fall in front of the white man. Starting towards the clearing with his rifle ready, he stops quickly as two Mohawk warriors step into the clearing calling out greetings.

Retreating out of sight into the dense underbrush, he takes a quick glance at the cave then back at the white man and the two Mohawk Warriors, who are scouring the ground as they advance towards the cave. St Georges glances around him as there is little time. Soon they will follow his tracks back to the cave. There is neither time to return for the girl or warn the Shawnee Warrior guarding her. Turning, he vanishes silently like the coyote, disappearing back into the depth of the forest, taking the trail that leads north to the Shawnee Village.

St Georges is beside himself with rage. The raid was a complete failure with the exception of killing a few of the hated British settlers and stealing a few trinkets from their homes. The Black Panther, chief of the Shawnee Village, where he is now in route, is probably dead. All of the warriors that stay with him are probably dead. The Frenchman shakes his head in disgust, it is a waste of time and even the captive white women are all lost. Now his head could be next if the Shawnee leaders do not believe what happened.

The white long hunter he watched kill Mad Wolf is a mere boy but he manages to ruin all of St Georges plans for a combined raid of the tribes on the encroaching settlements. The Frenchman shakes his head in dismay. How did this youngster manage to kill Black Panther and his warriors? He rescued the white women and now he follows them alone from the English Settlement. He somehow kills Mad Wolf, one of the best knife fighters in the Shawnee Nation. Looking back one last time as he passes over a ridge in the mountains, he shakes his head in disbelief. Perhaps the Indians are right, perhaps the Medicine Woman carries great power and is helping this white. St Georges berates himself for such thoughts. He is not superstitious, nor did he believe in the woman's power. This is not finished yet! He will still have his revenge on the settlers and the young white hunter.

Lance with Ravenhair and Blue Elk, backtrack the Shawnee, Mad Wolf, to the hidden cave where Satia is held captive. Blue Elk stops momentarily and points out where St George stood, watching them from the woods near the cave. His tracks are evident among a stand of Cedars where he was waiting and watching the finish of the fight. They also see his tracks where he fled north. Without warning, the last Shawnee of the impending danger approaches the cave.

Stealthily, without making a sound, the three slip to the entrance of the cave. With the coiled spring of a hunting cougar, Blue Elk launches himself into the cave as he confronts the surprised Shawnee. Ravenhair and Lance are at his elbow with their weapons drawn.

"Drop your weapons Shawnee, or die." Ravenhair pushes in front of Blue Elk holding back his enraged son, "now!"

"I am dead already, Mohawk," the warrior stands defiant. "I helped steal your Medicine Woman."

The girl, though totally exhausted, manages to regain her feet. "This one helped me to this place, he did me no harm."

Blue Elk glares as Ravenhair holds him back. "No one is permitted to touch a medicine person."

"Do not harm him. Let him go in peace." Satia places her hand in front of the enraged Blue Elk. "This is my wish. To harm him will bring bad omens on our people."

"Who else was here, we found tracks of another outside?"

Satia waits for the Shawnee to answer, seeing the warrior will not speak, she answers. "There is another called Mad Wolf somewhere outside. A Frenchman named St Georges just left here. He brags that he led the raid on the white settlements. They captured me when I became lost as I was trying to find you."

Ravenhair studies the Shawnee for several seconds then steps aside. "Go back to your village and tell them Black Panther and all of his warriors are dead. Tell them this Frenchman, St Georges, led them to this and he is bad luck. Tell them the Mohawk people will kill this Frenchman and any Shawnee found with him because of dishonoring their Medicine Woman."

"I am called Small Turtle. We tried to tell the Frenchman not to take the girl but he would not listen to our words." The warrior looks over at Satia. "I will tell my people not to follow this one anymore."

Ravenhair restrains Blue Elk as the Shawnee exits the cave. "Go quickly Small Turtle before my son Blue Elk kills you; tell your people we are still at peace."

"No, he is mine." Lance steps in front of the Shawnee preventing him from leaving the cave.

Ravenhair steps beside Small Turtle and looks at Lance. "He has helped Satia. It is her wish that he leave this place unharmed."

Lance studies the face of the Shawnee, then steps aside. "Look for me always Shawnee. One day I will be there and one day you will die by my hand."

The Shawnee studies the hungry face of the young white and nods. He can read the hate in this one; he knows this white does not lie. Never until the white is dead will he be able to sleep in peace.

Watching as the Shawnee disappears into the thick forest, Lance shakes his head. "He will not do as he says."

Ravenhair agrees with a nod of his head. "This is so, but he helped the woman, we cannot harm him against her wishes." Looking at the girl Lance turns from the cave and without a backward glance, he disappears. Blue Elk steps to the entrance of the cave. "He goes after the Shawnee."

Ravenhair nods. "This white has much hate for the Shawnee. I think if he does not die, he will kill many before his thirst for vengeance is satisfied and his blood has cooled."

"For one so young, he is a dangerous enemy." Blue Elk looks out into the darkening day. "You are right my father, this one thirsts for revenge. His eyes are red like the enraged Wolverine, perhaps he is crazy."

Ravenhair shakes his head. "No, he is not crazy; he is young and has lost his people. Until his lust for blood is sated or he is killed, he will follow and kill his enemies."

"I have seen him kill; he is like the lobo wolf, bloodthirsty," Blue Elk agrees. "I would not wish him after me. I believe his hate makes his strength greater than normal men."

Ravenhair changes the subject. "We will let Satia rest here tonight, then take her to our village with the coming of the sun."

"What of Otter?"

Ravenhair shrugs. "If he lives, he will return to us."

"Maybe the white one killed the Otter." Blue Elk stares out into the rain. "He hates all Indians."

"No," the older Mohawk shakes his head. "No, I looked into the white's heart. He hates the Shawnee and the Frenchman but he gave his word to me. No, even as great as his hate is, he is still a man of honor. He would not kill the Otter."

Blue Elk pokes at the small fire and scoffs. "He would kill me easily enough."

"This is true my son. There is bad blood between you and him. Do not underestimate this white. He is young yet, but he has strong medicine. I think he is a great warrior."

"All the more reason I should kill him now." Blue Elk shrugs, "before he grows stronger."

"He will never be killed," Satia mumbles under her breath. "No mortal will ever kill this one."

"Blue Elk has more problems than the white." Ravenhair looks over at the girl nervously when she speaks about the white.

"If the people find out how she became a prisoner of the Frenchman and why, do you think they would kill me, my own people?" Blue Elk questions then looks over at the girl.

Ravenhair nods. "She is big medicine to them, it is forbidden for her to have feelings for a mere mortal."

"What will we do, my father?" Blue Elk asks then looks over at Satia. "We have great feelings for each other."

"You will forget about her and say nothing of this, ever." Ravenhair frowns at his son. "It is the only way."

Blue Elk again let his eyes fasten on the worrying girl. "This I cannot do."

"We will sleep now. Tomorrow we return Satia to the village." Ravenhair looks at both of them. "This cannot be. You cannot be as one. Sleep and study your hearts, my children."

"What about the white?" Blue Elk again stares off into the oncoming darkness.

"His blood runs hot and thirsts for vengeance. He goes on a blood trail now. Only death can turn him from the Shawnee."

"I see much death and blood for the Shawnee." Satia surprises the two warriors as she suddenly speaks again. They know her medicine is strong. They know she can see into the warrior's future and foretell what is to come. "I see the deep hatred the young white hunter carries in his heart and eyes. He lusts for blood. He will kill anyone who crosses his path; even the Mohawk. Someday he will take a wife, a light haired woman and father many children. He will never die."

"You said he will never be killed." Blue Elk looks at her down-turned face.

"Not by an Indian's hand."

"Perhaps by a white man?" Blue Elk questions the girl. "Tell me."

Satia closes her eyes and turns her back, silent as the flames of the fire.

Ravenhair pretends to sleep, stirring slightly in the night, then watches through half-opened eyes as Blue Elk and Satia slip silently from the cave. Sitting up, he shakes his head sadly. "Goodbye, my son; run far. From this night forth, you will always be an outcast in the Mohawk Nation."

Chapter 8

Otter stands outside the settlement gate as Tracy, Iona and May Lynn place biscuits and side meat in the leather pouch hanging about his shoulders. His leg wound needs time to heal but he can bear weight on it, enough to walk. He is eager to start back to his village and the Mohawk People. He shakes his head declining all of their pleadings to stay longer.

They stand waiting as Angus Hale hobbles slowly towards them. "Mister Hale, ask Otter if he will watch for Lance and send him home to us. We want to be sure he understands what we are asking."

The old man was a long hunter and trapper long before settlers moved this far west. Now a cripple, from a life of hardship and cold, he hangs on around Frazier's Hollow helping out when he can but mainly living on the charity of the people.

His value to the settlement is well worth it, as his knowledge of the tribes saved the settlement many times. Signaling quickly with his hands, he nods and watches as the warrior answers. "He says he will do as you ask. If he runs across the young white hunter, he will tell him what you said." The old man nods. "He also says thank you and he will forever be your friend."

The girls all surround the bashful Otter and touch his arm. Already the Mohawk was at the settlement for two weeks recovering from his wound. Now he is ready and eager to return to his own land with the Mohawk people. Most of the settlement treated him kindly and now they stand about the gates, watching as the Mohawk limps slowly off towards the North, disappearing from their sight.

Iona felt a lump in her throat, as the warrior passes from view into the deep forest. "You know, we only knew him for three weeks, but he seems like family."

Angus Hale looks oddly at the girl. "He may seem like family gal, but that buck would cut your throat as quick as you could blink."

"Mister Hale, you said he would always be our friend," Iona questions the old man.

"His words Missy, not mine." Hale starts away. "You wanted me to interpret what he said."

"I don't believe you."

The old hunter stops and turns. "There's lots of bones laying out there in the woods, belonging to folks that didn't believe me either."

"You're wrong about Otter," May Lynn chimes in. "He's our friend."

"Humph," is the only reply that comes from the old man as he hobbles across the dusty ground towards the store. "Women. I'll never understand the critters."

Small Turtle does not know someone is following him as he heads north, disregarding the falling sleet and rain. He is still young, intent on reaching his people. The warrior only thinks of hot food and the warm blankets that will remove the chill from his bones. Two times, as he follows the Shawnee, Lance reaches for the bone-handled knife of his father's but then he changes his mind. He needs this warrior alive to lead him to the Frenchman. Later, with his usefulness gone, the warrior will pay with his life.

He knows the Frenchman, St Georges, was within his grasp back at the cave and again he escaped. Lance wipes the rain from his face and runs on to the north. For now the Shawnee will live, to lead him to the village where the Frenchman will be. Shawnee Warriors from this village killed his folks but the Frenchman is the one who leads them. He is the one Lance wants most; the one man responsible for their deaths. St Georges cannot travel far enough or fast enough to escape his wrath, not even if he travels to the far northern woods of Canada.

Lance hates to seek shelter and take a chance of losing sight of the warrior, however the Shawnee finally slowed down. For Lance, soaked to the bone, the day was long and miserable and the night will be the same. He traveled at a fast trot all day. Tiring, he found a dry cave to lie in for the night. The pure hate that burns deep in his chest for the Frenchman and Shawnee keep the cold of the night from seeping into his body. Wrapping a deer hide around his shoulders, he squats under the branches of a Cedar, close enough to keep the cave in his sight throughout the night.

For three days, Lance follows Small Turtle to the north. With no time to hunt or cook meat, Lance makes do on the small patches of wild onions and dried berries he finds in passing. On the third day, after he crosses several small creeks and valleys, he smells the faint odor of wood smoke on the air. Small Turtle does not change his course once; he comes straight here to this place, it is his village, Lance can sense it. The Shawnee, in his haste to return to the village, did not check behind him to see if someone is following. Now he led Lance straight to the Frenchman or at least to the Shawnee Village.

After smelling the wood smoke, Lance slows his pace, letting the Shawnee race forward out of his sight towards the village. He traveled hard with little rest or food. Now he watches from afar as the warrior trots into the outskirts of the village.

Entering the village, Small Turtle is immediately recognized by the villagers, causing a loud shout to sound out across the valley. Preoccupied with their returning warrior, the villagers gather in mass around Small Turtle, allowing Lance to crawl unnoticed into the underbrush alongside the excited village. The ground underneath the brush, where he lay, is soaking wet and cold but it matters little to him. He finally spots his prey. St. Georges appears outside one of the grass lodges, looking curiously as the commotion of Small Turtle's arrival is heard throughout the village.

Sighting along the barrel of the long rifle, Lance can feel his finger itch in anticipation of the shot. Finally, he relaxes and lowers the weapon. The shot is just too far and he cannot be sure of killing the man. He does not fear dying but he has to be sure St. Georges is also dead. Then and only then, can he rest in peace and then his folks can rest in peace too. He watches the excited red warriors leaping about the village as they greet Small Turtle. It made the haunting memory of his butchered and mutilated mother return so vividly to his young mind, he cannot shake it.

He watches as St. Georges speaks with Small Turtle briefly before the warrior pushes him away roughly and enters one of the lodges. The Frenchman glares at the warrior before following him but not before turning to scan the nearby woods. Lance watches the hated Frenchman as he stands momentarily outside the lodge. The man is wild and cunning as a wary wolf. He seems to smell the air, testing it, as if he can sense Lance is out there somewhere.

The white hunter smiles, the look on St. Georges hairy face is worry, perhaps fear. He looks like the fox caught in the henhouse. Lance heard his father say on several occasions, while he was telling his tales of fighting wars with the French and Indians, the bravest of men sometimes fear something they cannot explain or understand. Perhaps, the Frenchman is spooked. He lost all of his Shawnee and some Seneca warriors on his retreat from the white settlements. Even the great Black Panther is dead.

Perhaps, living among the Shawnee causes their natural fear of the unknown to rub off on St Georges. The warriors who followed him on the raid against the settlers near Bacons are all dead. Who killed them and who is responsible? Surely not the young white he saw kill Mad Wolf, one of his most dangerous fighters back near the cave. The white is just a youth. To kill so many battle-tested warriors is something he cannot fathom.

Lance recalls the cool reception the Shawnee warrior, Small Turtle, gave the Frenchman. Maybe if he is lucky, the Shawnee People will save him the trouble of having to kill the man. No, he does not want that, he wants the man to fall under his knife, to feel the Frenchman take his last breath knowing who is killing him. There will be satisfaction if the man dies by his hand. If the Shawnee kill him, it will not be the same.

He knows the Shawnee will not turn on the Frenchman, in that he has no worries. Lance heard his father and others speak of the wild tribes need for the French, their weapons and supplies. The Shawnee will not turn on the Frenchman no matter how many men he loses, not yet anyway.

Lance looks up at the sun; it will be down soon. He needs to move away from the village and find something to eat. He will set his rabbit snares then build a fire to get warm and dry his clothing. Pulling back from the village, Lance scouts around for a dry place of concealment; a cave or large cedar with overhanging branches, any place he can safely build a fire.

Small Turtle points a long accusing finger at St Georges, across the fire where the elders of the tribe sit gathered in council. "This one took the Medicine Woman of the Mohawk against her will, then without warning me the white long hunter was near the cave, he left the woman and me behind to be captured." The warrior glares hotly at the Frenchman. "All of our warriors are dead, including our chief the Black Panther. Also many Seneca are dead."

"Who killed these warriors?" the Elder of the village questions. "Tell me, who has done this thing, who is responsible?"

"It has to be the young long hunter of the whites, the one at the cave with the Mohawks." Small Turtle looks across at St Georges and nods. "But this one is responsible, he is the reason this white devil killed our people and our Chief."

St Georges leaps to his feet with his face contorting in rage. "Small Turtle lies! Have I not always led the Shawnee to victory over their enemies? Have I not always shared the hardships with my blood brother's, the mighty Shawnee?"

The heavily crowded lodge becomes deathly quiet as every warrior looks to where Small Turtle rises to his feet, pulling his knife. To call a bloody warrior of the Shawnee Nation a liar is the greatest insult that is given. The round gourd of the Elder rattles its warning as the bony fingers of the old Sachem point at both men. "This lodge is sacred; there will be no bloodshed here." The Sachem looks quietly at both men. "Sit down. We have enough problems with this white hunter stalking us without fighting among ourselves."

"Why would Mohawk Warriors travel with a white long hunter? They are enemies," a large warrior they call Tinnaman questions.

"The Mohawk do not travel with the white. The Frenchman takes their Medicine Woman against our advice. They track her to the cave and now they have her back but they may come against the Shawnee for revenge."

"But they did not kill the white," Tinnaman is confused. "Why is this so?"

"They seem to know him," Small Turtle replies, shrugging his shoulders. "But, they let me go free; they do not come to kill Shawnee, only the white long hunter does."

"The Mohawk have what they come after, the woman. Now they will return to their own lands," St Georges speaks up. "Small Turtle saw this white with his own eyes; he is much too young and inexperienced to kill the Black Panther."

Small Turtle smiles coldly. "He may be young Frenchman but you know it was this white that did the killings. He also killed Mad Wolf in single combat with a knife. You saw the fight yourself."

"What happened to Black Panther?" A warrior sitting near the fire speaks up.

"Our Chief Black Panther had eyes for only one of the white women; the tall one with the dark hair that he took captive near the white settlement. He was fascinated with her, blinding our great Chief to the danger around him and the one that followed our trail."

St Georges smiles and looks at the elder. "You see, Stalking Cat, it was not me that got these warriors killed, it was your own Chief. I found the women captives later."

The elder looks back at Small Turtle. "Is this true?"

"That part is true. He did not know of our Chief's death until we watched the women Black Panther took captive enter the settlement fort with this white and one Mohawk warrior."

"Tell us Small Turtle, how does this prove to you that Black Panther and his men are dead?"

Small Turtle looks across at the Elder Shawnee. "Our Chief Black Panther now walks among his ancestors; he would never release the white woman unless he was dead."

"What about the Medicine Woman of the Mohawk?" The Elder's dark eyes turn back to the Frenchman. "Why did you take her? Why did you not leave her as Mad Wolf and Small Turtle told you?"

St Georges shrugs his bulky shoulders. "I don't know, maybe it was her medicine. Maybe she put a spell on me."

"St Georges knows it is against our custom to touch a Medicine person of any tribe, for any reason."

The Frenchman shrugs again. "The whites do not have medicine people. It is not the custom of the whites. If I took this woman back to the Mohawk they would show their gratitude and they would join the Shawnee in our raids on the settlements."

"Perhaps St Georges is right," exclaims Stalking Cat as he looks into the fire spreading his hands. "But now, we must choose another War Chief for our people. Our new war chief will make the decision of what will be done."

"I say we follow this one and the French no more." Small Turtle lunges to his feet. "I have seen the white villages. They are heavily armed and they will destroy us if we continue to raid them."

"Enough." The Elder shook a gourd rattle at the warrior. "You are young yet Small Turtle, too young and inexperienced to have a voice in this council of Elders. We will settle this later after our new Chief is picked."

For two days, Lance lies in his place of concealment, watching as the village turns into a mass of excitement and a craze of hysteria. The elders elect a new chief and then parade him on the shoulders of several warriors through the throng of villagers.

To elect a new war leader is traditional and a good excuse for the Shawnee to celebrate with dancing and feasting for several days. On several occasions, Lance saw the Cherokee and the Delaware celebrate for several days when a new chief begins his reign. The Shawnee are the same. He knows the village will dance and sing throughout the nights to follow. He also knows in the morning after celebrating and feasting all night the people will be exhausted. The village will not wake up early, as was their custom but much later in the day. Touching the hilt of his knife he thinks, perhaps while they are asleep and there are few guards, he can reach the Frenchman.

Chapter 9

Only the lingering smoke from the huge bonfire that the people danced around during the night, showed any sign of life on the quiet village floor as the sun started to rise over the lodges. As Lance figured, the village slept late. No human life, only the village dogs move about the lodges. Hiding his rifle inside a dead stump, he follows the cut-bank of a small creek to the edge of the village. Now will be his best chance at the Frenchman. If St Georges were dead, perhaps it will satisfy his hate and thirst to avenge. Then he will be able to return to the settlements with a clear mind and conscience.

During the long night and noisy celebration, Lance watched the Frenchman enter the same lodge several times. The structure may be a bachelor lodge of some kind, as only young men enter and leave the lodge. After dancing and partaking of the white man's firewater all through the night, they finally pass out.

The sun is beginning to bring new life on the earth as Lance silently slips from lodge to lodge like a ghost. Several minutes later, he works his way to the entranceway of the huge lodge undetected. Pulling a green deer hide from a drying rack, Lance wraps it across his shoulders, then ducks quickly through the door. Several bodies lay scattered about the lodge, some snoring loudly. Lance squats in the darkness of the room letting his eyes become accustomed to the gloom. After his eyes search every face carefully, he cusses; the Frenchman is not in the bachelor quarters. Backing slowly from the lodge, making sure not to wake any of its occupants, Lance drops the deer hide from his shoulders and turns.

"You." St Georges yips in shock and surprise as he recognizes the young white holding a long skinning knife almost at his stomach.

Surprised at the Frenchman's sudden appearance Lance throws himself across the space catching the Frenchman completely off balance as he knocks him into another bark lodge. St Georges yells as he flings himself sideways away from the knife that rips through his hunting shirt. Lance starts to advance on the frantic Frenchman. He then hears the noise of several excited voices coming from the bachelor lodge, as St Georges' frantic yelling alerts its occupants.

"I'll return for you, Frenchman." Lance glares as he spit the words at the cringing St Georges. "You're a dead man."

"Who are you? Why are you trying to kill me?" St Georges regains his composure and yells at the fast disappearing back of Lance. "You're the dead man!"

The Frenchman looks about him nervously, as the sleepy eyed warriors spill drunkenly from the lodge. He breathes a sigh of relief, thankful that no one saw him shrink backwards away from the madman coming at him from the lodge. St Georges is no coward, but he was ashamed that he showed fear. Anyone would be scared, surprised as he was with the white's sudden appearance.

The dark eyes of the warriors follow the Frenchman's trembling finger as he points and waves at the retreating back of the white man. The red puffy eyes of the warriors try to focus on the racing figure. They are in no shape to respond to the demands of the Frenchman, yelling for them to take to the trail of the escaping white.

Small Turtle stands nearby watching, as Lance disappears into the safety of the forest. Smiling, he looks over at the pale face of the Frenchman. He knows the man was scared. He can smell it and he can see the knife cut across the shirt of St Georges. The warrior knows this young white is brave. He comes unafraid and alone into the enemy hunting grounds and then he follows the Frenchman here into the large Shawnee village to kill him. He almost succeeded.

Several of the younger warriors, too young and uninterested in the all-night partying, quickly gather, ready to take the trail of the white. Small Turtle shakes his head sadly. The untried Shawnee, who are planning to take the trail of the white long hunter, are much too young to chase after such a dangerous enemy. If the white should turn on them, they could all perish by his hand. Small Turtle frowns, they will never overtake the white but if they do catch up to him, there will be many more dead Shawnee, thanks again to the Frenchman.

The warrior watches the younger warriors as they race after the white. They disappear out of his sight and then heed the beckoning of their new War Chief as he summons the Elders, along with St Georges and the older warriors to the council lodge.

The older warriors of the tribe elect Tinnaman as their new leader. A white hater and warlike Shawnee, Tinnaman dislikes any tribe or people that do not follow the Shawnee in their wars. A huge warrior, standing head and shoulders above any warrior in the Shawnee Nation, Tinnaman is a half brother to Black Panther. Now, he too has reason to hate the young white that just entered his village unafraid. The same long hunter who, he was told, is responsible for his brother's death.

Small Turtle watches his new Chief as he stares out at the tall forest that surrounds the village. He knows Tinnaman, now with Black Panther's death as an excuse, will listen to the Frenchman and together they will attack the white settlements.

Both Tinnaman and Black Panther are his uncles, but they are only half brothers. He remembers they never were close as brothers usually are. Tinnaman was always jealous of Black Panther's status as War Chief of the Shawnee, but now he will use his death as an excuse to follow the Frenchman against the whites.

"Go," Tinnaman points at the warriors arriving at the council lodge and orders them to go after the white hunter before entering the large lodge. "Bring me this white long hunter back alive."

Small Turtle shakes his head and watches as more young warriors retreat to their lodge to get weapons and a small supply of pemmican. "Small Turtle, my nephew, does not approve?" Tinnaman turns his attention on his nephew.

"The white is more dangerous than an enraged bear, my uncle, and he kills with no feelings." Small Turtle stares across at the new Shawnee Chief. "You are sending these young men to their death."

"He is alone. What could he do against so many warriors?" St Georges growls. "There is always safety in numbers."

"He was right before you Frenchman, on two occasions, yet he still lives." Small Turtle shakes his head in disgust. "You yourself lost many full-grown experienced warriors to this one. Why do you not go with them?

Let us see how brave the French are or do you fear this young white?"

"We need the older warriors to attack the settlements." St Georges glares at the warrior. "I must lead them."

"And perhaps, it is safer here with the older warriors." Small Turtle sneers. "You are a coward Frenchman; I can smell fear on your body."

Knives appear in both men's hands as they went into a crouch ready to lunge. "Enough." Tinnaman steps between the two. "Come, we go to the council lodge. Soon, there will be enough fighting."

"This insult cannot be forgiven, Tinnaman." This time St George has to show courage. Too many heard the heated words of Small Turtle and too many faces are looking at him.

"Small Turtle is young; his words are spoken in haste before he thinks." Tinnaman looks over at his nephew. "You should apologize to our friend and ally, Small Turtle."

St Georges relaxes; the Shawnee Chief already apologized for the young Shawnee who stood wooden faced. He could overlook the insult and not lose face among the warriors. Small Turtle grits his teeth and turns away without a word.

The Shawnee Council Lodge is the biggest in the village, almost four times larger than the bachelor lodge. As Tinnaman enters with the Frenchman and Small turtle following closely behind, the new chief can see the cream of his warriors are already gathering slowly inside the lodge. In less than a few minutes, at least eighty older warriors and elders sat packed about the hide-covered floor.

Small Turtle watches the mood of the gathered warriors change, as the Elders of the tribe work them into a frenzy. With the death of the Black Panther and his warriors while they slept, the men are already in a rage. They thirst for blood against the whites. The same long hunter, who now enters their village, is the same white who the Frenchman said slipped in among them and cut their throats while they slept. St Georges stands off to the side and smiles smugly. He knows now he will have no trouble talking them into taking out their vengeance on the white settlements to the southeast.

Small Turtle has no feelings one way or the other about the whites. He always made war against the English and other tribes that are the enemies of the Shawnee. Fighting his people's enemies is part of the responsibilities of a young warrior. It is something they expect of him. This is no different; he will do as the Elders decide. If they decide to war against the white settlements, he will follow the warlike Tinnaman. Nevertheless, he dislikes St Georges and now he smells fear on the Frenchman. Two days earlier, St Georges ran away and abandoned him back at the cave, where he guarded the Mohawk Medicine Woman. To follow one such as he on the war trail is folly.

Sitting before the council, Tinnaman watches stoically while the Elders whip the warriors into a blind fury. As the yelling and screaming reach a crescendo, the big warrior stands and raises his great arm, hushing the noisy din inside the lodge. Small Turtle saw this same spectacle played out many times before but the sudden deathly silence always makes him blink.

"We will travel to the forts of the whites. We will take captives to trade. We will take their weapons, their children and their spirits. The ones we do not kill will leave our lands forever." The Chief hesitates as he studies the assembly of warriors. "Who will follow Tinnaman? Who strikes the war post with me?"

In a mass exodus from the lodge, the warriors yell their loudest, screaming and dancing like banshees around the blood red post. The Frenchman smiles as he stands next to a frowning Small Turtle.

Looking over at the warrior, he grins wider. "My young friend does not approve?"

"No, but I will do as my people bid me and we will kill many whites." Small Turtle acknowledges, "But, you know as well as I, Frenchman, the whites will never leave our lands. They are like the leaves on a large tree: they are without numbers. Frenchman, from this day forward, I am not your friend."

"So be it, but Small Turtle is a pessimist, we too have many warriors."

"You mean the Shawnee have many warriors," Small Turtle sneers. "I saw many dead Shawnee on the field of war, but I have yet to see a dead Frenchman."

St Georges frowns. "The French have always been a friend of the Shawnee. Why do you talk as you do? Don't we give you everything to make war against your enemies?"

"You supply many weapons, but the Shawnee supply the blood."

"This is your hunting grounds that we protect."

"Whites are all the same. They only bring death to my people." Small Turtle walks away without looking back.

St Georges touches the hilt of his skinning knife, squeezing it until his knuckles turn white. He senses the disgust in the warrior's voice and actions.

He knows the warrior saw fear in his face as the white hunter ran from the village. He knows the Indian, any Indian, can smell fear in a man's sweat and they detest a coward. Shrugging, he turns his attention to where the warriors are dancing around the war post. Who wouldn't show a little fear or surprise? The white comes upon him so unexpectedly, lunging at him with the razor sharp skinning knife. Had he not shown his courage in many battles with the Shawnee?

Small Turtle is a lesser warrior in the Shawnee Warrior Society and he is still young. St Georges knows if he survives long enough, the Shawnee warrior may one day become a great war leader of his people. He is the son of a great warrior who is now too old to take the war trail. He is also nephew to Tinnaman. Small Turtle's father is now an elder of the tribe and one day his son will take his place as a war Chief.

The Frenchman knows Small Turtle has little respect for him and will not follow him blindly against the white settlements, as the others do. Already the young Shawnee is known for his wisdom when he speaks with the calmness he already displayed in numerous battles. If the warrior speaks out strongly against him and the other warriors heed his words, his efforts to wipe out the white settlers of the British could fail. The Shawnee may refuse to follow him. Stroking the wooden handle of his knife a wicked smile comes across the man's face. Perhaps Small Turtle will meet with an accident in the coming days.

Lance races easily through the forest, the ferns and tall grass raking against his legs as he runs. Small limbs and dead leaves snap and crackle under his moccasins as he crosses the virgin timberland, staying well away from the worn game trails. He knows he is leaving a trail a blind man can follow but that is what he wants. He wants the warriors following to be able to trail him easily.

Behind him, he can hear the catcalls of the Shawnee, keeping their positions known to one other as they follow. He knows there is no need for the warriors to worry about losing his trail. They can see his tracks plainly in the soft ground. Spread out in a fanlike pincher behind him, the warriors know it is just a matter of time before they spot their quarry. All he can do is run, staying ahead of them until dark; then he will change direction and lose them.

He knows the Shawnee will think he is racing to the white settlement for safety. They have no idea of his stamina and running ability. Usually they run down their quarry after a few miles. Only a few whites reach safety or lose the red warriors when they are as close to their victim as they are to Lance. It is a game to almost every tribe. They love the chase but the Shawnee love it even more. They take pride in their running ability. Over the years, many captives were turned loose to run for their lives, enabling the young warriors to practice their tracking ability and running stamina during the chase. In their heated pursuit, the young warriors learn to enjoy outrunning and outsmarting the enemy. Very few times the prey slips away from even the youngest of the pursuers.

As the trailing warriors close the distance between them, Lance's face becomes serious. He has no intention of being run down and caught. He also does not intend to run for safety into the settlements and take a chance of losing St Georges trail. No, if they do not overtake him by sundown, he will circle behind them and return to the Shawnee Village. He swore an oath to himself; the Frenchman will die by his hand, even if it means his own death in return. He runs his hand softly over the smooth walnut stock of the rifle. If the young warriors are foolish enough to catch up to him, that will be their mistake.

Lance lopes easily along the flat bottomlands of the valley he is crossing. Occasionally he kneels to scoop up a handful of water from the numerous small streams that cross the meadows. There is no need to try to conceal his tracks or even his presence, nor did he want to. With the soft earth from the last rains and the surprised deer and wildlife he startles, he cannot hide from his pursuers. They know he is ahead. From the sound of their calls, he can tell they already are closing the distance behind him. They are excited and their yips show it. They yell in delight when they get a glimpse of him ahead, darting through the timber.

It is a game to the Shawnee to chase their quarry, anticipating the capture and torture the person would endure; it thrilled them. Lance's father told him the Shawnee and other tribes follow a quarry for days. They follow close behind, tiring a man down until he staggers in his tracks, taking away his courage sometimes making the man babble in fear. Eventually, their quarry will give up in despair, completely broken, knowing the torture they were about to be subject to. When their man is completely exhausted and scared out of his wits, they close in, springing from all sides and beating their foe with their war clubs.

Smiling slightly, Lance listens to their excited voices as they call to one other. On several occasions, he purposely slows down so they can see him ahead, staggering through the heavy timber, as if he is exhausted. The race lasts many hours, covering many miles across valleys, mountains, and streams. The day is almost over. The afternoon sun is slowly setting in the west and soon it will be dark.

Lance looks to the western horizon. When the sun completely disappears, he will turn back to the north and slip through his pursuers. Several times, he spots the Shawnee following him as they race after him like a hound on a rabbit's trail. They are young warriors, not like the experienced older warriors. They will be intent on catching him, not expecting him to turn back on their lines and head north.

Lance's hunting shirt is soaking wet with sweat from his exertions of the long run throughout the day. Slipping the heavy garment over his head, he carefully spreads it out on a limb for the Shawnee to find. Tonight, when the sun goes down and the cold comes, he will miss the warm shirt but wet as it is, it will take hours for the buckskin to dry. Now he intends to travel fast. Leaving the garment in plain sight for the Shawnee to find is just his way of insulting the young warriors.

Concealing his tracks carefully he travels another half mile. He hides his long rifle under a pile of leaves then climbs up into the branches of a huge sycamore tree. Cautiously, he keeps his body concealed behind the wide trunk out of the searching eyes of the warriors. The slightest movement high up in the sycamore will quickly focus the sharp-eyed Shawnee immediately on him. The sun lowers slowly, leaving the heavy foliaged tree in darkness.

Hiding in the heavy leaf covered limbs that camouflage his presence from the warriors, Lance watches as the Shawnee pass beneath him in a steady ground-eating trot. Only his blue eyes move as he scans the dim forest floor counting eight warriors. He knows there could possibly be more Shawnee trailing him but eight are all he spots from his vantage point. He is right, they are all young men, some even younger than he is. Waiting several minutes, after the warriors pass, Lance slips quietly back to the ground and retrieves his rifle. He watches for a few minutes longer before turning back to the north.

Being cautious, he makes sure he leaves no sign for the warriors to find in case they double back. Lance searches out a small cave just large enough to fit into and then inches his feet first into the opening. Pulling a pile of brush in behind him, he checks the valley floor then relaxes. He was running all day covering many miles; he has to rest. Tomorrow he will return to the village and waylay the Frenchman somehow.

The floor of the cave has a deep covering of sand and blown leaves. He rakes as much of the dead leaves and sand as he can, on his bare torso, to ward off the chill of the night. He takes one final survey of the woods in the valley below him, before drifting off into a much-needed sleep.

Chapter 10

Otter's leg is healing and it becomes stronger every day but at times, the slightest strain can cause him pain. He is far from home. The land he now crosses, both red and white men inhabit, either one could be hostile to a lone Mohawk far from his hunting range. At last, his spirit lifts, as he is free of the confines of the crowded white settlement. He can now travel to his own village and the warmth of his family and lodge.

The whites fed and treated him as a welcome guest. Even the hostile ones finally take to his laughing, good spirits and happy-go-lucky smile. The Doctor's medicine was strong, healing his wounded leg, almost as good as the Mohawk Medicine Man could have. Now, after two weeks at the white fort and another week on the trail, he is at last heading home to his people. He will travel slowly, using caution not to run into any hunters or raiders that may inhabit these mountains. He is still lame, if discovered he would not be able to outdistance the slowest of enemies.

The Otter is young and healthy and with every mile he travels, his leg grows stronger and has less pain. Cold is once again here; it is the time of the falling leaves and the beginning of the crisp frosty mornings. Soon the heavier snows of winter will fall in earnest covering the forest, making it harder to hide his tracks and more dangerous for a lone hunter to travel alone. The young Mohawk knows the danger of hurrying and accidentally running into hostile hunters, either red or white.

Mohawk lands lay due north and east. The warlike Shawnee and Seneca are between his village and the area where he travels. Otter is enjoying his journey through this wild and dangerous country; subsisting on rabbits and squirrels that he brings down with his bow.

The meaty hind leg of a swamp rabbit almost touches his lips when the unmistakable sound of a voice carries across the flat bottom where he stops to rest. Otter falls quickly to the ground and slips silently into the heavy underbrush. He crawls forward until he sees the long line of warriors making their way south along the same trail he is traveling as he heads north. His mind races to his passage, did he kept his presence hidden or did he accidentally leave a sign of his passing?

Shawnee! Otter can see the distinctive markings and headdresses of the Shawnee Tribe. Then his eyes widens as he spots the Frenchman, St Georges trotting along effortlessly at the front of the warriors. A tall, large-framed warrior is in front of the white man, leading the war party. "Tinnaman!" Otter exclaims softly.

There is little doubt, with the warrior Tinnaman leading them; this is a raiding party, heading south to strike the whites. Which fort are they going to attack? Otter knows when they reach the banks of the Delaware River, they could turn in several directions and each path will lead to a different settlement.

Otter has no way of knowing Tinnaman was elected to replace his brother Black Panther as war leader of the Shawnee; nor did he know the Elders elected to follow St Georges advice and attack the white settlements along the Delaware. The young Mohawk's village is far away from the Shawnee. Ravenhair, his tribal chief and the Elders of the tribe, keep them apart from the other warring tribes. He knows little of the fighting between the French and British, nor does he know of the French's desire to control the tribes and the Ohio Country.

Chewing slowly on the rabbit, Otter watches as the last of the war party passes from sight, then flips the bones away. Rising slowly, he studies the surrounding forest for any more of the Shawnee before trying to decide what course to take. Should he go to his village or return to the settlement called Frasier, to warn the whites?

Finally, he decides to follow the warriors to the south, keeping well off to the side of the trail. He will travel as far as the Delaware River to determine which settlement Tinnaman will attack first. The whites or their forts meant nothing to him, but the faces of the white girls and the way they took care of him keeps flashing before him. There may be at least one hundred Shawnee warriors and he also counts six French white men in the party. If the fort where the girls are staying suffers a surprise attack, they could all be killed. Otter could not let this happen. He will follow and see which fort Tinnaman intends as his first target. If the Shawnee turn away from Frasier, then he will return to his homeland and his village. If their target is Frasier then he will go on to warn them.

With the fast pace the war party is traveling, they will reach the river quickly. They are no further than three days away. Otter's leg still pains him some, but he has no choice, he will have to keep up with the hard traveling Shawnee. Otter is curious; no other tribes from the federation are going to the war trail with Tinnaman. Usually, there are two or three different tribes brought together for a big raid so there will be plenty of fighters. Perhaps others will join him at the big river that lay ahead.

Otter's attention is focusing on the warriors ahead. He fails to see the warrior slipping through the heavy timber to his rear. Whirling at the last moment, Otter pulls his war axe and skinning knife and prepares to defend himself as Blue Elk steps from behind a large Cedar Tree.

"Ah, my brother," Otter let out a sigh of relief. "You startled me, what do you do here?"

"Looking for the Otter, who has grown slow and careless to let us get behind him so easily." Blue Elk smiles, "We followed you many miles."

"We?" Otter sees Satia standing alone and silent behind the Cedar. "What happened, my friend. Why is she here?"

"We come to find you, then we travel north to the land of our brothers, the Ojibwa."

A frown comes over the face of Otter as he looks at the girl then back at Blue Elk. "Where is Ravenhair? Does he know you intend to take our Medicine Woman to the Northland?"

"He knows she is with me, but I do not know where he is." Blue Elk shrugs. "We slipped away from him as he slept."

"This could cause much trouble for the Mohawk People." Otter looks again at the girl, "perhaps for you, Blue Elk."

"What happened to your leg?" Blue Elks asks.

"A Shawnee arrow," Otter looks down at the bandage that was dirty and ragged on his long trek from the settlements.

"Why would a Shawnee attack a Mohawk?"

"As you know, I was leading the whites back to the South and their fort," Otter explains. "The one that shot the arrow will not shoot anymore arrows."

Blue Elk looks into the warrior's dark eyes. "Did you kill him?"

"No, the young white hunter, the one they call Hawkins killed them."

"Where is he?"

"After leaving us at the white fort he heads to the north, back to the land of the Shawnee."

Blue Elk nods. "He still follows the Frenchman, St Georges."

"You have seen him?"

"Ravenhair and I found him as he killed Mad Wolf, the Shawnee."

"Did you look into his eyes? They are vacant as a clear sky. He only thinks of revenge for his dead people." Otter looks off to the south. "Maybe he has lost his mind. I see nothing in his eyes except the look of death. This one feels nothing and fears nothing, neither death nor torture. He just thinks of killing the Frenchman and the Shawnee and now you say he killed Mad Wolf."

"Why, with your leg hurt do you follow the Shawnee and French on their war trail?" Blue Elk looks off to the south.

"I follow the Shawnee only to the big river to see which way the Frenchman and the Shawnee warriors travel."

"Again they attack the fort at the place the whites call Bacon's Crossing."

"Why will they go there?" Otter questioning, "The fort where I left the white women is closer."

"Perhaps, but a Shawnee warrior named Small Turtle told my father Ravenhair, the Frenchman St Georges hates the whites at Bacon's Crossing and wishes to kill them all."

"Why does he hate these whites so?"

Blue Elk shrugs. "I do not know this thing but I do not think this Shawnee would lie."

"Then the white women will be safe at the Frasier Settlement?"

"Perhaps, but if St Georges is successful at the first settlement, he will attack Frasier on his way back north to Shawnee Lands."

"Tinnaman is with the Frenchman."

"Tinnaman!" Blue Elk tenses. "He is a dangerous warrior; crazy and mean."

"He is not like the Black Panther. He lives only to kill the whites." Otter agrees. "Also he is sly like the fox."

"Not only does he kill the whites, my friend." Blue Elk turns keen eyes again to the South. "He kills any who are his enemies."

"I go now," Otter replies.

Blue Elk looks at the girl and nods. "We will go with you."

"Satia must be returned to our people," Otter states as he looks back at the girl. "She must not be put in danger."

"Satia is my woman now. She is no longer the Medicine Woman of the Mohawk."

"This cannot be. You cannot do this thing, my friend." Otter looks across at Satia. "Think of our people. They will sicken and die without her."

"Come, we go," Blue Elk said as he looks hard at Otter. "We will speak no more of this woman."

Otter looks over at the girl. "Satia, have you lost your love for our people?"

The young woman only shrugs then turns her gaze from him as Blue Elk speaks. "She has spoken."

"Why do you go with me Blue Elk? You have no liking for the white's at the settlements?"

"Satia sees the Shawnee attack the white people in her dreams. She wishes that we help the white women that were kind to her."

Otter agrees, "We will follow, but when we find out where the Shawnee go and the white women are safe, then you will take Satia to safety."

Blue Elk nods then takes the lead to the south following the trail where they last saw the Shawnee.

Lance wades for almost two hours and several miles, in the cold waters of a small creek that meanders to the north, after leaving the cave. He left the Shawnee far behind as they passed earlier underneath the tall Sycamore without an upward glance they lost his trail. Backtracking, they discover where he climbed the tree. With dark coming, they wait until morning to trail him to the cave.

Finally, coming to the small creek in the early morning they lost his trail completely. Mostly young with little inexperience, they argue among themselves. They give up in disgust and turn in the direction they know the raiding party will take on their way south. They will waste no more time on this lone white. They will rejoin the warriors heading south. The warriors are young. They want to be in on the raid and fight the whites, to make a name for themselves.

Emerging from the cold water, Lance changes into the extra dry moccasins he carries. He then heads north, towards the Shawnee Village with renewed energy after the good night's rest in the cave. The face of the Frenchman flashes before him several times, as he approaches the village.

Again, slipping silently into the same hiding place he found on his first sighting of the village, Lance crawls quietly under the overhanging shrubs and grass. Scanning the village carefully, he is stunned and surprised at the absence of any full-grown warriors among the villagers. Only old men and boys stroll about the village. Squaws are busy working over their cooking fires or scraping on deer hides preparing clothes for their men.

After watching the village from his place of concealment for two hours, Lance knows the warriors are gone. He returns too late, the Frenchman once again escapes and they are all gone. Where did they go; he has to find out. He will wait until full dark and then slip into the village.

He ran from the village before the war party formed. He knows the Frenchman is probably leading the Shawnee south, against the white settlements but first he has to be sure. If he hunts for their trail, he could probably find it quickly. He wants to find out their intentions, if he can, before following a blind trail. He needs a hostage, someone to tell him exactly where the warriors are and what direction they took upon departing the village.

Lance blinks in surprise, as a young woman carrying a water jug walks towards the clear running stream that borders the village. Listening to her happy singing Lance smiles slightly, he knows she holds the answers he seeks. With the stealth of a stalking cougar, he glides silently through the tall trees of the valley slipping closer and closer to the unsuspecting girl. She is young but Lance has no compulsion in forcing the information he wants from her but if need be, he will kill. The settlements depend on him to warn them. The girl may be of some use, maybe she knows where the warriors are heading. Unknowingly, she has fallen into his hands. He touches the long knife, as he is thinking she will talk or die.

She appears small to him as she bends down to fill her earthen jug from the cold stream. Stepping quietly behind her, to prevent her from crying out or trying to run, Lance waits until she pulls the jug from the water and turns to face him. Shock, surprise and perhaps a little fear shows on the smooth brown face but to her credit, the girl never tries to flee or call out a warning to the village.

"You need not fear, little one," Lance said stepping closer, "I mean you no harm."

"You are the Shawnee killer." The girl asks with fright, "What do you want with me, are you a woman killer too?"

"Where have the warriors gone?"

"You are the white killer our warriors followed from the village yesterday."

"I am. Now tell me. Where is the Frenchman?"

She watches as his fingers close around the knife. "The Frenchman leads them to the south."

"Where to the south did they go, which white village?"

The girl shrugs as she moves the heavy water jug in her hands. "This I do not know; I am but a squaw."

Her dark eyes follow his hand as Lance pulls the knife from its sheath. "Tell me!"

She points to the main trail heading south. "They went there. This is all I know. Kill me if you must, white dog."

Lance studies her eyes for several seconds, then turns suddenly and disappears into the dense forest. He knows she could warn the village but who would follow him, the old men or the boys? No, there is no one left in the village to cause him concern.

Chapter 11

The war party travels in single file, their shaved heads bobbing up and down, as they trot quietly along the forest trail. Almost ghostlike, they pass silently past where Blue Elk lay camouflaged beneath a pile of brush. They are close to the big river, their turning point, depending on which settlement they meant to attack first. No words pass between the warriors; none are needed. They know their voices can carry far in the silent bottoms and they know what to do. Blue Elk blinks his eyes; if his eyes did not spot the warriors, his ears would have betrayed him.

Blue Elk's blood races through his body. The urge to run and go raid the whites with the Shawnee is strong but there is always another day. He did give Otter his word. Today the whites are safe, today the Shawnee are his enemy. He will go with his friend to the white settlement. He will take Satia and turn back towards the Seneca lands.

Thinking of the look Otter gave him upon seeing the woman, Blue Elk blushes as the blood going up his neck makes him turn darker. He knows he is doing wrong. The girl should be with her people but his love for her is strong. He also knows wherever he goes, he will always be an outcast because of his actions. Even his father, Ravenhair, will be against him now. He wonders, when Satia is safe, will his friend Otter challenge him?

Otter with the tired girl find Blue Elk waiting for them farther up on the trail. Blue Elk can see she is exhausted, her face is drawn and her moccasins are worn almost through. His eyes took in the disheveled girl and the crippled foot. Her entire life the tribe pampers her so she never knows unhappiness or hunger. His heartaches as he looks at her, is it worth it?

"She cannot travel further, my friend," Otter said looking back where the girl collapsed.

Kneeling beside the girl, Blue Elk starts to reach out to her but the strange look in her eyes made him drop his hand. Something in the last few days comes between them. He did not know what she thought or felt, perhaps he never did. Satia is always quiet, using her powers to translate her wishes to him. Now, she will not even look directly into his eyes.

"Otter is right, she needs rest." Blue Elk rises and steps back from the quiet girl. "And you're leg has begun to bleed again."

"In the dark, I ran into a sharp limb and reinjured it." Otter nods. "It is nothing."

Blue Elk turns his eyes, from one to the other and then places his hand on Otter's shoulder. "I have done our people a great wrong. She knows it and now I know it. If we return her now, all will be as it once was, no one need know."

"A wrong can be made right," Otter agrees with his friend. "What will we do?"

"Neither of you can travel fast enough to keep up with the Shawnee." Blue Elk drops his hand. "You will return Satia safely to her people."

"What about the white girls?" Otter asks.

"I give Otter my word. I will go to the white settlement and warn the whites the Shawnee are coming to raid their settlements."

"Blue Elk has never lied to me." Otter nods, "nor I to you, my friend, I will take Satia home."

"Be careful Otter, this land holds many enemies."

"She will be safe." Otter looks over at the girl. "Our people depend on her."

Removing his brave heart charm from around his neck, he slips it gently around Satia's neck. Alarmed, she looks at the good luck piece and shakes her head. "Wear it always and remember me to our people." Blue Elk nods at Otter and turns to the south in a fast trot, never turning or looking back.

A quiet sob comes from Satia.

"What is wrong woman?" Otter asks.

"He will not return from this journey." The sad eyes of the girl follow the disappearing back of the warrior. "Neither I, nor his people will see him again in this life."

Otter follows her eyes and then helps Satia to her feet. "Perhaps you are wrong this time." He knows the Medicine Woman's predictions are never wrong; she is the Medicine Woman. Her powers to foresee the future cannot be false but perhaps, this one time.

"No, he will not come back." She shakes her head. "The Mohawk lost a great warrior."

"We go." Otter shivers uncontrollably as he looks into the deep brooding eyes.

The broad Delaware River flows smoothly and softly down the great valley of the mountains. The water is emerald clear, showing the small rocks that lay beneath its surface, covering the bottom of the riverbed. Along its banks, Tinnaman and his warriors gather in a group, staring across the wide expanse of water.

St Georges steps beside the tall warrior and waves at the river. "It's shallow; no more than three feet deep here at most."

"We will cross and turn east."

"East?" St Georges turns on the Chief. "We're headed for Bacons. East will take us to Frasier."

"We will attack the nearest white fort first and then we will go on to the others."

The Frenchman looks disgustedly out across the Delaware. "Our plans were to go to Bacons."

"I have spoken. We will attack Frasier first." Tinnaman glares at the Frenchman and then waves his hand to start across the river. "We go."

After leaving Otter and Satia, Blue Elk travels at a hard pace finally catching up to the vanguard of the Shawnee War Party as they reach the banks of the great river. From a good place of concealment, he watches as Tinnaman and the Frenchman stood on the banks and motion at the water. He thought they were arguing but he could not be sure because their faces turn away as they wade into the water.

Looking up and down the river, Blue Elk searches for a place he can cross so no one will spot him in the open water. The Delaware is wide and straight at this point. It makes it almost impossible to stay out of sight of probing eyes if one of the warriors happens to look back over his shoulder. Blue Elk slips into the river as the Shawnee left the Delaware and head to the east, their backs turned to him. He knows they are heading for the place the whites call Frasier, it is the closest to the east. The white settlement where Otter said he left the white women.

He needs to cross fast and hurry on to the white fort if he is to keep his promise to Otter and save the women. Blue Elk hates the taste in his mouth. He has no wish to warn the whites and turn against his own kind. Nevertheless, he did give his word to Otter; he will keep his promise to help the women if he can reach them in time.

Lance's powerful legs carry him in a long lope, along the same trail the Shawnee War party took only hours ahead of him. He is gaining on the raiders, but his mind only focuses on the Frenchman. St Georges is becoming an obsession with him. His mind pictures the man's cruel face and his thoughts put strength into his efforts to catch up. It is as if the hate in him fuels his legs, making them run on without tiring. His lungs and legs seem to work in tandem as he traverses the valleys and mountain trails, never slowing from the fast pace.

He cannot understand the Frenchman; he is white. How can a white man lead the cruel, heathen Shawnee against other whites, then watch while they murder and torture people in their own homes. Unknowingly, Lance's knuckles turn white as they grip the stock of the rifle as if they are choking the life from the Frenchman. St Georges will pay, if it is the last thing he ever does; he will pay.

Blue Elk exits the great river and turns east, his great stride takes him quickly to the rear of the Shawnee column. He has no fear of the warriors ahead discovering him. Their attention is focusing ahead, eager to attack the white settlement. Skirting far to the side of the long line of warriors, Blue Elk races onward towards Frasier as if the devil himself was in pursuit. He has to reach the fort in time for the whites to gather themselves and prepare a defense. The war parties he was with were always successful when surprise was on their side. The whites are brave men and good fighters. If the warriors know they are aware of their presence and are ready to fight, they would veer off to another settlement. War leaders like Tinnaman do not want to lose men by attacking fully armed settlements that are on the alert. Blue Elk was on raids where the raiders turned back without lifting a scalp because of a bad omen or because the whites were forewarned and were ready to defend their fort.

War leaders, such as Tinnaman, know they will lose prestige with the tribe if too many warriors are killed while on a raid. They fear this as they fear nothing else. Maybe the warriors will not follow them on the next raid. Maybe they will no longer be Chief, something a proud man like Tinnaman could never tolerate.

Frasier's Settlement stands less than a hundred yards across the open field where Blue Elk stands, gazing into the open gates. Everything seems peaceful and calm, no alarm sounds. The whites are unaware that danger lurks just minutes behind him. He wonders if the whites will shoot their long rifles at a lone Indian coming towards them. The Mohawk calls out in a loud voice as he starts across the open field.

"It's the Indian coming back. Something must be wrong." Benjamin McDowell heard Blue Elk's call and hollers down from his place beside the gate. "Get Tracy Trent."

Blue Elk trots quickly towards the gate as several of the settlers start gathering outside as word of his appearance spread. Walking the last few feet slowly, Blue Elk studies the faces before him.

Tracy Trent and Iona step forward and look hard at the warrior, recognizing him. "It's not the Otter, it's another Mohawk, named Blue Elk."

"What does he want?" McDowell steps forward.

"Can't say, but he keeps looking back; he's bound to have something on his mind." Tracy looks around for Angus Hale. "Where's Mister Hale?"

"Here I am." The old hunter steps forward beside Tracy.

The old hunter listens closely as Blue Elk speaks in his guttural tongue. "According to this warrior, we got real trouble coming close behind him, Benjamin."

"You trust him, Angus?"

"I do." Tracy looks across at Blue Elk. "He is a friend of the Otter."

"He says the Shawnee have a large body of warriors and several French coming this way right on his tail." Hale looks over his shoulder at the near timber. "Mister McDowell, you better pass the word; we best fort up."

"Sound the bell," McDowell yells at one of the men. "Close the gates and make sure the water barrels are full."

Hale translates as Blue Elk speaks quickly to Tracy. "The Mohawk says to bring all the men, older boys, and women out front carrying rifles and let the Shawnee see them. He thinks they might turn aside to another Fort that hasn't been warned."

McDowell looks around as the bell began to sound and toll out its summons for the settlers to hurry to the fort. "Alright, sounds like it might work."

"He says to hurry, they are near." Hale looks at the Mohawk curiously.

St Georges stares out from the woods in disbelief, cussing under his breath when he finds Frasier's Hollow armed and ready for the attack. Somehow, someone is warning them that a raid is coming. A body of armed men stood in formation; ready to engage the Shawnee should they appear.

Suddenly the large bell hanging in the stockade starts ringing out, sounding its alarm for everyone in the valley to hear. Within minutes, while the Frenchman and Tinnaman watch in disbelief, several wagons loaded with people from the outlying homesteads, along with two-wheel carts, horseback riders, and people on foot start converging on the palisades from every direction. The Frenchman glares, his face turning crimson as he watches as the armed men form into a skirmish line in front of the gates then start forward towards them.

Tinnaman stands looking out across the open flat, his face a mask of consternation. This is his first raid on the white settlements as War Chief of the Shawnee. He has to have victory to secure his place as Chief. The huge arm of the Chief rises in the air preparing to order the attack.

"It will be suicide to send our warriors out into the open against that many guns," St Georges argues. "We must go and leave this place as we found it."

Tinnaman growls deep in his chest. "I will lose face if I retreat without bloodshed."

"If you attack, my Chief, you will lose many men," St Georges argues, "these whites are deadly with their long rifles."

"What would you have me do, Frenchman?"

"Leave this place and move on to another." St Georges suddenly became interested in something near the gates. "Look Tinnaman, that is Blue Elk of the Mohawk with the whites."

Tinnaman's dark eyes seek out the Mohawk. "You are right, it is the son of Ravenhair. Why is he with the whites?"

"This I do not know but it seems he warned the stockade and has betrayed us."

Tinnaman lowers his great arm and turns. "This is bad medicine; you are right, we go."

"You are wise, my Chief." St Georges agrees as he tries to smooth over Tinnaman's rage. "We will attack another settlement and fight another day."

"Wise? No Frenchman, a wise man would not have come this far without sending out scouts first." Tinnaman turns once more to look at the fort. "Nor would a wise man trust a Mohawk; something I will never do again."

Angus Hale yelps in glee as he watches the last of the Shawnee trot out of sight and retreat towards the Delaware. "We fooled them boys, we sure did. Those red buggers didn't know we were fixing to retreat back inside the walls."

Blue Elk eases silently through the deep woods, his eyes following the tracks of the raiding party. He did as he promised; he saved the white women. Now he will return home to face the judgment of his people. He could go alone to the Ojibwa people but he knows that is the coward's way out. He took Satia; he would not live as an outcast. He will return to his village and face his punishment and Ravenhair, his father.

He lost her. It matters little to him what happens now but he would not be shamed or called a coward, never. First, he will follow the raiding party to make sure it is no trap and to make sure they will not return to the white fort at Frasier and catch them again by surprise. Blue Elk has little respect for the whites, except their accuracy with the long rifle. To him they are like children, always forgetting the danger of the frontier, then paying the price with their lives.

After traveling in a ground-eating trot for two days, Lance arrives near the crossing of the Delaware. He is just in time to see the Shawnee pass along a single game trail only yards below where he waits. He knows they are returning from the direction of the settlement at Frasier. None of the warriors appears hurt and there are no captives or blood covering them.

He is so close he can see the frown on the face of the huge warrior that leads the column. Apparently, something went wrong since there was no attack. Now the column pads west towards Bacons. It is only a guess on his part but there was advanced warning at Frasier somehow because they were ready. His skin tingles as he studies the cruel face of the Frenchman who follows closely behind the warrior that leads the column.

"With your long rifle you could kill the Frenchman from here." Blue Elk somehow senses Lance's presence and slips quietly behind him.

Whirling, Lance relaxes as he recognizes the Mohawk. "You! What is Blue Elk doing here so far from your village?"

"The Otter asked me to see that the women were safe."

"Are they?"

Blue Elk nods. "They are safe at the white fort."

"Why didn't the Shawnee attack Frasier?"

"The whites were ready." Blue Elk looks off towards the trail. "The Shawnee are not fools; they will not attack and lose many warriors."

"You warned the settlement?"

"I gave Otter my word; no harm will come to the women."

Lance nods. "For this I thank you. How is the Otter's leg?"

"He grows stronger, but he still wasn't well enough to come this far to warn the fort." Blue Elk looks at the young white saying nothing of Satia. "What will you do now?"

"I will kill the Frenchman."

"There are many with him."

"It will only take one bullet."

Blue Elk looks into the hollow eyes of Lance. "Then why didn't you kill him now? I have seen the white gun speak death from far away."

"I do not wish him dead quickly." Lance fingers his father's skinning knife. "He will die but it will be a slow death."

"Is he more important than the white people at Bacons?" Blue Elk questions, "Or has your hate and taste for blood blinded you, white man? Are you thirsty for more blood as the women said?"

"What do you mean blinded me?"

"For Tinnaman to save face he must attack somewhere, he must have captives to keep his warriors happy."

"Bacons?" Lance looks off down the trail. "He will attack Bacons."

"It is less than two days away. Tinnaman will rest his warriors tonight, then travel through the next day and attack early in the morning."

"Blue Elk is right; I have been blind with hate, the Frenchman can wait." Lance frowns, he did not want to let St Georges escape, but he has to warn the settlers at Bacon's Crossing that the Shawnee are coming.

"What will you do?"

"Will Blue Elk help me one more time?"

The warrior thought of the Mohawk village and Satia then shrugs. "Blue Elk is dead anyway. What do you wish?"

"Are you sure Tinnaman will rest tonight?"

"Yes, he will not attack at night." Blue Elk nods. "His warriors have traveled a long way. They must have rest and food the same as us."

"You say the people at Frasier know you." Lance asks as he picks up a straight stick then wipes a clean spot on the ground. "Does Blue Elk know the place the white's call the Devil's Hill near Bacons?"

"I know of this place." The Mohawk places his finger on the place Lance points to. "A small stream runs at the base of it."

"I want you to return to Frasier and bring all the men they can muster to this place as fast as you can."

"What will Hawkins do?"

"I will travel through the night and bring the fighters from Bacons to this place before the night falls again."

"We will have the Shawnee caught between us, if we hurry." Blue Elk nods. "It is a good plan."

"Will Blue Elk fight against the Shawnee?" Lance questions the warrior.

"Blue Elk will bring the whites but I didn't say I would fight."

"Fair enough," Lance nods. "I'll see you at the Hill."

"Blue Elk will keep his word."

"Thank you my friend."

"Friend?" Blue Elk looks puzzled at the young white.

Lance smiles. "For what you have done this day, from now on we're brothers and friends." Blue Elk seems to blush. "Stay wide of the Shawnee; they will have scouts out on their flanks."

"Thanks to you, my brother, I am no longer blind." Lance smiles. "I will be careful."

Lance passes the strung out raiding party early in the afternoon with no one noticing him. Traveling steadily, he knows he can reach Bacons before sun up early the next morning. Lance's long legs carry him through the night, bringing him outside Bacon's Crossing two hours before daylight.

Banging on the first wooden door he comes to, Lance can hear the sleepy voice of someone stirring around inside the house. Slowly, a firing port opens and a voice sounds from inside.

"Who are you? What do you want?"

"It's Lance Hawkins, Mister Johnson."

"Glory be, Lance Hawkins!" The door swings wide open as a short man clad in a long nightshirt and cap step out onto the porch, squinting at the tall figure that looms before him in the dark. "Gads lad, we about gave up on you being alive."

"I'm alive, sir." Lance steps closer to the door. "We've got to hurry now, or we might not be."

"What's wrong Lance?"

"There's no time to explain." Lance looks across the dark settlement. "Saddle your horse and spread the alarm. Get every man here as fast as you can."

"Injuns!" The little man squeaks, "Not again."

"They're close Mister Johnson, we've got to hurry."

"I'll sound the bell."

Lance grabs an arm as the man starts around him. "No, they'll hear it! We've got to be quiet and surprise them."

"What'll you do, Lad?"

"I'll start spreading the alarm here." Lance turns. "We'll have the women and children fort up inside the stockade, just in case they get past us."

"That's a good idea." Johnson agrees. "I'll go bring 'em in right away."

"Hurry Mister Johnson," Lance exclaims as he steps clear of the door. "We've got very little time."

Chapter 12

Bacon's Crossing fills up quickly as news of the impending raid spreads among the inhabitants. Every man able to walk helps spread the alarm and then hustles their families inside the stockade. No one dare shirk their duties; they know the punishment will be severe. When summoned, each man knows to immediately drop whatever he is doing and hurry to the stockade, armed to the teeth. There are penalties for not coming on the run when the bell rings, the wooden stock or several lashes with the whip.

Lance stands off to one side with Samuel Wilson and Ben Thompson, the leaders of Bacon's Crossing, watching the stockade fill with men, women, children, and their assortment of dogs, horses, and cattle. The commotion is making a noisy din inside the stockade, as barking dogs, braying mules, and children running about underfoot. The yelling men and women in their haste trying to corral the children, only adds to the confusion.

A tall figure limps slowly to where the men are talking. "Lance Hawkins, is it really you?"

"Lucas!" Lance steps forward and bear hugs the thin figure of his brother. "I thought you had gone under."

"Pert near, it was touch and go for a spell." Lucas smiles, "Those heathens dang near done me in for sure, but Miss Piffle and the good doctor pulled me through."

"I can't believe it, Lucas." Lance holds his older brother at arm's length looking at him embarrassed. "I should never have left you back at the farm."

"You did what you had to do, brother." Lucas shrugs his bony shoulders and smiles. "Were you able to find the girls?"

"I did, brother. They're safe at Frasier's Hollow." Lance thought Lucas would faint as the news sinks into his thin frame.

"Safe? How did you do it?"

"There's no time now to explain." Lance turns back to the two men. "We'll talk when this is over."

"I'm here to help."

"I know, but you're still too weak to travel fast."

"What do you want us to do, Lance?" Wilson interrupts the family reunion.

"We'll take half the men and leave half to protect the Fort." Lance stares through the dimness at the two leaders.

"Is that wise?" Thompson is doubtful. "Should we leave the safety of the stockade?"

"I've got men from Frasier coming up behind the Shawnee." Lance nods, then motions with his finger in a cutting motion across his throat. "We'll set our trap and be ready for the red heathens at Devil's Hill, when they start across Acorn Creek."

"You mean we'll have them in a trap?" Wilson agrees with a smile, "Between both forces and out in the middle of that miserable creek."

"We will, providing the men from Frasier get here in time."

"And if they don't?" Thompson rubs his chin.

"We'll be on our own." Lance looks over at the man. "If things go bad, we'll retreat back here to the stockade."

"You think we got'em, Lad?" Wilson looks over at the tall youth he watched grow up around Bacon's Crossing but the man before him changed. "You're certain."

"I'm dead certain." Lance nods. "It'll be a total surprise if we hurry."

"We've heard things here from other hunters. We've heard about the Shawnee being killed so mysteriously." Thompson looks at the bloody and tattered buckskins. "Now I see why. We'll follow you, Lance Hawkins."

Lance turns to Lucas and helps him back to a seat beside one of the houses. "We'll talk when I return brother, then I'll go bring the girls home."

"You do that, brother." Lucas sits down weakly. "I wish I could go with you."

Turning, Lance almost bumps into the small figure of Piffle Wilson standing just behind him.

"Piffle, it's good to see you."

The bright blue eyes took in the bloody buckskin shirt and the thin frame before her. "Lance, you're alive."

"Miss Piffle, I'm alive. I want to thank you for helping Lucas."

"He's your brother Lance and I would do anything for you."

"I must go now, Piffle but I'll return."

They call the place Devil's Hill for the treacherous terrain it covers. The trail leading up and over the small but dangerous divide is rough. However, is easy compared to the crossing at the small creek that flows swiftly through huge boulders at the bottom of the steep hill. With the arrival of the settlers years ago on the banks of the raging creek, many days of cold water and hard backbreaking labor was spent clearing a road through the rocks. In the spring, the creek is a mad rushing torrent. In the summer with the clearing of the boulders, the road is passable for the heavy wagons coming west.

Rocks, loose gravel, and deep gorges from heavy rains over the years cover the length of the hill. With no other way around or over the mountain, travelers have to navigate the trail or travel many days to another crossing of the creek. Lance knows the Shawnee; the creek will be no problem for strong warriors on the war trail. They are familiar with crossing rough water so he knows they will cross at the base of Devils Hill.

Dispersing his thirty men and boys in the deep ravines that line both sides of the creek, Lance nods absently. The trap is ready, now all the Shawnee have to do is walk into the cold water. His hands flex in anticipation causing the muscles in his forearms to bunch under the ragged hunting shirt.

The ambush he lays for the raiders is perfect, almost foolproof providing the Shawnee do not smell a trap. Now all he has to do is bide his time and hope the Shawnee do not sniff them out with their uncanny sense of danger. If the men from Frasier arrive in time, it could become a complete rout. At this rough crossing, few of the raiders if any will be able to escape their rifles.

The Shawnee are courageous warriors poorly arming themselves with the trade muskets of the French. His men have the long rifles of the colonies and they are expert marksmen, the best on the frontier. If they are lucky, they will catch the warrior's waist deep in the water as they cross the creek.

The men from Bacons wait quietly, not daring to move or slap at the terrible flies swarming in hordes about their faces, biting into their exposed flesh. To add misery to their predicament, even the nighttime mosquitoes buzz about the waiting men.

Lance's palms sweat slightly where he holds the long rifle. Not from fear as in most cases. No, he relishes the thought of meeting the warriors in combat. The thought of the Frenchman standing before him is what makes them sweat; he grips the rifle in anticipation. His dark eyes and ears strain to their breaking point as he tries his utmost to see or hear the enemy approaching.

Blue Elk leads the small party of settler's in a slow trot following the path of the Shawnee ahead of them. The whites are not the long hunter's he fought against in the past. No, these are farmers and merchants, men who take the trail only to strike a blow against the hated Shawnee. He was surprised the whites followed him into the forest. Some argue it could be a trap, a trick to lure them into the open and leave the fort undefended.

Tracy Trent comes to his assistance, shaming the men for cowards if they do not go with Blue Elk after he saved the fort from the raiders. Finally, the cooler heads prevail and thirty-five men follow him towards Bacons leaving the remainder to guard the stockade.

The men are not the hardy warriors of the Shawnee or Mohawk; still they travel well, keeping up with his pace until they come upon the fresh trail of the raiders. Seeing the tracks the whites become eager, hungry to catch up with the warriors, mete out the punishment, and to avenge for the past killings and savage attacks.

Blue Elk nods in understanding as he watches the cold, hard faces of these men. Now he understands they will never drive the whites from their lands. Unlike the Indian, these people cover the ground like locusts, multiplying quickly. In addition, they are strong warriors, equal to the red men; he knows they are here to stay. Not even with all the warriors from the Shawnee and Mohawk Nations combined; they will never be strong enough to run them from their hunting grounds. Ravenhair was right to keep his people far from the white settlements; to fight the whites would be the end of the Mohawk Nation.

Once he thought to abandon the whites after showing the trail of the Shawnee, not now. These whites are to be trusted, perhaps it is time for the Mohawk to become allies with the English and abandon the French who are forever pushing them into war. Blue Elk kneels and studies the fresh tracks of the raiders.

"How far ahead are they?" Phillip McKay looks over the shoulder of the warrior as another white interprets his question in the guttural speech of the Mohawk.

Blue Elk studies this white man as he speaks, surprised the man can speak so fluently in his native tongue.

"I am Isaac Kenton." The man can see the warrior's interest.

"Tell him we are less than a short run behind the warriors." Blue Elk shrugs. "Tell him the place where the one called Hawkins is waiting, will be reached soon."

"Will we reach Devils Hill in time to help the others?"

"We will hurry now and come up close behind the Shawnee but not close enough to give them alarm."

Lance senses the raiders before he sees the long column, then suddenly they appear in plain sight. The warriors stop to congregate on the top of the hill and study the swift running creek before starting their descent down. The Frenchman leading the column, moves quickly ahead haranguing the Shawnee to hurry, cross the creek, and attack the fort before someone discovers them.

"Let them get into the water before we open fire." Lance whispers, then the word passed up and down the waiting men.

"They're stopping." Johnson touches Lance's arm and whispers back. Lance watches as Tinnaman holds up his huge arm stopping the line of warriors. Nodding his head the great war chief motions at two warriors then points across the water. If the warrior's discover the Bacon men, the trap he laid was useless. Having to cross the rough water, the Shawnee will be stopped alright but the complete route of the raiders will not be as he figures, most would be able to retreat back over the ridge.

Fording the creek, the two warriors step out onto dry ground, the water dripping from their legs as they survey the surrounding terrain.

The Bacon men hide well, clinging tightly to the ground, in hopes no one discovers them. Only Lance's eyes move as he watches the two Shawnee start slowly towards them, their noses seem to sniff the air. The two reminds him of a pair of hunting dogs testing the wind. Lance recognizes Small Turtle as one of the lead scouts.

Less than twenty feet from where the whites huddle in the ravine, the warriors stop and look back to where Tinnaman and the Frenchman wait expectantly. Suddenly Small Turtle throws up his arm in warning and points at the ridge high on the hilltop.

Lance follows the man's finger and grins as several rifles fire a rain of death and destruction down on the Shawnee. He aims dead center on the

Frenchman as he darts forward trying to get away from the deadly fire from above. Lance swears as a warrior jumps in front of St Georges taking the bullet that was intended for the Frenchman.

Rifle bursts roar from the ravines as the men from Bacons join the fray causing the Shawnee to bolt in every direction. Bodies line the creek banks as others float quickly down the flowing water. Lance reloads several times, firing quickly at the fleeing Shawnee. Unable to locate the Frenchman, he let his smoking rifle rest.

Bacon men watch in awe as Lance rises from his place of concealment and rushes forward, slashing at the Shawnee warriors with his war axe and knife. They were in fights with the Indian warriors before, but no one ever witnesses anything as brutal and fast as they stood transfixed, their eyes unbelieving. Several red men fell before the crazed white before the rest flee with Tinnaman and make their escape. Lance kicks at a dead limb in a rage cussing himself for letting the Frenchman slip through his fingers again. The man is like a cat with ten lives.

Blue Elk appears at his shoulder and studies the hard face of the young long hunter. "The Frenchman and Tinnaman run towards the east when the rifles begin to speak."

"I saw Tinnaman, not St Georges." Lance looks down at Small Turtle. "This one won't kill anymore, where did you see him last?"

"I see them both." Blue Elk nods. "They go there." The long finger points at a rough ridge covered with scrub timber, heavy brush, boulders, thistles and bunch grass. Almost impenetrable, only a few animals run through it, mostly rabbits. Lance starts forward as Blue Elk takes his arm.

"If you go in there, they will be waiting for you." The dark eyes look up the hill. "You will die."

"I'm going."

Blue Elk shrugs. "If your wish is to die, then go but if you die the Frenchman will live, you will not have the revenge you seek."

Lance knows Blue Elk speaks the truth; still it chagrined him to let St Georges escape once more. "What will Blue Elk do?"

The warrior looks around at the dead bodies. "Tinnaman loses face with his warriors; he led them into a trap and lost many. If his people allow him to still be their Chief he will seek revenge against this place. If you wish your people to be safe from his revenge, he must be killed."

"How?"

"We will circle to the north and intercept him on his way back to the

Shawnee Village. Some of his warriors are wounded, they must travel slowly, and Tinnaman will not leave them behind. We will overtake them."

"Blue Elk is going with me?"

"I must go, Tinnaman watched as I led the whites down the hill." Blue Elk nods. "If I do not kill him, he will attack my people the same as the whites."

The two groups of fighters from Bacons and Frasier settlements gather on the banks of the small creek and shake hands. The whites take only one casualty in the short battle and it was not from enemy fire. One man wounded himself when he tripped charging down the hill and fell on his own knife.

The leaders from both forts gather around Lance and Blue Elk as they emerge from the woods. Patting the two men on their backs as they approach, they praise them for their leadership and courage. Lance is surprised; the older men look at him with deep respect, as if he is their leader.

"Let's take in after them heathens and finish those buggers off." Eli Johnson yells encouragement at the men. Lance looks over at Johnson as he harangued the men from Frasier and shakes his head. "No sir, Blue Elk and I already discussed that."

"Then what will we do?"

"We'll head back to Bacons and resupply our powder and shot, then you men from Frasier head home and protect your people."

"What about the Shawnee?"

"Blue Elk and I will go after them." Lance looks at the man. "The rest of you need to protect your families."

"You're a thinking they'll be back, ain't you?" Another settler speaks up.

"Blue Elk thinks so and that's good enough for me." Lance looks over at the warrior. "They've taken a whipping here but their pride's been hurt bad."

"An Indian can't stand to lose face." Another man replies looking at Blue Elk. "He's played fair with us so far, I'll do as he suggests."

"If ya'll are going after those Shawnee, I'll be going with you." Isaac Kenton speaks up.

Lance looks at the big hunter. "You must have an axe to grind?"

"I have, with that renegade St George, the Frenchman that was with them red sons." Kenton swears softly, "but mainly with Tinnaman the Shawnee."

"Alright, we'll be glad to have you." Lance nods. "Let's go get supplies and get on their trail."

Bacons is a stir with excitement as the men approach the closed stockade. Cheering and hand clapping rang out, as the gates swing open to welcome the men as returning conquerors.

"You boys get yourself some food and supplies and we'll be heading out quick." Lance looks over the settlement then walks to where Lucas sits beneath a porch.

"We'll be ready." Kenton shakes his head.

Lance approaches to where his brother is rising painfully to his feet. "How are you, Lucas?"

"I'm mending, little brother." The thin man limps slowly to the edge of the porch. "Slow, but I'm getting there."

"Brother, I'm glad you're alive." Lance sits down easily. "Awfully glad."

"I should be going out with you."

Lance nods. "You are with me Lucas, every step of the way. You've taught me all I know."

"The men buried the folks beneath the big cottonwood tree near the orchard." Lucas nods towards the far orchard. "Then the Wilson's took me in and cared for me."

"That's good of them."

"The girls?" Lucas worries as he looks over at Lance. "Are they okay, they weren't harmed?"

"They're all fine. Like I said, I'll bring them here when I return."

"You're going out again, I reckon?"

"I'm going; the Frenchman responsible for our folk's death is still alive."

"St Georges?"

"I aim to kill him Lucas, I have to." Lance looks away from the prying eyes of his brother. "I have to."

"Don't let hate engulf you, little brother." Lucas Hawkins almost did not recognize the brother sitting before him. He can feel the coldness; Lance seems old, older and harder than the men that run the forest, hard as an iron bar. "Don't let the taste for blood ruin your whole life."

"I aim to kill that rogue, then I'm gonna take me a bath in his blood." Pure hate emits from his blue eyes. "My life brother, if you haven't noticed, is already ruined."

"Lance, he ain't worth it."

"Are you saying Ma and Pa aren't worth revenging?" Lance stares hard at his brother. "Say it Lucas. Is that what you mean?"

"You know that's not what I'm saying." Lucas shakes his head; he cannot believe this is the fun loving younger brother he used to know. "But they wouldn't want you to turn renegade yourself."

"I already have, brother."

Lucas changes the subject. Somehow, he knows the brother he once knew no longer existed. "Okay brother, just bring the girls and yourself back safe."

"We'll be back."

"And you, little brother." Lucas touches Lance's shoulder. "We still ain't killed that old grizzly that keeps destroying our traps."

Just for a fleeting moment, a smile comes across the haggard face, a smile Lucas remembers and then it quickly vanishes.

Lucas stands propped up against the wooden gates as the two white men and one Indian trot quickly back towards the river crossing and towards Frasier's Settlement. Several men stand nearby watching the retreating figures. "Well, I for one wouldn't want him on my trail."

"Amen to that, brother." Another speaks up. "I've never seen anything as bloody and ferocious as he was today."

"Did you see his face?"

Eli Johnson nods. "I seen it and I'll remember it for the rest of my life."

From his place beside the palisade gates Lucas listens to the men and shakes his head sorrowfully. Perhaps the brother he knows and loves will never return to him.

Chapter 13

Tracy Trent looks over, shocked at the bloody scarecrow of Lance as he enters the small cabin's doorway she and the girls share at Frasier's Settlement. Lifting Iona and May Lynn from the floor, he hugs them to him almost squeezing them too hard. Tracy can see he has grown haggard and worn, thinner and even bloodier than when she saw him last.

Except for the brief instant, he greets the girls as he hugs them and he shows no emotion. The haunting look out of his eyes is blank, nothing showing, only the wild almost insane look of a bloodthirsty hunter. She saw the look in other men before, after their people were massacred. It almost makes her shiver to look at the young man she knows so well. To her he appears to have grown in height and width, heavier through the shoulders and chest. However, there is no warmth in him, nothing only coldness.

"Your brother Lucas is alive and waiting for us at Bacons." He hugs both of his sisters again. "When I return we'll go get him and return to our farm."

"Lucas is alive!" Both girls yelled at once. "He is for a fact." Lance tries to grin. "You'll see him soon."

"I want you to give this foolishness up and take us home, Lance." Tracy glares at him, "Now!"

"I can't." The eyes bore into the girl he knew so well, the girl he hoped one day would be his wife. "Tracy, this will be over soon, I'll be back, and then we will go back to Bacons."

"Your folks and little brother are dead, the same as mine are, there's no bringing them back."

"You're a woman, this is a man thing." Lance looks from one girl to the other. "You just don't understand."

"Don't I, Mister Hawkins? Look at you. You're covered in blood." Her eyes bore into his. "You're not going because it's your duty, you're going because you have to kill, you've grown to like killing, you like the taste of blood!"

"That's enough, Tracy." Lance steps towards her causing Iona and May Lynn to cringe back in fright.

"Enough! What are you going to do, kill me too?"

"I said I'll be back."

"If you leave, don't bother coming back." Tracy clenches her fist. "I won't be here when you get back."

Lance looks over at his two sisters. "You two stay put until I return."

He suddenly notices Piffle Wilson standing in the doorway listening to the exchange of words. How did she get here from Bacons? Stepping back as he walks through the door she reaches out and takes his arm.

"You go, Lance. I'll be here when you come home." Piffle smiles softly and looks over to where Tracy stands fuming. "No matter how long it takes."

"Piffle, what are you doing here at Frasier?"

"Pa needed supplies of powder and lead after the fight, we followed you here in our wagon with some other men."

"Tell your Pa to be careful on your way back to Bacons."

"We will but he said we'd have to wait here for the supply wagons to come." Her hand touches his sleeve as she smiles.

Lance shakes his head slightly confused at her sudden forwardness. She is a little younger than he is, he never thought of her rather than a friend. Tipping his head, he nods as he walks away. Blue Elk follows Lance from the stockade at an easy trot. He witnessed the words between the white woman and the young hunter. He has no way of knowing what they were saying but he knows the tall dark haired woman was upset about something. Isaac Kenton stands and joins them as they pass by where he sat resting beneath a tall oak.

"I about gave up on you two." The big hunter notices the dark scowl on Lance's face. "I must have missed something back there."

"No, you didn't miss a thing." Lance glances back towards the stockade. "Nothing at all."

Piffle leans back against the log wall of the porch as Tracy and the girls exit the room. Tracy catches the slight start of a smile just as she reaches the girl.

"He's yours, Piffle Wilson, if you want him so bad." Tracy stops and glares at the girl. "But you better remove that silly grin from your face now."

"I know he's mine, Tracy. He always has been." She nods, "and I think you just made it final. He's a lot of man or hadn't you noticed?"

"I noticed." Tracy balled her fist. "I also noticed he's become a crazed killer, lusting for blood."

Piffle shakes her head sadly. "You don't believe that Tracy, any more than I do."

With Iona and May Lynn in tow, Tracy whirls and leaves Piffle behind. "You should have slapped her, Tracy."

"No, May Lynn. We're supposed to be ladies. We're a little old to be having schoolyard fights. Don't you think?"

The younger sister frowns as she looks back to where Piffle stands watching them. "I guess, but she deserved a good slap."

"No, it's me that deserves the slap."

"Tracy, what for? You didn't do anything."

"You'll understand someday, May Lynn. I promise."

Blue Elk has no problem picking up the trail of Tinnaman and the Raiders as they travel north back in the direction of the far-off Shawnee Lands. Occasionally, the warrior finds blood spots scattered along the path, showing some of the warriors are badly wounded. Drag tracks on the ground show where some of them are being supported as they walk.

Blue Elk nods. "Many are hurt. We will overtake them soon." Lance thinks back to what Tracy said about not being there and shakes his head. He is not the killer that she believes he is, he just wants this over but killing the Frenchman is something he has to finish. He promised it over his mother's dead body, he swore and nothing will change his mind. He hopes they find the Shawnee Chief and St Georges soon, very soon.

"Is the Frenchman still with Tinnaman?" Isaac Kenton studies the ground for signs then looks across to where Blue Elk watches.

"I see the tracks of many white men with Tinnaman." Blue Elk shrugs his broad shoulders. "I do not know if St Georges is with them."

"He's with Tinnaman, he will go back to the Shawnee and try to get them to raid the settlements again." Lance heads on not waiting for an answer.

"The warriors will cross the big river and then they will bear off towards Blue Mountain."

Lance nods. "Blue Elk is right; Tinnaman will take to the mountains. He cannot take a chance on being discovered this close to the white hunting grounds with his wounded."

Tracy Trent watches angrily as Isaac Kenton and Blue Elk follow Lance along the dirt path that leads back towards Bacons and the Delaware River. Her face quivers slightly making her turn away from the girls. She warned him that she would not be at Frasier when he returns.

"I'm going back home." She looks again out the stockade gates as she speaks to the girls fighting to hold back the tears. "I'm not waiting, he's plain crazy."

Iona looks at her curiously. "You mean home to Bacons?"

"Yes, are you two coming?"

"But Lance told us to remain here and don't forget the Shawnee are out there somewhere." May Lynn argues.

"Don't you want to go see your brother Lucas?"

Iona nods her head. "Yes, but we don't even know the way."

Tracy looks about her. "I'll get Shawn Brady to lead us home."

"But Lance said to stay here." May Lynn repeats herself. "Why don't we wait and travel with Mister Wilson when they return to Bacons?"

"I won't go anywhere with Piffle Wilson." Tracy shakes her head. "I'm leaving now."

"It'll be okay, little sister." Iona pulls at May Lynn's arm. "When he returns we will have our homes cleaned up and ready for him."

"I don't know Iona, the Shawnee."

Tracy turns on the girls. "You heard the men say they whipped the Shawnee good and sent them packing back north."

"I would like to see Lucas and the other people at Bacons." May Lynn finally gives in.

"Good. Then I'll find Shawn and we'll prepare to leave." Tracy walks away.

"Lance is gonna kill us all." May Lynn agrees to go, but she is still not convinced. "I don't think we should go, at least we should wait for Mister Wilson."

"We are going, May Lynn." Iona pulls together their meager possessions.

Both Wilson and McDowell argue with Tracy against her decision to leave the protection of Frasier until they are blue in the face. Both are dead set against the girls leaving the safety of the stockade but Tracy insists she is going. Both men know she is a strong willed girl. They know that once she makes up her mind, there is no changing it.

Shawn Brady and another long hunter agree after several refusals to lead them home to Bacons. Both hunters return from a hunting trip and assure Tracy the Shawnee are whipped. They did not see any signs of Indians but they still have reservations about escorting the girls to Bacons. Early next morning, McDowell shakes his head sadly as he watches the small party disappear into the forest.

"They'll never make it."

"Shawn Brady is a good man."

"Yes sir, Mister McDowell he is but he is only one man." Wilson agrees. "I have a very bad feeling about this whole affair."

St Georges and the three Frenchmen that survived the ambush at Devil's Hill sit huddling about their small fire watching the hind leg of a small deer sizzle.

"That was a fine mess we walked into." One of the French pokes at the fire. "We lost three good fighters for nothing."

St Georges nods slowly. "The young white hunter who tried to kill me is responsible."

"Why does this one follow you?"

"We raided two farms outside of Bacons, killing many settlers there. I figure he is related to them. We never saw him but apparently, he followed us when we retreated to the north with our captives. Somehow he slipped in and killed the Black Panther, his warriors, and took the three white women we took captive."

"So now he hungers for your hair huh, mon amie?"

"He almost got it twice now."

"He was at the ambush?" Sergeant Boyer looks strangely at St Georges. "I saw him holding back his fire; he was searching for something or someone."

St Georges nods. "He was there alright, I saw him and it was me he was searching out."

"This one sounds like a dangerous enemy to have against you." Another Frenchman speaks up, "Very dangerous."

"He is dangerous. It's as if he has a magic charm protecting him."

"You surely don't believe that nonsense like the heathens do?" Boyer laughs.

"No," St Georges shakes his head. "I don't believe in charms or evil spirits."

"Perhaps my friend, you have been out here too long." Another laughs jokingly.

St Georges looks at the man seriously. "Yes, we have been here many years but we are still white men, who do not believe in silly nonsense like spirits. The Shawnee do and we need their help."

"What will we do then?"

"We will not go back with the Shawnee. It will do no good until I can prove to them I have killed this young long hunter and the Mohawk that is helping him." St Georges punches at the small flame. "The Shawnee are superstitious pagans. Now with the Black Panther dead, they will not dare go against the settlements until we can prove he has been killed."

"Where do we find this Englishman?" Another Frenchman asks.

St Georges smiles like a wolf over a kill. "We will return to Frasier. I saw the tall, raven-haired woman standing by the gate when Tinnaman detoured to Bacons. They thought they were disguised in their men's clothes but it was her alright. Her beauty and her thick dark hair cannot be hidden by clothes."

"Why do you want this woman? There are many women out here." The Frenchman laughs.

"I think she is his woman, he protects her too well." St Georges nods. "Where she is, he will be close. If I have her, he will come to me like a lamb to slaughter."

"Perhaps you are right." The Frenchman looks closely at St Georges. "Are you sure you don't want her for yourself?"

St Georges glares at the speaker as he stands. "I will tell Tinnaman our plans and where we go and then we will return to Frasier for this woman."

"The Chief must take Jean with him, he is hurt too bad to travel with us."

St Georges agrees, "I will pay him well to see after our friend and get him back safely."

One of the Frenchmen shakes his head. "It is sad mon amie, these are our allies but we have to pay them for everything."

"Yes, if we pay them, they will be sure to get him back safely and they will stay on our side."

"You do not trust these Shawnee either, my friend." Boyer frowns. "Do you think they would go over to the English?"

St Georges looks at the Sergeant without answering then rises and walks slowly to where Tinnaman sat beside the fire. The Frenchman knows he has to be careful and form his words well. The Shawnee War Chief is in a killing mood, he lost his brother and many men and he has many wounded. The slightest word could set him off.

Chapter 14

Two days later, unknown to Lance, his party passes St Georges and the two French regulars with him less than a quarter mile on another game trail heading back for Frasier's Settlement. Blue Elk is following the trail of the Shawnee, not realizing the French turned back to the south. As they pass on different trails, neither party is aware of each other's presence.

Lance and Isaac survey the forest with eagle eyes as they follow Blue Elk, as his full attention centers on the track of the Shawnee. Tinnaman, his warriors, and their wounded are close, almost near enough to smell them. Blue Elk promises they will come upon the raiders before another sun comes and goes. The wounded have to rest, to continue without rest would kill them.

Late in the afternoon, almost at sundown, Blue Elk cautions Lance with a wave of his hand, then motions him forward. Tinnaman and the raiders are near; he can smell the smoke of their campfire.

Tinnaman paces the camp like a caged cougar, his sharp eyes going repeatedly to the silent forest that surrounds them. He does not want to stop but some of his warriors and a Frenchman are badly wounded. Too weak to travel further, they could die unless he makes camp and lets them regain their strength. He lost too many to refuse rest to the wounded and race on to the north would show cowardice.

The War Chief is already on shaky ground as his warriors are in a dark mood because of losing so many. Tinnaman knows even a war chief such as he could be killed if the warriors sense fear in him. However, since St Georges and his men left to return to Frasier, the big warrior senses something is wrong. Nothing shows that someone is following them. However, the forest about him is too quiet, too eerie, and something or someone else travels the woods, perhaps stalking them at this very moment.

The others scoff at their Chief's worry, thinking he is acting like an old woman. Nevertheless, as they make camp, the warriors become nervous as they wonder who is out there. Tinnaman wanted the French to stay with them at least until they got the wounded home but St Georges insisted on going back after the dark haired woman. The same woman his brother, the Black Panther, died because of her. The war chief has a bad feeling; this is an omen from the spirits.

His mind races, he knows little of the whites. He has heard the tales of whites burning their own women at the stake further to the north, perhaps this dark haired woman is what the whites called a witch. Maybe she put a curse on the French; maybe even now she lurks out in the dark waiting to drink of his blood. The Shawnee burns captives but not their own women.

Tinnaman has a cold chill run down his spine as he stares into the darkness. His superstitious Indian nature would not let him dismiss his thoughts of the woman. Tinnaman is a great and fearless leader but no mortal man can stand against the spirits. He lost Black Panther, then he lost the great battle, and now something tugs at him from the darkness. He wants to run, to flee the woods but his pride holds him back. He cannot abandon his wounded; he will not, to do so would be his end.

Maybe the Frenchman is right. If the young, white, long hunter dies, maybe the Great Spirit will once again smile on the Shawnee and give them strength against the whites. For some reason, this long hunter is following St Georges trail and because he follows, this may be the reason why the Shawnee are losing many men. Perhaps, this one has great magic; the spirits seem to smile on him. Tinnaman does not want St Georges to go back after the woman but maybe he is right. The white hunter has to die and the woman will be the bait.

Lance and the others kneel silently in the darkness and study the small fire and the warriors lying about it. Their eyes follow Tinnaman as he paces the camp.

"This one who walks is Tinnaman, brother of the Black Panther, the warrior you killed many days ago." Blue Elk whispers quietly in the dark.

Lance nods. "I saw him once at the Shawnee village when they elected him Chief and then again in the battle."

"I know who he is." Isaac growls from where he kneels. "He is the one that led the raiding party that killed my wife."

Blue Elk looks over at the long hunter with curiosity. "You have come here to kill Tinnaman because of your woman?"

Isaac pulls open his shirt to reveal a long scar across his chest. "Many moons ago the Shawnee attacked a party of travelers and killed many men and women. My wife, my children are all dead because of this one. I was wounded severely, so I crawled into the thickets like a coward and waited for them to leave. Now I have finally found him."

"There are no Frenchmen down there." Lance searches the camp. "Where are they?"

Blue Elk counts the warriors that sat or laid about the camp. Eight warriors not counting several wounded were all that was left of a war party of eighty or more. Blue Elk shakes his head, there were many killed back at Devil's Hill but he did not think so many. As Lance does, he too wonders where the Frenchmen are.

"They must have split from the others." Isaac counts the warriors himself. "There should be more Shawnee."

"We killed many at Devil's Hill." Lance is also studying the camp.

"We did not kill that many." Isaac put in.

Blue Elk agrees, "In smaller parties they are harder to track, that is why they split up."

Suddenly, without saying a word, Isaac stands and steps forward in full view of the warriors around the fire. Shocked, the Shawnee rise to their feet and draw back slightly as he approaches. Lance and Blue Elk follow only feet behind him. Tinnaman stands in front of his wounded warriors; his feet spread wide and his right arm brandishes his great war axe. His eyes went first to the huge white man that stands before him only yards away, next he focuses on the Mohawk, then the younger white.

"You!" the Shawnee Chief looks directly at Lance in shock. "You are the one that follows the Frenchman!"

"I am the one." Lance steps beside Isaac. "Where is he?"

Tinnaman looks at the young white incredulously, for one so young to come forward in plain sight of so many enemies. What was this white, a phantom spirit that could defy the might of the Shawnee? First killing the great Black Panther, then coming into the village after the Frenchman, the battle where so many perish, now here, coming into the Shawnee enemy camp unafraid, with so few. Could one so young be a spirit person?

"He has gone; he seeks the dark haired, white woman." Tinnaman shuffles his feet nervously. "The Frenchman says she is your woman."

Sensing the unease in their chief, the other warriors step back hesitantly. The Shawnee are a brave and noble enemy fearing nothing. Years of teachings by their tribal medicine men make the warriors fear the unknown.

"You are but two white men." Tinnaman steps forward his great war axe swinging a wide arc as he regains his composure. "You are not spirits and we are many."

"No, but you soon will be a spirit, Tinnaman." Isaac steps forward brandishing his war axe. "Fight me and your warriors can all go from this place in peace, even the wounded."

"You are the great long hunter, Simon Kenton." Tinnaman looks across at Isaac. "I know you, white man."

"You are wrong, Shawnee. I am Isaac Kenton, the brother of Simon."

Regaining his confidence he lost when seeing the whites materialize from nowhere, Tinnaman steps forward to meet the big hunter.

"First, tell me white man. What have I done for you to wish my life?" Tinnaman was curious, he knew Simon Kenton. All the tribes know the great hunter but this one he has never heard of.

"You killed them all."

"Who do you speak of?" Tinnaman laughs. "I have killed many."

"My woman, my children," Isaac states as he steps closer to the fire, "at Salt Flats on the trace."

"I remember the place, we killed many that day." Tinnaman sneers again and looks to where Blue Elk stands. "And you Mohawk, why do you join these weak whites against your brothers?"

"I have given my word to help these long hunters."

"Then you will die after I kill this one." Tinnaman steps forward. "I will feed your flesh to the buzzards."

The sun was setting as the two giants clash with a shrill ringing of their war axes. They come together as the failing sunlight filters through the branches of the mighty oaks; the fighters struggle in the light of the fire. The two men are both powerfully built, strong as bulls and both possess the courage of the mighty grizzly. The two fighters are the pride of manhood in strength and courage from both red and white races.

The Frenchman travels in a mile-eating trot back towards Frasier's Settlement. The young white is on his mind. St Georges knows the long hunter has luck running on his side, several times now he managed to surprise and ruin his plans. The white has to die, before the Shawnee and other tribes became scared and refuse to go to war against the white settlements. St Georges has no idea where the man is. He did not have the time to run him down yet somehow this young white will have to be lead into a trap. How could he know the raid on a few settlers would bring this hot head after him? He kills the great Black Panther and his warriors, travels into enemy hunting grounds, and even comes alone to the Shawnee village.

Never, in all the years St Georges has been fighting on the frontier, has he known fear like this young long hunter made him feel back in the village. The white must die. He will use the girl as bait and then St Georges will kill him and erase his shame. St Georges lived with the Shawnee for many years; perhaps Boyer is right, maybe he is getting as superstitious as the Indians are.

The girl at Frasier is the quickest way to find him and maybe the only way to coax the long hunter into his trap. The white came after her before; he will come after her again. The Frenchman wants to lead the Shawnee against the white settlements soon, before the great snows but he knows this white has to die first before Tinnaman can take up the war trail again.

Shawn Brady and another white dressed in greasy buckskins lead the three girls along the rough road leading to Bacon's Crossing. The morning was clear and crisp as they wave good-bye to Wilson, Johnson, McDowell and a few others at the stockade gate.

"I wish you girls would reconsider and wait at least until spring." McDowell looks down into the firm face of Tracy. "This is a very dangerous time to travel with the Shawnee out and all."

"We have been here too long already." Tracy looks to where Iona and May Lynn waited. "The girls want to go home."

"We can't spare any men to go along with you, Lass." Johnson looks over at Brady. "You should wait until Wilson and his party returns home."

"Don't worry Mister Johnson; we'll get'em there." The tall lean hunter grins through a shaggy beard.

McDowell looks over at the two scouts and warns them. "You know if you go through with this and anything happens, Lance Hawkins will be on your trail quicker than you can blink."

The taller man grins even broader. "Uh huh, we know."

Piffle Wilson and her father shake their heads sadly, as the small party disappears down the wilderness road that leads to Bacons and out of sight of the settlement at Frasier.

"They should have waited." Piffle looks up.

"A few days wouldn't have mattered," her father said.

A day's hard walk from Frasier, the Frenchman holds up his hand and crouches beside the wilderness road that grew up from lack of use. Nothing stirs as his grey eyes survey the surrounding woods and underbrush that line the winding, lonely trail that the settlers call a road.

Rough-cut stumps stand silently, their quietness telling the story of the hastily hewed out thoroughfare, as the settlers made their way into the hunting grounds of the Shawnee. They finally found their way down into the flat, rich valley where the stockade now stands.

Normally the sandy road is covered in wild flowers, fern, and tall green grass that grow abundantly along the trace. Now, fall is in the air and the first frost of the year killed out the sweet aroma of the flowers and turned the grass brown. St Georges knows this country like the back of his hand. The stockade rests in a large valley less than a days walk to the west. By morning, he will be outside the stockade hiding and then he will have to find a way to lure her into his hands.

Shawn Brady leads the small group, his sharp eyes missing nothing as he moves down the road. Tracy and the girls follow in single file as the other white man, Louis Springer, guards the rear. Tracy worries, Lance was never this careless; he would never let them be so visible or vulnerable on the trail as they are now.

Picking up her pace, Tracy touches the man's fringed sleeve and stops him. "I'm worried Mister Brady, we're walking down this road in plain sight of anyone who might be hiding in the brush."

"Now Lass," Brady laughs lightly. "Don't you fret; old Brady will get you there safely. Besides, we've sent them heathens back home with their tails between their legs, didn't we?"

Tracy is doubtful, then falls back to walk several yards behind the man. She does not like it, neither one of the men seem the least bit worried or afraid of being ambushed. Brady is too sure of himself; she should have listened to the men back at the stockade instead of going off half-cocked and mad at Lance as she did.

A shiver goes up her spine, as fear starts to penetrate her mind, sending cold chills clear up into her hairline. She is not completely sure Brady is wrong but she is scared for Iona and May Lynn. The two men either are complete fools or dead sure of themselves. If anything happens to the girls, she would never forgive herself for getting them into this mess and she knows Lance would hate her for life. Slowing her pace, she let Iona catch up to her.

Taking the girl by the hand, she pretends to be helping Iona walk. "If I say run Iona, you duck into the woods and hide. Now slip back and tell May Lynn the same thing."

Iona looks about the woods her eyes as big as a frightened doe. "Why Tracy, why should we run?"

"You just be ready, if I yell do it and stay hidden. Then make your way back to Frasier quick as you can." Tracy grasps her hand in a strong grip. "Do you understand?"

"I understand." Iona nods. "What about you, Tracy?"

"I'll be with you. Now tell May Lynn to stay alert and ready to run like the wind."

St Georges kneels beside the wagon road and stares in disbelief. His mouth wide open in surprise, as the white man leads the same girl he is coming after, down the middle of the road in broad daylight as if he is going to a Sunday social. He cannot believe his luck. He and his men along with a single Shawnee tracker intersect the road almost halfway between the two settlements. They were waiting for the warrior to scout out the road when the two men with the women between them come walking right into his sights.

Resting his rifle softly on a branch, the Frenchman takes careful aim on one of the men's chest. Squeezing lightly he hears the roar and then feels the recoil against his shoulder. Looking through the smoke, he can plainly see the white man is down. Blinking, he watches as one of his French soldiers charges the other white, only to be cut down by the long rifle the man holds.

Tracy screams, "run" as soon as the rifle roars and watches as Iona and May Lynn race behind Brady and disappear into the woods. She was right; that feeling as if they were walking into a trap, they were just too exposed. The lone Shawnee, one of the attackers, is preoccupied with cutting the man

St Georges shot to pieces and taking his rifle, he never looked up as the girls fled.

St Georges looks through the dark smoke of the rifle and stands up. Two of the girls and one white man disappear right before his eyes. He should have waited to let them get closer. No matter, with the Shawnee tracker they will not get far.

Curiously, the dark eyed girl does not try to flee; she stands where she was as he approaches. He admires her spunk; he knows she is trying to give the others time to hide.

"Well Mademoiselle, we meet again." The Frenchman smiles, "I have come looking for you and you walk right into my arms for the second time."

"I assure you Sir, I had no intention of seeing you ever again." Tracy glares at the man. Her face fills with hate, "You call yourself a civilized, white man?"

"Yes, I am white but not civilized." The Frenchman waves his hands about the road as the others gather around Tracy. "This country took anything civilized out of me."

The Shawnee walks up and speaks to St Georges. "I will follow the others."

"No, let them go back to Frasier and warn the settlement." St Georges changes his mind.

"You wish to warn them, Sir?" One of the other Frenchman looks at him in surprise. "May I ask why?"

"Not necessarily to warn them, Sergeant Boyer." St Georges looks at the girl. "I want them left alive so they can return to Frasier. That way the young long hunter will know we have his woman."

"I am not his woman."

St Georges looks at the girl and smiles. "Maybe not but he's covered a lot of miles and killed a lot of men getting you back."

"I don't blame him, Sir." One of the men laughs and moves closer to Tracy. "She's a mighty, pert, looking young thing."

"He didn't kill for me, Frenchman," her dark eyes blazing. "You killed his folks and burned down his home. It's you he comes after."

"You mean the farms near Bacon's Crossing?" St Georges is curious. "That's what this is all about. What's his name?"

Tracy averts her eyes and refuses to answer his question. The Shawnee lifts the bloody scalp of Stringer and holds it in front of her face.

"I've seen scalps before." Tracy pushes the scalp away.

"What's his name, girl?" St Georges steps closer to Tracy and touches her smooth face.

Pushing his hand loose, she spits in his face. "You'll find out when he kills you."

Sergeant Boyer steps forward. "She may not be his woman Sir but she's sure protecting him."

Wiping his face, the Frenchman smiles evilly, "No, now she's my woman, but only after I kill the young white."

"You'll never kill him, Frenchman."

St Georges whirls, his face crimson. "We go, you'll tell in time."

"Where are we headed?"

"There," the Frenchman points due west and north.

"Why there's nothing out there but mountains and a forest full of heathen Indians," another Frenchman adds.

"Exactly what I want, he'll follow us there. We'll be sure to leave a trail he can't miss." St Georges speaks to the Shawnee. "We'll have him out there alone, just us and him."

"You sure that's what you want, Frenchman? He'll have you out there all alone." Tracy laughs slightly. "Why don't you just wait here for him and save us all a long walk, maybe you're afraid."

The slap resounds throughout the clearing causing Tracy to land hard on the ground. The strong hand of St George rips at her dress as she tries to rise.

"One more word girl and I'll forget I am civilized." He shakes with rage as he releases his hold on her. Even the thought of someone thinking him a coward sends the Frenchman into a rage. "Not one more word girl or I swear I'll turn you over to these men and the Shawnee."

Tracy shudders, as she looks at the leering, lust filled faces of the men around her. For the first time she is scared; the Frenchman means what he says.

Brady watches from where he and the girls lay hiding far back in the woods as St Georges knocks Tracy to the ground. His hand tightens around his rifle but he knows he has to protect the two sisters. To try and fight would be complete folly and could get all the girls recaptured. He was a fool. He should have known better than to travel the road so carelessly but he knew the Shawnee were beaten and retreating back to their villages. Brady did not figure in the Frenchman. He knows St Georges and what he is capable of but he thought St Georges was with the Shawnee.

Brady watches as the French, along with their prisoner, follow the Shawnee warrior due north. St Georges turns once and looks directly to where he is hiding behind a dense cedar tree. Too far to make eye contact, Brady can almost feel the dark eyes of the Frenchman feeling his hiding place out. The man appears to smile and wave before disappearing from his sight. Returning to where the girls are hiding, he hurries them towards Frasier in a slow trot. He still can almost feel the Frenchman's eyes boring into him, laughing at him. Why did he want Brady to know the direction he took away from Frasier? Brady cusses; he was a fool. Now Tracy Trent is once again the prisoner of St Georges and at the renegade's mercy.

Chapter 15

Tinnaman circles slowly to the right of Kenton who turns with him. Both men are bleeding, small wounds made as razor sharp knives slash forward like the head of a striking serpent. The two are warriors; strong and experienced in knife fighting as most men on the frontier are. Tinnaman fights because of the challenge of this white man and does not want to lose face before his warriors. Kenton fights solely to kill the warrior before him for hate and to avenge his family.

Lance watches as the two men charge back and forth across the small clearing slashing at each other. Both sides watch the fight as it is playing out, neither of the combatants giving an inch. One or both of these fighters will die here in this clearing without making a sound.

Arm and shoulder muscles cord as the two men try to wrench free, each trying to break the powerful grasp of the other. Both equally matched in size, strength, and both are fearless. Quick as a cat Kenton hooks his leg behind Tinnaman's leg and shoves him backwards as he lands on top of the Shawnee. With unbelievable strength, the warrior tosses Kenton from him like a rag doll but not before Kenton stabs the warrior through the shoulder.

Rolling quickly to their feet, the fighters circle each other warily. Kenton lunges forward, his knife opening up a long slice across Tinnaman's shoulder. Again, the men circle as blood runs in rivulets down both men. None of the wounds are serious but the blood makes both fighters slick and hard to hold on to.

Tinnaman throws caution to the wind and rushes forward, his knife slashing at the retreating white man before him. Both fighters extend much in the fight; they are tiring, weakening from their exertions, and losing blood.

Blue Elk steps near Lance as the two fighters sink wearily to their knees, their hands locking together.

"Tinnaman tires, his warriors will attack us, be ready."

Lance also saw the wild look in the eyes of the warriors as they watch eagerly as their chief starts to tire. "I'm ready." Lance watches both the fighters and the Shawnee warriors step near the combatants. Suddenly both men lay exhausted, their will to fight still intact but their stamina depletes completely. The two fighters crawl forward, neither willing to give up the fight but neither able to rise to their feet and continue.

Both men are bloody from many minor wounds but still they fight on. Lance watches the two men stab feebly at each other, without doing any damage. The fight for now is finished. Kenton protests, cussing weakly as Lance drags him away from Tinnaman who the Shawnee is dragging backwards.

"You are finished for today, Isaac." Lance looks down into the pale face of the long hunter.

Shaking his head slowly the big man can only utter a few words. "No, I've got to kill him."

"I know, my friend, I know." Lance knows exactly how Isaac feels.

Blue Elk returns to where Kenton lay and nods towards the Shawnee. "They will return to their village and not fight us."

"No!" Lance steps towards the small fire where Tinnaman lay.

"I have given my word, Hawkins." Blue Elk takes him by the arm, "My word."

"But not mine."

"What do you want here, white man? We have agreed to return to our village without any more fighting." One of the Shawnee Warriors questions Lance as he approaches.

"You have a Frenchman with you, leave him and I will let the rest of you go to your village unharmed."

"What will he do with this white man?" The warrior questions Blue Elk who stands behind Lance. "You gave us your word, Mohawk."

"This one is crazy, touched by the evil spirits." Blue Elk shrugs. "Leave him Shawnee or you will all die."

Lance watches as the able-bodied warriors help the wounded to their feet. They disappear into the night, only the wounded Frenchman is lying near the fire. The hickory, handled skinning knife slips quietly from its sheath as Lance approaches the cringing man. Returning to where the wounded Kenton lay, Lance looks down and shakes his head. "He cannot travel, at least not until he rests and his wounds are treated."

Blue Elk nods in agreement. "I have never seen two men fight so hard with the knife and neither die."

"Me either." Lance looks at the warrior. "I must go back to the white settlement now."

"And you wish for me to remain with this one?"

"If Blue Elk thinks the Shawnee will keep their word and not track you, then I must go. Tinnaman says St Georges goes back for the white girl." Lance frowns in thought. "She is in danger."

"The Shawnee gave me their word, they will not break it." Blue Elk looks down at Kenton. "This one has lost much blood but he is strong. He will be able to travel in two days."

"You have helped the women twice now. Will Blue Elk help one last time? Stay with Kenton at least until he can defend himself."

The Mohawk studies the still form of Kenton and nods slowly. "He is a brave man; we had great respect for his brother Simon. Yes, I will stay with him until he is out of danger."

"Water," Kenton whispers.

Both Lance and Blue Elk look down at the wounded man. "We thought you were out of it."

"I will get water for him, you go." Blue Elk starts to turn for the creek. "Hurry, the Frenchman has a great lead and he is a dangerous foe, my friend."

"I owe Blue Elk." Lance places his hand on the warriors shoulder. "Good-bye, my friends."

Both men watch as the young hunter trots from sight. "That's the first time I ever seen the young one smile."

"He hasn't had much to smile about lately," Kenton replies weakly. "I know how he feels; my family was massacred the same way. Now how about that water."

"He didn't have to kill the wounded Frenchman." Blue Elk looks towards the fire.

Isaac nods. "Yes he did. I would have done the same if I was able to get to the wounded Shawnee. Besides, I have seen your people do the same, perhaps even worse at the burning stake."

Blue Elk disagrees, "I am not weak and I do not kill that way."

"You would, if Ravenhair or your mother were killed in front of your eyes," Kenton replies.

Brady follows Iona and May Lynn as they stagger out of breath through the gates of the Frasier Settlement. Several villagers warned by the gate sentry rush to surround them, all firing questions at the same time. Johnson and Wilson can only shake their heads as they listen to Brady tell about what happened.

"I told you, you dang fool." Hale pushes to the front glaring at Brady. "You wouldn't listen, no sir, you young, whipper-snapper. Now the fats in the fire for sure."

Brady's face turns red as he listens to the unbraiding the old hunter is giving him. "I thought the danger had passed."

"Tell Springer's family that." Hale spit. "It'll make them feel real good, I bet."

"I'm sorry." Brady drops his head. "I just figured the Shawnee were headed north, didn't figure on the Frenchman."

"You should be sorry." Hale shakes his head in disgust. "At least you got two of them back safe."

"It was our fault too." Iona steps in front of Hale. "He warned us not to go but Tracy said we'd go alone if he didn't take us."

"You're all fools." Hale will not let Brady off the hook. "If he had of talked you girls out of this foolishness at least Springer would still be alive, and the girl would be here safe."

"You don't know that Mister Hale." Johnson steps to the front of the gathering crowd. "Could be the Frenchman and his men were planning to come in here at night and take the girl anyway."

The old hunter looks across at Johnson and Brady. "You two tell that crap to Lance Hawkins when he gets here and hears what happened."

Lance trots swiftly back towards Frasier, his mind racing with Tracy's face flashing through it. She has been through so much these last few weeks, now St Georges is threatening her again. How far ahead was the Frenchman, and did he reach Frasier already? Was she already in danger and in his clutches again? The dead leaves crunch under his moccasins as he trots across the flat bottom that leads to the settlement. His eyes and ears honed sharply onto anything that does not sound right to him but he did not slow his pace. Frasier is another day traveling across the mountains. The young hunter did not have time to hide his tracks or muffle any noise he might be making.

The night is black, black as a cave. Lance cannot see to travel so he slips under a large cedar tree and builds a small fire. Pulling deer jerky from his bag, he bites casually into the tough meat hardly tasting it. Not actually wanting the food but he knows he will need energy for the coming day. His body is young, hard as a Hickory limb but he has been on the trail of the Frenchman now for a solid month. He does not have time to rest for long but at least he can eat.

The little blaze crackles and pops as the small squaw wood is eaten quickly by the flames. Lance can feel the comforting heat from the fire as he stares hard into the flames. Many times his father warned him about the danger of looking into the blaze of a fire at night but tonight he does not care.

The fire mesmerizes him, relaxing him with its warmth, helping him forget the aches in his body and the aches in his heart. He fixes his eyes on the blue flames that send an occasional spark into the heavy branches overhead. Why did he leave Tinnaman alive? Why did he not attack the Shawnee warriors instead of letting them retreat to their villages? He held the hated Shawnee lives, killers of his people, right in his hands and let them go. Why?

A huge, northern horned owl hoots from somewhere far out in the woods, then another one answers. The low sound reminds Lance of the sound he and his brother Lucas used to make when they cupped their hands and blew into them. He enjoys the musical sound like the tooting of a deep horn as they call to each other from across the valley. It seems like years ago but actually, it was only a month ago that they were a happy loving family before the Frenchman destroyed their lives.

Lying back on the sandy ground, he studies the stars through the branches as they twinkle overhead with an occasional shooting star darting swiftly across the dark sky. He wonders about Tracy, the girls, and what the days ahead will bring. Lance awakes with a start as the morning light brings life to the surrounding woods. A light frost shows on the valley floor. Shivering as he looks at the dead fire, he lets his eyes seek out any unwanted company before pulling himself from under the tree. The new buckskin shirt he acquired at Frasier is warm but not heavy enough for the early morning crispness of the mountains. Winter is close; he will have to buy himself and the girls heavy coats before they start back for Bacon's Crossing and their own farms. A grey squirrel barks at him as he emerges from his lair under the cedars. Lance stretches as he watches the little ball of fur scamper from limb to limb, as it watches him. Hopefully the Frenchman will go back north and let him take the girls home safely. He blinks, is his hate for St Georges weakening and is he growing soft?

St Georges follows the lead of the Shawnee as they cross a high range of the Allegheny's. This is north of his range but he was here on two occasions before. Somewhere ahead there is a pass letting them cross into a huge valley that spreads out for miles with tall timber and wide open valleys.

He remembers the tall grass of the lush valley that grows head high on a man. The mountains are home to bountiful herds of deer, buffalo, and all kinds of small game that can feed hunters even in the worst of times, which is why the forest here is full of hostile tribes from several nations. Stopping, he looks back over the range of mountains they just descended as he studies their back trail.

"Are we being followed?"

St Georges shakes his head. "I hope so, Sergeant but not yet."

"Soon maybe?"

"Maybe." The Frenchman motions with his hand. "He'll come, meanwhile we've got all of this to enjoy."

"Yes Sir." The Sergeant looks nervously around the huge valley. "I just hope we're the only ones enjoying the view around here."

St Georges laughs. "Scared, Sergeant?"

"Well Sir, there's only three of us left and we're a long way from home."

"I wouldn't worry none about who's out here with us, no Sir. I'd worry about the one who follows us."

"Is he that dangerous?" St Georges nods his head thoughtfully then looks over to where Tracy is sitting on the ground listening to them. "He is, that is why I want him to die."

"He'll kill you all." Tracy spit at them, "You will never leave this place."

"And you want us to turn you loose?" St Georges sneers, "You think he'll turn back once he has you and spare all of us?"

"No, I don't want loose. I want to be here when he kills all of you. It was my folks too that you and your Indian friends massacred. It doesn't matter about me; he won't turn back as long as he knows you are alive." Tracy looks over to where St Georges seems nervous, looking about the clearing uneasy. "Once I tried to get him to stop but now I don't want him to."

Sergeant Boyer looks curiously at the girl, then over at St Georges. "He's just a man."

"He's more, he's become the devil." Tracy looks towards the ground, then straight at St Georges. "I know him, he's crazy for revenge and he'll kill any man with this one when he finds him."

"Shut up!" St Georges takes a step towards Tracy with his hand raised but then he changes his mind. "Stand up woman, let's travel."

"Maybe we should return to the Shawnee village instead of heading further into this unknown land." Boyer looks closely at St Georges, "At least we'd have numbers on our side."

"No, we're gonna travel to the north until he finds us." The Frenchman whirls. "And he'll find us Sergeant, you can bet on it."

"That's what I'm afraid of." Boyer whispers softly and then looks over at the hate emitting from Tracy's face, "If his hate is half as bad as yours."

"It's far worse, Frenchman." Tracy stands and follows St Georges and the Shawnee along the little traveled trail. "I heard the people at the settlement now call him the avenging angel of death."

Lance studies the closed gates of Frasier's Settlement for several minutes before crossing the open stump strewn flat. Trees near the post were cut and used for the stockade walls and it left the area around Frasier a clear field of fire in case of attack.

Stopping before the huge gates, Lance bangs his rifle butt against the wood posts then steps back to where he can see the top of the stockade.

Two faces look cautiously over the palisade.

"Who are you and what you be wanting, stranger?"

"It's Lance Hawkins, you know me, George Hale." Lance looks up at the old hunter.

"Lance Hawkins, I didn't recognize you boy under that hide you got on your head." Hale cackles. "Open the gate."

Lance walks through the gate as Hale makes his way slowly to the ground. He has known the old hunter almost since he was born. Many a time the long hunter left venison hanging in their dog run without saying a word, then other times he comes in for a visit. The old hunter is his own man, never married except maybe to a Delaware woman once, no children and too stubborn to know he is getting old. Many times he brought warning of a raiding party then stayed to help fight them off.

However, age finally caught up with his old bones forcing Hale to seek the comfort of Frasier doing what he could to pay for his keep. His eyes are still sharp as a hawk and this morning McDowell and Johnson set him to watching for any unwanted company.

"We been expecting you, Lance Hawkins."

Lance replies, "Why?"

"We've been hearing things." Hale looks the new arrival over closely. "You've grown some."

"Reckon it is all the home cooked meals I've been getting." Lance is sarcastic not wanting to take time for idle talk. "Are the girls here, George?"

"Two of them are here."

"Two?" Lance questions.

"The Tracy girl's been took." Hale looks away dropping his old eyes from the cold hard stare that turns red as fire. "Three days now."

"The Frenchman, St Georges?"

Hale nods slowly. "That's what Scott Brady said. St Georges, three of his men, maybe just two now, and one Shawnee."

"What's Brady got to do with the girls?" Lance looks around the settlement.

"Let's walk over to the store and see McDowell," Hale turns towards the general store.

Lance glares, "I asked you a question."

Hale looks back at the hunter. "I heard you boy, now let's go talk to McDowell."

Piffle stops cleaning the shelves of the store as Lance follows Hale through the door. Her green eyes took in the buckskins covered in mud and the worn out look on his face. How many miles did he travel in his quest to run down the men that killed his parents?

"Lance," the name slips from her lips almost in a whisper. Her head starts to swim as she looks at him in shock. "You're here."

"Piffle," Lance takes in the surprised look in the girls face. "Where are the girls?"

"In the back, I'll go fetch them."

"Thank you." Lance watches the lithe body of the young woman as she hurries from the room.

McDowell and Wilson appear from another end of the long store both men extend their hand. "Lance Hawkins, I wouldn't have recognized you. You've sure grown."

"Yea," McDowell takes in the broad shoulders of the hunter. "He has at that."

"You've seen Piffle?" Wilson looks around for his daughter.

"She's gone to get the girls for me."

"Good." Wilson nods. "We'll be heading back to Bacons come morning light."

"Watch your back trail, Mister Wilson." Lance fidgets. "That Frenchman is mean."

"I've got several men traveling as guards with us."

"Alright Mister McDowell tell me, how did the Frenchman get his hands on Tracy Trent again?" Lance looks over at Hale with a frown. "Some folks seem to have a tight mouth."

McDowell runs his hands through his thinning hair and motions for Lance and Hale to sit. "The girls wanted to go home, we couldn't change their mind."

"Did Scott Brady take them out of here?" Lance slaps his leg hard with his leather cap. "All alone, he knows this country and the Shawnee. He should have known better."

"Now son, don't go getting your hackles up at Brady." McDowell sees the change coming over Lance and pales. "Tracy was going alone if necessary; no one could have stopped her."

"Is she dead?" McDowell shakes his head. "No, I don't think so. Brady thinks St Georges took her to get you to follow him into the North Country. He said the Frenchman made no attempt to capture Iona, May Lynn or follow them back here."

"North Country, you mean the Ohio Country?" Lance asks.

"Exactly, some of the wildest country you've ever seen."

"My father said that's Abenaki Country." Lance looks off to the north. "Well, he'll get his wish as soon as I finish with my business here."

"Business?" McDowell shrugs. "What business?"

"I need supplies if you'll take my marker until I have time to hunt and gather some furs together."

"Certainly I will." McDowell is relieved, "Is that all?"

"I want Brady here."

"He tried his best." McDowell cannot meet the cold eyes that now stare right through him without any emotion whatsoever. "I'll have no trouble here."

"You've got trouble; you shouldn't have let the women leave this place." Lance touches the hilt of his knife. "If she's dead I'll cut your heart out along with Brady's."

"I told you, Brady made a mistake but at least your sisters are safe." McDowell looks incredulously at the figure before him. He cannot believe the change in the young Hawkins.

Iona and May Lynn rush into the store throwing themselves into his arms. Lance is shocked, both girls have grown and matured. How he did not know, for it was such a short while since he saw them last but they were not the same little sisters he had known.

"Oh Lance, now we can go home at last."

Lance looks at May Lynn. "You mean you want me to leave without trying to rescue Tracy?"

"No. Of course not, you know better." May Lynn stammers. "I mean after we get Tracy back."

"I'll be going out as soon as I see Scott Brady." Lance steps back from the girls. "When I return, we'll go home."

"You promise, as soon as you return?"

"I promise May Lynn, as soon as I return."

Nodding May Lynn smiles, "I'll fix you something to eat and some pone for the trail."

"Why do you want to see Scott?" Iona looks up at her brother.

Lance studies her upturned face in disbelief. "Why? He's put all of you in danger, got a man killed, Tracy is in the hands of the Frenchman and you ask me why?"

"He's my man, Lance." She steps in front of Brady as the hunter walks into the cabin, placing her hand in his. "Mine, and you won't harm him, you hear me? He was trying to help us is all, we asked him. He tried to warn us but we wouldn't listen. It wasn't his fault."

Lance stares in shock at the girl who suddenly matured into a woman. He then wipes his face as the passion of rage passes. Looking over at the stocky hunter, he shakes his head. "We've known each other for quite a spell, Brady. I should kill you; thank her for your life."

"I'll go with you Lance to help bring Tracy back." Brady looks at the tall youth he no longer knows. "It was my fault."

"No, you won't follow me or I'll kill you for sure." Lance turns and walks through the stockade gates without looking back.

Iona steps up close to Brady. "He's changed, I no longer even know my own brother."

George Hale nods solemnly. "Well one thing's for dead certain, Scott Brady."

"What's that George?"

"This little woman just saved your life."

"I s'pect she did alright." Brady pulls Iona close. "Thank you."

May Lynn stands holding an oilskin bag filled with cornbread and side meat. "He didn't even eat."

"He can't wait to get back on their trail." Iona drops her eyes as tears roll down her cheeks. "Tracy was right; he's turned cold, no more than a bloodthirsty savage himself."

"Go easy on him, Lass." Hale watches Lance trot out of sight. "To survive what he has, a man has to be tough and hard. If it wasn't for him we'd all be dead now."

Lance cast back and forth studying the ground where Brady told him to look for St Georges trail. If the Frenchman wants him to follow, the trail will not be hard to find or follow. At least until he closes the distance between them, then he will have to be wary of an ambush. He knows St Georges alone is a dangerous enemy and he has a Shawnee tracker with him to help. The Frenchman has been on the frontier for many years, he fought many battles, and a man does not survive the things he has without being smart and hard to kill.

Lance is not a fool, he knows he is no match yet for either St Georges or the Shawnee in the wild but it did not matter. The Frenchman will die by his hand before this trail is finished. He knows what Tracy and the girls think of him, yes, he has grown cold but he is not bloodthirsty as they thought. The blood of his folks call out to him, he cannot turn back even if he wants to.

Maybe his inexperience and youth will help him. He needs to use caution and not rush headlong into a trap. He knows St Georges wants him dead, kidnapping Tracy proves it. She is the bait that lures him on into the wild. He will go slow, taking all the time he needs. The Frenchman's death in the end is all that really matters or is it?

Tracy's beautiful face, the soft smile that she always graced him with before their folk's death, all this flashes across his mind. Is she safe in the Frenchman's hands, can she endure the hardships of the trail after all she has been through already? He knows she will be safe and alive, at least until St Georges captures or kills him.

Chapter 16

Blue Elk studies the front gates of Frasier's Settlement as he eases Isaac and the travois to the ground outside the stockade. The wounds of Kenton are much more severe than he first thought. The many knife wounds crossing the big, long hunter's body are infected and now for the last three days he has been racked with fever and unable to walk.

Lance was gone for more than a week by the time Blue Elk is able to get Kenton back to the settlement. As the days pass, Kenton gradually weakens until finally the high fevers set in. The Mohawk fashions a drag out of light poles and pulling the wounded man tediously along the game trail, he manages to get the man back to the white settlement.

Tying the white, under-skin of a rabbit to his bow, the warrior waves it until one of the sentry's on the gate discovers them and hollers out a warning to the settlement.

Immediately the place is a hubbub of activity as people lining the stockade wall. Finally, the heavy gates open slightly, allowing the old hunter, Hale, to limp out alone to where Blue Elk waits with the fevered Isaac Kenton.

"Isaac Kenton, what has happened to you?" Hale looks at the Mohawk then kneels beside the wounded man. "Man, you're cut all to pieces."

"Is Lance Hawkins here, George?" Kenton rasps feverishly, barely able to speak loud enough to make himself understood.

"He was but he's done lit a shuck out of here about four, five days back."

"Where did he go?" Kenton asks.

"Due north, through the Iron Springs Pass." The old hunter touches Kenton's forehead. "Dang fool went after the Frenchman alone; he's got more fever in his head than you do, Isaac."

Kenton's dark eyes look to where the Mohawk stands. "You know the place, Blue Elk?"

"I know this place." The warrior nods. "It is the dark land, all tribes, enemy or friend, hunt this bloody ground."

"Track him down and bring him back, do this and my rifle is yours." Kenton whispers hoarsely, "Hurry, Blue Elk."

Nodding the warrior looks down at Kenton and then takes off like a shot never looking back as he disappears from their sight.

Hale watches the warrior disappear. "I've seen a lot of things in my old life but I never thought I'd see a Mohawk hurry to help a white man."

Kenton mumbles weakly. "Blue Elk's one of a kind George, he gave his father his word to help young Hawkins and I reckon he aims to keep it, plus I have something he wants."

"I heard what you said." Hale helps Isaac to his feet. "It still don't figure to me, risking his life to help a white."

"He wants my rifle and I owe Lance Hawkins my life, as you all do, so we struck a deal." Kenton's feverish eyes look towards the forest. "Sides, I think he kinda likes Lance, maybe wants to help him."

Hale shakes his head again as the people from the settlement come from the stockade to help. "Ain't natural, I'm telling you, a red heathen helping one of our'n."

Blue Elk's long shambling trot is deceiving like the lumbering Raccoon. Looking slowly, he covers the ground at a pace that he could hold hour after hour without tiring. He shakes his head in disgust as he tracks Lance through the flat heavy timbered valley. The white youth is brave, but foolish. He and the Frenchman left a trail a squaw or child could follow. Perhaps if Lance Hawkins survives this long trail, one day Blue Elk will teach him how to conceal his tracks better. Providing of course the Frenchman does not kill him first, which seems likely as careless as he is lately.

The Mohawk traveled the war trail with St Georges many times, he knows how cagey the Frenchman can be and St Georges is sneaky like the grey fox. Blue Elk reads the signs on the ground; the Frenchman left a trail the white youth could follow easily. A blind squirrel could follow the trail; this is a trap using the white woman to lure the long hunter to his death and he is falling into it.

The smell of a storm is in the air, the clouds are banking dark and low, perhaps a heavier storm of winter is coming with a vengeance. Blue Elk glances skyward and frowns, if it snows hard he will lose the trail and perhaps he would not find Hawkins in time to help him. The storm is close, tall oaks and pine start to sway gently as the wind begins to build.

Small whirlwinds stir the dead leaves that lay about the forest partially covering the game trail Blue Elk is following. He has to hurry; the tracks show Hawkins getting closer to the French, but still a few hours ahead of where he stands. If the weather worsens and the French stop to make camp, perhaps then he can catch up in time to help the young hunter.

Blue Elk does not know why but he respects and likes Lance Hawkins even though they only know each other for a short time. The Mohawk people always place great value on a courageous and brave warrior and this white proves he is both. Blue Elk knows life has a funny way of working out, he remembers their first meeting when he challenged the white hunter to fight, now he finds himself hurrying to help him.

St Georges stands with his long rifle across his arm watching in shock as several warriors walk from the woods towards them. He knows these warriors, at least he knows their tribe, they are completely ruthless and not to be trusted. They are the dreaded killers of the far north woods, the dreaded Abenaki and now several of the warriors stand only yards from him in a semicircle. St Georges cusses under his breath but still keeps his cool holding up his arm in the universal sign of greeting. He foolishly walked right into the midst of an Abenaki hunting party. He saw the marked up warriors at most trading posts along the frontier. Their scalplocks, the narrow faces covered with facial tattoos, and their dress give away their tribe's identity. Also the eyes, eyes which are more slanted than most, eyes that smolder from their deep sockets and stare at you with a dead look, giving most men a nervous feeling. The Abenaki are generally a smaller boned people but loaded with endurance, courage, and they are fearless on the war trail.

St Georges knows of no deadlier enemy to the whites than the warriors of the Abenaki. All are bloodthirsty, all are great fighters and the Frenchman knows none of this tribe could be trusted to keep their word about anything.

Loyal only to their blood kin, even then he has known them to kill their own people when in a state of drunkenness.

The stockier of the Abenaki steps silently forward, his dark snake eyes shifting back and forth in the skintight face. St Georges remembers this warrior from the battle of Bard's Creek and from Fort Niagara where the Abenaki trade. The tattoos and facial scaring from smallpox set him apart from all others. Before them stands one of the worst of the Abenaki, a subchief, if St Georges memory serves him right. The man is a white hater, a warrior who hates anybody or anything that is not from his tribe.

"Tell me, white man. Why do you bring an enemy of the people here to this place?" The short warrior nods towards Trail Runner, the Shawnee tracker, who stands watching without emotion. The Shawnee are sometimes allies of the Abenaki but caught here alone in their hunting grounds he knows his life and the lives of the men with him could be in danger. The slender warriors are dangerous; an outsider never knows what they will do. The Abenaki before him struts as he crosses the clearing and stops before him. The warrior is arrogant, even though he is shorter than the Frenchman, his demeanor and smugness seem to make him taller.

"My friends the Abenaki, it is good to see you again." St Georges ignores the question. "We have come looking for you."

"We are not your friend and this one comes into our country like a thief in the night." The warrior hisses looking over at Trail Runner. "And I do not think you were looking for the Abenaki. I think the Abenaki found you!"

"The Shawnee have been your allies in war against the whites; he has brought us here for a parley." The Frenchman argues knowing full well if the Abenaki kills Trail Runner they will next turn their blood thirst on them. St Georges knows they are all in grave danger, no one can determine what an Abenaki will do, not even themselves. The taste of blood enrages them into a killing frenzy. "We have come looking for you; we have many presents for the Abenaki."

"I do not see any presents." The slanted eyes look about the whites. "This Shawnee dog will die and maybe you too."

St Georges steps forward leveling his rifle at the warrior's midsection. "And maybe you will die too, Sastook."

"You know my name?" The short warrior ignores the rifle but looks in surprise as his name is called out.

St Georges relaxes then smiles. "You do not remember me; I fought by your side far to the east when we fought the British Militia."

"You!" The warrior seems shocked as he looks over at St Georges then down at his arm. "I remember now, you put medicine on my arm when an enemy cut it with his long knife."

"Yes, the French helped your people then. Now I have come asking for your help." The Frenchman lies as he studies the warrior. "And for this help I will reward my friends the Abenaki handsomely."

Sastook flashes his smoldering dark eyes at Trail Runner. "What do you wish?"

"There is a white, long hunter following us, we lured him here to this place." St George looks towards the woods where several more warriors appear. "I wish my friend Sastook to capture this one and bring him here to me."

"And for this one, lone white, you will pay us?" The warrior looks nervously towards the approaching warriors. "What will you pay, white man?"

"Rifles, lead, powder, and cooking pots for your women." St Georges nods. "Providing the one I want is alive when you bring him to me."

"So much for one white hunter?" Sastook looks suspiciously at the French. "Why do you not capture this one yourself and save paying us?"

"He must be captured quickly. The Shawnee will not take the war trail against the white settlements until he is dead." Sastook looks at the Shawnee. "Does he speak the truth, Shawnee?"

"He speaks the truth, except he didn't tell you this white is very dangerous."

"He must be a great warrior if the Shawnee people fear to fight against him." Sastook watches the eyes of the Frenchman. "Why does he follow you to this place alone, against so many?"

St Georges shakes his head then looks back at Tracy who stands quietly behind him. "She is his woman, he wants her back and he will follow and try to rescue her. We do not know if he comes alone, more warriors may be with him."

A subdued murmur arises among the gathered warriors as they separate and let a taller warrior pass through their ranks. The man is heavy with tattoos across his face, down both arms, legs, and across his broad chest. St Georges does not know the warrior, never saw him before but he knows what the proud aristocratic carriage and fearsome markings on the man means.

The way the other Abenaki step back and cower at his approach marks the tall warrior as a mighty warrior with much prestige. He must be a chief of some kind, maybe even a Sachem of the Abenaki.

"It is Tenkiller." Trail Runner becomes pale. "Very seldom is this one seen by strangers."

"Tenkiller," St Georges heard of this Abenaki Chief but never saw him. No one he knows has ever seen him and lived. All he knows is this is the mightiest of the Abenaki, held in awe by his tribe and feared by all. This one holds the power of life and death over anyone or anything in his hunting grounds, his word is law and final. He always thought Tenkiller was a myth of the Abenaki. The saying is the ten slashes across the man's left shoulder symbolize the death of ten enemy warriors he killed in single combat on one day. After the fight the young warrior was renamed Tenkiller.

"So this is the great Tenkiller?"

The tall Chief steps inside the circle of men and stares into the Frenchman's eyes. The dark eyes study each of the whites for several seconds as if he is seeing deep into their souls. Finally, he focuses on Trail Runner and then he looks down at Sastook making the shorter warrior drop his gaze. Turning his dark eyes on St Georges, he steps closer to the Frenchman who appears to hold his ground fearlessly. "You Frenchman, you have brought a Shawnee into my hunting grounds."

The voice is deep but clearly speaks from a man of deep intelligence, a man in total control of his surroundings. Sastook steps between the Chief and St Georges as the Chief reaches to draw his hunting knife. The knife clears its scabbard and snakes forward cutting a thin line across the Abenaki's stomach as the warrior steps into its path.

"You would kill me, my Chief?"

Tenkiller's broad nose flares, his hate for intruders into his lands is well known, now his blood lust is enraged, he wants to kill St Georges. "I did not mean for the knife to bite you Sastook; I meant it for the whites. But you Sastook, you should have already killed them all for entering our lands without permission."

"He is a Frenchman, an ally, he fights with us." Sastook raises his badly scarred arm. "Once this one saved my life."

"No one comes into our lands uninvited, no one." Tenkiller shakes with rage. "You have heard my words spoken many times Sastook."

"He will pay with many rifles." Sastook stands his ground as blood trails down his stomach. "Our people need rifles, my Chief."

"The Abenaki need nothing from these whites." St Georges can see the anger in Tenkiller's eyes, the lust for blood, and the need to kill.

"Then kill me too, my Chief, for I have given them my word to help."

The knife wavers as the dark wide eyes of the Chief glares at his tribesman. "Do not tempt me, Sastook."

"Will not the great Tenkiller, Chief and High Priest of the great Abenaki people at least listen to his friends, the French?" St Georges speaks quietly hoping to defuse the situation. He has no doubt, if Sastook dies under Tenkiller's knife, they will all die. Pulling tobacco from his pocket, he pushes it towards Sastook. "Let us smoke together and hold council."

"We will talk white man and then you may die." Tenkiller's eyes focus on the form of Tracy standing with the other French. The dark face stares for a long time taking in the beauty of the girl. "Now I will listen to your words."

The ground is brushed clear of snow where a small council fire is built then carefully fed enough small sticks in a pyramid to keep it burning but not enough to throw any heat outwards. Several brooding warriors sit about in a circle while snow falls around them causing the flames to hiss and sizzle. The wind blows without letting up, throwing an icy cold breeze across the valley.

Tracy watches the warriors as they prepare the fire then quickly averts her eyes as Tenkiller, Sastook, and St Georges remove all of their clothing before taking their places by the fire. All three men sit naked and none flinch or shake as their bare bodies make contact with the snow and cold ground.

The Abenaki place much emphasis on important councils, baring their bodies shows they are baring their souls and speaking the truth. Tenkiller wants to see if the white skin of the Frenchman can withstand the freezing wind and snow or will he complain in front of the Abenaki.

Several times, Tenkiller looks across at her, pointing his long brown finger and nodding. Finally, the warriors and St Georges stand and replace their clothing. Tenkiller approaches where she sits with her head lowered then suddenly jerks her roughly to her feet seemingly as easy as he would lift a child. Speaking gruffly to her, he looks her up and down then abruptly shoves her back to the ground and walks away.

"What did he say?" Tracy turns to where St Georges stands.

The Frenchman smiles cruelly. "You are now a princess, sweet lady."

"What are you talking about?" Tracy fears what they will tell her.

"His name is Tenkiller. He is the big, boar hog around these parts and I just traded you to him along with rifles and powder."

"For Lance," she asks.

"You are correct, my dear." St Georges grins. "I think you will look very handsome in deerskin and beads."

"You coward, too scared to do your own killing." Tracy spit at him as Tenkiller looks on from where he stops and turns to listen. "You're a pig!"

"Oh, I'll be the one that kills him alright." St Georges grins again wickedly. "Soon as he is brought here, that is."

"You haven't got him yet, Frenchman."

"It's just a matter of time, just a matter of time." St Georges laughs lightly as he walks away. "These Abenaki are like bloodhounds on a track, nothing can escape them. You're gonna make a beautiful squaw, Tracy." For the very first time Tracy felt terror, stark deep terror. Before she was only frightened, not now, this Abenaki Chief now owns her; she is his to do with as he pleases. She shudders underneath her dress, everything about the man, his face, the slanted eyes, and taught skin speaks of cruelty and it revolts her.

St Georges laughs again and looks at her shocked face. "Don't worry Tracy, my dear, you're safe at least until Tenkiller delivers your boyfriend."

Shocked, she barely hears the words as another warrior pushes her roughly towards the woods and orders her to gather wood. Looking around at the hostile warriors that reminded her of green lizards, she staggers towards some dead wood laid piled under a fallen tree. Why did she not stay at the settlement as she was told instead of getting herself captured? Now she is the property of this crazy Abenaki Chief. Tracy shudders when she thinks of the cold haughtiness of Tenkiller. She can still feel the roughness of his hands when he touched her; the smell of him makes her sick. Now not only is she his captive and maybe his squaw, she is endangering Lance who she knows will try to rescue her.

"You aim to let that heathen have the girl, Sir?" Sergeant Boyer watches as the girl picks up dead branches of wood as if she is in a trance. "You know what she's in for with him."

St Georges follows Boyer's gaze then laughs lightly. "She won't be the first white woman that one has taken to his blankets."

Boyer shakes his head in disgust. "No Sir, but this one is different."

"How's that, Sergeant?"

"She's a lady."

"They all were, for a while anyway." St Georges laughs again and walks away calling back over his shoulder without a backwards glance. "You better hope he captures the long hunter and takes her, Sergeant or he might just take our hair."

Boyer shakes his head sadly. He has come to like the girl, the proud way she carries herself, the fearless courage. Already she starts to change just knowing what could be in-store for her.

Tenkiller looks one last time at Tracy then calls the Abenaki warriors around him. Slowly after their Chief dismisses them, the warriors drift from the camp in small groups trying not to be noticed. The Frenchman St Georges notices, then smiles wickedly. The white hunter who has caused him so much trouble is now in trouble himself.

Tenkiller sends his men to hunt for the trail of the young, white hunter. Soon the hunter, the source of all the Frenchman's problems, will be captured and then he can lead the Shawnee against the settlements without further interference. Perhaps he will try to trade the woman back. If that fails, he will go back to the Shawnee with the scalp of the white, or he might take his captive back alive to prove he was captured. The woman is beautiful and she would warm his lodge but whether or not he got her back from Tenkiller did not matter in the end.

Sergeant Boyer watches from the fire as the warriors in two's and three's depart from the camp and disappear into the surrounding forest. Not all of the Abenaki are gone, a few stay behind standing guard over the camp but St Georges knows they are actually watching the whites. Tenkiller and Sastook disappear, neither are anywhere about the camp.

Lance looks skyward at the tall trees, watching the heavy limbs as they sway in the growing winds. He knows the stronger storm can come before morning and if he does not miss his guess strong winds, heavy snows and freezing cold will accompany it. Looking down at his thin, doeskin-hunting shirt, he knows he is in for a long, cold night.

Lance senses he is close to the French; their tracks are muddy and still holding water that seeped into them. He knows Tracy is near. If luck is on his side, she will be free before the day is out. He has no idea where the Frenchman and his men are but he knows he will have to be extra cautious as he advances. The winds grow stronger; there will be no warning from the animals of the woods if man enters their domain. Their instincts of survival force them to seek shelter in their hollows, nests and under the heavy branched cedar trees.

Crouching slightly, Lance is about to move forward when he spots them.

Five slender warriors, smaller formed in size than the Shawnee or the eastern tribes move almost undetected towards him keeping close to the trees. He knows instinctively they are scouting for him. There is no other reason for them to be moving so cautiously and they are studying the ground for tracks. He has no idea what tribe they are from, as he never encountered this type of people with the body tattoos before. Possibly St Georges put them on his track. The Frenchman knows he will follow but how did he contact the warriors so quickly? Ham Hawkins told his sons once of a tribe to the north, warriors like these with tattoos over their bodies. A tribe that is terrible in battle, bloodthirsty, skilled trackers, and great hunters. Lance figures they must be the fearful Abenaki he spoke of. With their sudden appearance, he knows his chances of saving Tracy become complicated.

Slipping from his place of concealment, Lance looks for a way to circle around the warriors without being spotted or of leaving tracks in the soft ground. He knows he can escape to the south but he came this far after Tracy; there is no way he is leaving without her. It suddenly dawns on him, the Frenchman has not entered his thoughts. He is no longer important, at least not until he rescues the girl.

Behind him the soft call of a dove sounds from the exact spot he just lain watching the strange warriors, they found his track. Lance stiffens as another call sounds off to his left. The warriors did not have time to separate, there must be more. Several calls come on the heavy wind as he listens and looks for a way to evade his enemies. They are converging on him in a half circle, almost like tightening a fishnet; he remembers his Father's words of warning concerning these small men. They are vicious and terrible in battle.

Sprinting from his place of concealment, he throws safety to the wind in his bid to outrun his pursuers. If he can break clear of the circle of warriors, he knows they cannot catch him, even if they run him in shifts. He needs to outdistance them long enough so he can lose them or find some kind of sanctuary. The loud cry of exuberance from behind told him they see their quarry in front of them. With a burst of speed unequal in the tribes, Lance races across the valley leaping fallen trees and small creeks in his flight.

The catcalls, from his followers, become dim as he sprints across the wet ground gaining distance on his pursuers. The snow starts to fall, first in lazy soft flakes then they grow larger and heavier as he runs. Suddenly looking up, as he clears a small stream and regains his stride, three of the Abenaki appear right in front of him, blocking his way. The warriors are too close, only yards distant from where he stands, there is no time to change direction or try to escape. Hoping the powder is still dry in the rifle, Lance fires point blank at the nearest warrior as he charges forward. The roar of the weapon going off reverberates across the valley floor. The heavy lead ball tears through its target flinging the warrior backwards onto the wet ground. The second warrior close behind the first has little time to dodge as the heavy walnut stock of the rifle caught him square in the mouth knocking him unconscious to the ground.

The third warrior slips as he tries to turn and flee from the demon in front of him but his feet betray him on the wet, muddy ground. Lance's blade almost decapitates the small warrior as the razor sharp blade did its gruesome work. Looking about for any more of the enemy the young hunter looks down in satisfaction at the dead bodies that litter the trail.

Reloading the rifle as he runs, his eyes seek out a likely place to hide, a way to conceal himself from his pursuers. Now he worries, he knows the other warriors saw him as he raced away from them. They will know he is the one responsible for killing the dead warriors. If Tracy is their captive, what will happen to her? Will they seek revenge on her for their tribesmen? He has to find a way to circle back to where he lost the Frenchman and try to rescue her from her captors.

The snow starts falling hard as Lance slips silently along the banks of a small river. If they discover him, he can always take to the water but as cold as it is with nightfall approaching, he does not dare swim the river for fear of freezing.

No sound is heard from the warriors trailing him except for a long piercing cry of despair when they find the bodies of their dead. Lance wants to sound his own yell of triumph and rage but he did not dare. This is a game to the warriors but not to him. Tracy's life depends on him finding her and getting her free from whoever now holds her, whether it is the Frenchmen or the Abenaki.

The turbulence of the snowstorm picks up making it almost impossible to see farther than a few feet ahead. Again, Lance thinks back to his father's teachings about the Indian. Their nature to hibernate is almost like the wild creatures of the woods, when bad weather strikes they retreat from the elements to the warmth of their own shelters.

Wrapping the rifles firing pan in soft leather, he turns back north and retraces his steps cautiously to the field where he killed the three warriors. The bodies are gone; Lance studies the faint trail of several warriors as they turn back the way they came, back towards the north. There are at least twelve warriors ahead, maybe more so there is no time for caution. The heavy snow obliterates their tracks. He has to follow quickly hoping the warriors are not waiting in ambush for him somewhere along the trail.

Minutes later, he slows his pace as he closes in on the warriors who are weighed down with the bodies of their dead. Their tracks in the new snow are plain to see as the warriors carry the extra weight causing their footprints to press deeper into the wet ground. Knowing they will soon grow tired from the weight of the bodies and the heavy snow they trudge through so he slows his own pace. Again, from the past he remembers his father saying an Indian is superstitious of anything they cannot understand. Touching his knife he nods knowing what he has to do, then with a sudden burst of energy he springs forward throwing caution to the wind. A lone man attacking them from out of a snowstorm could be just what he needs to spook the warriors and keep their minds away from harming Tracy when they return to their camp.

Over the storm the warriors hear a crazy eerie moaning of something causing the warriors to turn and look fearfully behind them. A shadowlike figure stands over two of their bleeding warriors, then the terrible noise comes again as the shadow disappears from their sight. Again the shrill scream comes as something ghostlike springs across their back trail then disappears as quickly as it appeared. The Abenaki are paralyzed with fear from this unknown aberration, causing the warriors to drop the bodies and huddle together. Several times out of the storm, a caricature or spirit seems to materialize and then disappear again right in front of their eyes.

No mortal could move with such speed or disappear before their very eyes. It has to be an evil spirit; the Abenaki must have made the spirits mad for them to come during the daylight. Finally, the warrior's superstitious minds can stand no more. Lance laughs lightly to himself as he watches the warriors drop the dead bodies then retreat in a dead run, racing away scared out of their wits. There is no hurry now; following slowly in their footprints, he knows they will lead him to Tracy and the Frenchman.

Blue Elk halts high on the ridge that borders what seems like a large valley. He heard the shot but with the wind and heavy snow pummeling him, he cannot tell exactly where it comes from. He could not even be sure it comes from Hawkin's rifle, maybe it is just a stray hunter looking for food.

Like a silent ghost, he slips down the steep ridge and makes his way to where he thinks the shot came from. The snow continues to fall, the Mohawk knows he should be close to the shots origin but the valley is huge, with the wind and blowing snow, he could not be certain. Traversing the bottom east and west, he finds no sign of anyone passing. No tracks, man or animal, show on the ground. The snow is falling too fast and too heavy.

There is no need to be careful, with the storm howling out its vengeance on anything caught in its fury, Blue Elk doubts any warriors are out. The temperature falls drastically as the storm gathers strength. His body bends over as he leans against the heavy gusts of wind that lash at him. Blue Elk does not notice the small lift of the snow covered ground until he trips over something under his feet.

Regaining his balance, he kicks at the mound until he removes enough snow to see what tripped him. With a grunt, he turns the already half frozen body over.

"Abenaki!" Blue Elk whispers through half-frozen lips as he examines the body. "You have been killed with the knife, not the rifle."

Looking about, he finds the other body only yards from the first. "Ah, my young white friend, you have been very busy."

Blue Elk knows it will only take minutes for the trail to disappear under the deluge of snow. The Abenaki were not dead long but the snow already covers their bodies. There is no sense looking for a trail, all he can do is pick an opening to the north and hope for the best. The Abenaki and French are ahead somewhere but Blue Elk is more concerned about running up on Lance. He does not know for sure, with all the snow and wind, if the young, long hunter will recognize him or shoot him on sight.

Seven of the twelve warriors that Tenkiller sent to capture the white hunter remain alive and return to camp. Fearing the evil Spirits are following just behind them, all are frightened half out of their wits. Superstition prevails; they cannot help themselves, as their teachings are too strong, instilled deep into their savage minds since childhood. Huddling up against the campfire in a silent group, none looks their chief in the eye as he looks down at them curiously.

"What has happened?" Sastook studies each face as Tenkiller and St Georges looks on. "Speak, tell me, where are the others?"

Trembling, one of the warriors look out through the blowing snow and then back at Sastook. "Five are dead."

"Five?" Sastook looks at each man. "Who did this thing? Where are their bodies?"

"The evil ones attacked them and then as we carried them here it attacked us again." Sastook watches as the warrior trembles. "We had to leave them behind or we would all die."

"Cowards!" Tenkiller steps forward, raging at the warriors. "You have run from one man."

"Not a man, my Chief." The warrior trembles before Tenkiller. "The one who did this is an evil spirit."

Tenkiller whirls and looks out into the darkened forest. "You fools have led him here to this place."

"We returned here trying to escape his wrath, maybe his blood lust is filled and we were not followed."

"How do you know this was a Spirit?" Sastook looks hard at the men. "You were too scared to look behind you."

"We could see nothing Sastook, in the spirit world a being cannot be seen."

"How far away are the bodies?"

"There." The warrior pushes out his chin, "Just a short run."

The warriors look off into the gloom, expecting the evil one to materialize again before their eyes. Normally they are brave and fearless warriors, not now; this is different as this is not a mere mortal. Standing huddled together near the fire they watch in fear, even the great Tenkiller cannot induce them to leave its protection.

Sastook looks once again in disgust at the petrified warriors before pulling a heavy elk hide over his shoulders and disappearing into the falling snow.

"He will not come back." A warrior spoke in a trembling voice. "The evil one waits to drink his blood also."

"Then he will die a brave man, not trembling here like a coward." Tenkiller looks with contempt at the scared warriors. "I am ashamed of you."

One of the older warriors squares his shoulders and points out into the darkening dusk. "Tenkiller speaks brave words here near the fire, let him go there and then still speak these words to the Abenaki."

Tenkiller glares at the warrior and is about to speak, then changing his mind, he returns to where Trail Runner and St Georges stand under the covering of cedar branches and poles. Unable to block the wind completely with the shelter at least the snow cannot fall on them and put out their fire as they wait.

"Is this one an evil spirit, Frenchman?" Tenkiller looks back to where the warriors still huddle and asks, "Or a man?"

"He is just a man, a white man from the smaller settlement on the great river."

"Sastook goes alone to find the man." Tenkiller nods his huge head. "He is a great warrior."

"Yes, Sastook is a brave warrior but he will need help, my Chief." Trail Runner speaks with respect not wanting to infuriate the Abenaki Chief further. "The one he seeks is not a spirit but a great warrior."

"Sastook is a great warrior also, Shawnee."

"Sastook will die; no lone man can stand against one such as he. You must send the others to help him."

"But you said he is just a man."

"He is just a man but he has killed many Shawnee, Seneca's, even Mohawks, and now Abenaki."

"I will not shame Sastook by sending him help; he will kill this white man." Tenkiller looks over at the larger fire where the warriors stand about nervously. "We have heard about the death of the Black Panther. Is this white the one that killed the Shawnee?"

"He is the one." Trail Runner acknowledges.

Lance follows the fleeing Abenaki closely. He watches the campsite from his place of concealment, watching as the warriors trot into the camp and huddle around the roaring fire. He can tell from their actions, they are reporting their story as they continually point back to the forest from where they came. As they finish and move closer to the fire, a tall warrior much larger than the others steps forward. The warriors cringe in fear as the big Indian berates them, waving his arms and yelling. After several minutes, another warrior pushes one of the frightened ones backwards, almost into the fire. He then wraps some kind of skin around his shoulders and trots away from the fire directly to where Lance is hiding.

Slipping further behind a large oak, he watches as the warrior passes unknowingly within feet of where he waits. As the warrior nears, Lance can tell his covering looks like elk hide. The warrior is not as tall as the one by the fire but he is heavily muscled and the look on his face is evil.

Trailing the warriors back to the camp, he stayed well off the trail away from the tracks of the Abenaki warriors. Still, he knows this warrior is backtracking his men and he will eventually discover his tracks as well. If he finds his tracks, the warrior will know it is no spirit, for the evil ones do not leave tracks. He knows this is a brave warrior to come alone after whatever scared the others into abandoning their dead and fleeing in fear back to the camp.

The wind and snow is miserably cold, biting through the deerskin shirt he wears as if it is not there. He should have taken clothing from the dead warriors but the weather was mild until today, they were dressed as lightly as he was.

Sastook trots back to the South, the wind biting and pushing at his back. His dark, sharp eyes continually survey the surrounding woods, back and forth, as he follows what is left of the snow-covered trail. He knows somewhere ahead either the white, long hunter or the evil ones wait for him. The hair on his neck stands on end as somehow Sastook senses something or someone's eyes on his back as he follows the trail south. The warriors said a spirit killed the dead Abenaki, could it be possible.

The storm shows no signs of letting up as snow falls heavily and the wind whipping at the trees intensifies. Sastook has to hurry and reach the bodies before daylight is gone. He does not want to encounter whatever waits ahead of him especially after the dark falls and hides the land. The Abenaki warriors call this one a spirit and perhaps they are right. Tenkiller is in a rage because he allowed the Shawnee and French to enter their hunting grounds unharmed. To appease the Abenaki Chief and return to his good graces he will find this spirit and bring his scalp back to the Frenchman. Sastook is not as superstitious as most of the Abenaki people. However he knows somewhere ahead is a dangerous foe, whether man or spirit, is waiting for him. Finding one such as he in this storm will be impossible, he will have to let the white hunter find him.

Sastook is no coward; many times, he proved his courage in battle. In his village, he is praised and highly respected but today the great Tenkiller threatens to kill him as if he is an unproven youngster. The many scalps, captives, and trade goods he took over the years in battle and brought back to his people now means nothing. His whole life, his reputation and status as an Abenaki warrior now lies before him; he has to kill this one. To do so will prove he is the greatest of warriors, greater than any in the Abenaki villages, even greater than Tenkiller himself.

Chapter 17

Lance watches curiously as the warrior passes before him with less than twenty yards separating them. It is almost dark, the snow falls hard covering the sun, making the night come quickly. Could this be a trap? Why would a lone warrior walk out alone away from the safety of the fire and his comrades?

This warrior did not interest Lance; he saw the Frenchman standing near the shelter, somewhere in the camp ahead Tracy Trent would be waiting. He did not see her yet but if St Georges is there, he knows she will be also. He knows most of the warriors are already spooked, superstitious as they are he does not figure they will come out into the oncoming dark. If they are as his father said, superstitious of the unknown, it will take little to scare them into retreating to their villages and leave the French to fend for themselves. What can he do to spook them even more? He needs to think like his father, what would he do if he were here?

Lance watches as the lone warrior trots ahead into the falling snow and gloom. Slipping silently along after the warrior, he stays off to one side of the trail keeping in sight of the man. The warrior never once looks behind him until he comes to where the bodies were abandoned. Turning, Sastook surveys the forest as best he can in the deepening darkness, then kneels down and brushes snow from the first warrior's frozen face.

Slipping underneath the shelter of a tall cedar tree where he can watch the warrior's movements undetected, Lance waits. The huge snow covered limbs provide him a perfect place where he can lie and survey the forest and the trail that leads back to the camp. If this is a trap, other warriors will be coming soon. Lance blinks in curiosity, as the warrior discards the elk skin then shouts out something to the forest.

Peering out from the tight limbs. he watches the trail back towards the other Abenaki to see if any movement comes down the trail. He still does not figure this warrior brave enough to come alone into the forest, somewhere close behind the other warriors could be slipping forward preparing to ambush him. The shouting from the warrior might be a ruse to get him to show himself. Whatever is going to happen should happen soon, as it is only minutes before complete darkness engulfs the forest.

He cannot understand the warrior's words but the way the man stands shouting with his feet spread wide and the motions of his hands, Lance knows he calls him to fight. The warrior is short but he is a magnificent specimen of manhood, either red or white. The naked, upper torso of the man is heavily corded with muscle that bunches in mass with every movement as the warrior flexes his muscles as he screams. The warrior is naked, wearing only a loincloth and moccasins, still he shows no signs the cold is affecting him.

He yells out challenging the white man or the evil spirit that killed the dead ones that lay there. The words almost make Lance leap to his feet in surprise.

Rolling to his side, Lance looks at the grinning face of Blue Elk who slips in behind him unnoticed as Lance has his complete attention focused on Sastook. "Blue Elk, you almost got yourself shot." Lance exhales in relief. "How did you find me?"

"How?" Blue Elk shakes his head. "You leave a trail a blind squirrel can follow and then you ask me this?"

"I didn't even know you were here. I thought you were with Kenton."

Blue Elk crawls up beside the hunter and stares out to where Sastook still yells out his challenge. "Kenton is at fort, I come here to help you get girl back."

"I'm glad you're here, I can sure use the help." Lance replies.

Blue Elk smiles but does not tell Lance of his promise to find the young hunter or of the trade for Kenton's Kentucky Long Rifle. "This Abenaki warrior is Sastook, he challenges you to fight."

"Why would he come out here all alone to fight a spirit?"

"Sastook was raised by the Black Robes. He is well educated by the white priests and taught their religion, he knows you are no spirit." Blue Elk parts the limbs slightly. "But to answer your question, this one is a great warrior. He must prove this by killing you or the spirit person. Then he will become even greater in the eyes of his people."

"So if he kills me and the Abenaki think he killed a spirit person, he will have even greater prestige in his village?" Lance questions. "Maybe even greater than the great Sachems?"

"Yes, you are right. Maybe as much as their great war leader and holy man, Tenkiller."

"I have heard my father speak of a warrior named Tenkiller almost as if he were a ghost."

"Tenkiller is a mighty warrior." Blue Elk looks towards the yelling Sastook. "No enemy sees him and lives to tell about it.

"I have to get Tracy away from the French." Lance studies the lone figure. "If this one is killed and doesn't return, perhaps the other warriors will spook and leave this place and then the French would be alone."

Blue Elk agrees, "It is a good plan and perhaps the others will be afraid but first you have to kill Sastook."

Lance rubs the stock of the long rifle. "I cannot use the gun; the noise would betray our presence." He grins, "I never heard of a spook using a rifle."

"Do not underestimate this one, young Hawkins, he is a mighty warrior."

"So am I." Lance hands the rifle to Blue Elk. "If he is such a great one, to kill him with a gun from hiding would also be the act of a coward."

"You are no coward, white man, but if you die here the girl will be lost."

"I will not die, Blue Elk, but if I do, you will save her and you can have my rifle." Lance starts backing out from under the tree. "You just watch for any tricks from any of his friends."

"There will not be any tricks, Sastook is an Abenaki and he is a warrior with great pride."

"Hope you're right."

"He challenges you to personal combat." Blue Elk assures him. "It would dishonor him if anyone interferes."

"I reckon we'll see pretty quick." Lance stands up and checks his war axe and his father's hunting knife as Blue Elk emerges from behind the tree.

"He is a great knife fighter and he is very powerful."

"Seems like you know old Sastook, as you call him very well."

"I have seen him in battle many times." Blue Elk nods, "May the great spirit go with you."

"What do you mean? I am the great spirit."

Blue Elk watches, as Lance walks away trudging through the deep snow. "Perhaps you are at that."

Sastook calls out to the tall ghostlike forest as the sun begins to set. "Come out Spirit or are you afraid of this warrior?"

Twenty feet separate the two men, one red and one white, before the warrior notices the tall white hunter approaching. Stepping forward away from the elk hide, Sastook drops his bow then pulls his knife and axe swinging them in small arcs in front of him. Not a sound comes from either man as they walk forward, closing the space that separates them.

Blue Elk watches the two fighters circle slowly, sizing each other up before closing the gap to within striking distance. The ringing of the blows sound out across the flat snow covered ground as the razor sharp weapons clash together. Several times the weapons miss their mark by only an inch or less. Sastook is the more experienced knife fighter but the white hunter is younger and perhaps faster in his reflexes. Blue Elk can see the pure hate coming from the white's eyes and the almost fanatical desire to lunge forward and kill his opponent.

Blue Elk watches the fight; the ghastly look on the long hunter's face almost makes him shudder. As the fight progresses he nods his approval and smiles, now he understands, Lance is not trying to kill Sastook. The young one is making fierce faces as if he has lost his mind, trying to make the Abenaki think he is indeed a spirit or one of the crazy ones.

For the first time in his life, Sastook has doubts about his superiority as he faces this white. His knife and war axe miss with every blow when they should have struck whatever stands before him. Sastook finds it hard to look at the thing before him. Maybe his warriors were right, perhaps this one is a spirit. He has never seen the look of craziness and hate on any living person as this one has. The paleface wavers before him then takes shape again. Sastook shrinks back, he fears no mortal man but this one is different. He stands eerily in the falling snow making no sound. Maybe this white is one of the mindless ones, a person no Abenaki is permitted to harm for fear of bringing destruction upon the Abenaki Tribe.

Sastook steps back as the white before him laughs with strange shrill noises and slobber coming from his mouth. Then Lance falls to the ground and rolls around before lunging up and striking at him again. The warrior knows his blade touched the one before him, yet no blood shows anywhere. Sastook looks at the clean knife blade then across at the madman crouched before him. He remembers the teachings of the Black Robes that Evil Spirits do not exist but maybe they lied to trick him.

Lance can sense the superstitious warrior is beginning to waver, becoming indecisive. The age old beliefs of his people are seeping back into his mind, beginning to play tricks on him. This warrior is no coward but to fear the evil ones of the spirit world is a spiritual thing to the Abenaki, not an act of cowardice.

Suddenly, Sastook looks at the phenomenon as if he is some kind of devil then bolts back towards the Abenaki camp. Lance straightens and watches the frightened warrior as he races away in the falling twilight. Nodding to himself, he picks up the elk hide and walks to where Blue Elk steps from behind the cedar.

"Don't run off Blue Elk, it's me." Lance notices the strange way the Mohawk is looking at him then at the back of the Abenaki as he races away.

Blue Elk looks sharply at Lance then once again to where Sastook disappears as he races away. "This Abenaki is no coward, he fears you because he thinks you are of the spirit world."

"And what does my friend Blue Elk think?" Lance can see the uneasiness for the first time on the Mohawk's face. "Do you fear me?"

"I have seen you kill many. The Black Panther was a mighty warrior and his men, the Shawnee back at the cave, the ones at the battle, and the Abenaki warriors. Now Sastook, who is a dangerous knife fighter, runs away without making you bleed. Perhaps you are of the spirit world."

Lance nods. "And spirit people don't bleed, do they?"

"Do you bleed, Lance Hawkins?"

Pulling his knife, Lance runs the sharp blade across his arm then reaches out showing the Mohawk where a trickle of blood sprang from the cut. "I bleed Blue Elk, just like any mortal man."

Relief shows on the warriors face as he grins broadly. "You scared Sastook out of many years of his life. Maybe Blue Elk too."

"Enough for him to scare the ones with him into returning to their villages, I hope."

"How did you do this thing?"

Lance grins and remembers when he and Lucas would scare the girls into hiding under their blankets. "It's called playacting my friend. Now we will finish it."

"What will you do?"

"Come, we will move closer." Lance turns back towards the camp of the Abenaki. "We will see what they do."

Chapter 18

Tenkiller and St Georges look in disbelief as Sastook races in from the darkness and stands trembling close to the other warriors. Unable to look any of them in the eye, he just stands near the blaze and shakes his head.

Tenkiller steps before the warrior and looks at him nervously. This is his most trusted warrior, one he knows to be fearless in battle, yet here he stands trembling before the fire just as the others did.

"What has happened, Sastook?"

Finally after much urging the warrior speaks. "Our warriors spoke truthfully; the one out there is a Spirit, the Evil One."

"You have seen this Spirit?"

Sastook nods, then shows the knife wounds Lance inflicted on him. "I fought this one; he did not bleed as my knife tasted his flesh. He just laughed as I cut at him and then rolled crazily on the ground before springing at me again."

Tenkiller looks at the cuts then about the fire at his warriors. "You fought an Evil One and you are still alive?"

"I could not harm him so I ran away." Sastook looks up at his Chief. "He did not try to kill me; he just touched my arms slightly with his knife. I do not know why."

St Georges stands by listening to the conversation but does not interfere. He lived with Indian Tribes from different nations; their Spirit World was one thing he did not understand. Still he knows better than to argue with them about this. In the past he saw what could have been a victory turned into a full-fledged retreat when a warrior proclaimed to see an evil one fly through the air or appear on the trail. The Frenchman knows to interfere with their beliefs or superstitions could cause the warriors to turn on him and his men.

Tenkiller looks out into the dark, visibly shaken. "Did the Evil One follow you here, my friend?"

"I do not know this, my Chief, but we must leave this place. We made him mad because we are here. We have disturbed the Spirits of this place in some way."

Tenkiller nods, "We will return to our village when the sun comes again."

From the heavy timber, Lance and Blue Elk watch as Sastook speaks with the taller warrior. They can plainly see the Frenchman as he stands nearby, the Frenchman keeps quiet. Despite the dark and snow, they can see the nervous way the warriors hug the fire shifting their shaved heads back and forth trying to see into the darkness.

"Our friends the Abenaki are afraid of the unknown." Blue Elk wipes snow from his face. "I understand their fear."

"Afraid enough to leave this place?" Lance asks.

"Perhaps but they will not leave while the Spirit ones can hide in the dark." Blue Elk nods. "We will see when the light comes again."

"You mean they could come back after us in the morning instead of going back home?"

"Maybe but I don't think even the great Tenkiller himself can make these warriors come after the evil ones."

"Look, Blue Elk," Lance grabs the Mohawk's arm, "There she is."

Tracy walks from the shelter into the light of the campfire. They watch as the girl adds wood to the fire then stands before Tenkiller as he speaks to her and the Frenchman. Blue elk watches the actions of the warrior chief and the girl then looks across at Lance. "She is the woman of Tenkiller now."

"What?" Lance stutters in shock. "What are you saying, Blue Elk?'

"His actions, she carries the firewood and stands beside him away from the Frenchman."

"What does this mean?"

Blue Elk shrugs. "Perhaps the Frenchman traded the woman to Tenkiller."

"That's crazy, why would he do that?"

"For you, my friend, to get Tenkiller to help kill or capture you so he can get back to the Shawnee and his wars on the white settlements, for this he trades the woman to the Abenaki."

"Not yet, he ain't." Lance looks through the gloom as she retreats to the shelter. "I'm not captured by a long shot and she's not his woman. No sir, she ain't, not by a long sight, no sir."

"Maybe this one is wrong, when light comes on the forest again we will see."

Lance and Blue Elk back further out of sight of the roaring fire where the scared Abenaki hover. Holding out the heavy hide, he stares down at the elk hide in his hands, then nods.

"What does Lance Hawkins do?"

"Let's give our friends over there a little shove." Lance half smiles. "They're ready to break and run, let's help them along."

Blue Elk watches in curiosity as he cut saplings and constructs a framework for the hide.

St Georges thoroughly disgusted with the heathen superstitions of these warriors, follows Tracy as they go back to the shelter away from the fire and the nervous Abenaki.

"Spirits, evil ones." The Frenchman cusses under his breath so only the girl and the other French can hear him. "All nonsense, it's only your boyfriend out there, the young long hunter, no spirits of any kind."

Tracy looks across at St Georges. "He ain't a spirit but he's out there Frenchman and he's coming for you."

St Georges raises his fist to slap the girl as she stands her ground glaring at him. "Shut your mouth woman or I'll give you to Tenkiller tonight."

"Let's leave here now, Sir." Sgt. Boyer steps between the girl and St Georges. "Let's go now while they're too spooked to leave their fire."

"Yes Sir, scared as those redskins are, they aren't about to leave that fire before sun up."

Another Frenchman speaks up, "They might run right into those spirits of theirs in the dark."

Boyer looks back at the glowing fire. "I've got a bad feeling; it's either the long hunter or the Abenaki come morning."

"What are you saying, Sergeant?"

"Haven't you seen the way Tenkiller looks at the girl?" Boyer looks over at Tracy. "He isn't about to leave her behind when he heads home."

St George stares into the small fire that glows hotly underneath the shelter then looks to where the Abenaki either sit or stand about the larger fire. Even half naked, the falling snow and intense cold does not bother them at all. He also notices that Tenkiller is doing as the Sergeant said; the warrior keeps looking over to where Tracy sits under the shelter. The look of the tall Abenaki speaks volumes. If they decide to return to their village, there is no way he would leave the woman behind.

St Georges knows the Abenaki are deadly; they will not hesitate to kill them all to get the woman. "Maybe you are right, mon amie." St Georges nods at the Sergeant. "We will pretend sleep, let the fire die out and then we will leave from this place."

"They will leave a guard to watch us." Boyer looks over at the fire and counts the warriors. "There are fifteen of the little heathens standing about over there."

"One of us will watch them until the fire dies; if any are missing, I will take care of him before we leave." St Georges touches his knife.

"If none die and we leave this place, we will still have allies with the Abenaki." Trail Runner looks at St Georges. "But, if we kill one of them we will have much trouble."

The Frenchman nods. "I know this. Perhaps we should leave the girl with them."

"No!" Boyer speaks louder than he intends. "We may need her to get us by this Spirit of theirs."

St Georges studies his Sergeant for several seconds than smiles slightly. "Ah mon amie, I think maybe you want the girl for yourself."

Blushing, Boyer turns from the fire and finds himself a place beneath the shelter. The Sergeant is young and inexperienced about women; he knows Tracy heard St Georges remark and it embarrassed him.

Tenkiller and Sastook sit immobile before the dying fire as daylight peeks slowly through the snow clouds that cover the skies. Neither slept, Tenkiller contemplating what he will do come morning and Sastook reeling from the shame of running from the Spirit or Evil One he challenged.

Suddenly from around the fire excited voices raise eerily into a high pitch fervor as warriors point out into the gloom of early morning fog and fallen snow. One of the warriors shrinks back as he mumbles incoherently.

"It is the Evil One, he waits there." A warrior wails stepping closer to the fire.

Tenkiller rises to his feet as the figure move sideways slightly. The snow is coming down hard and the distance to the shadowy figure is many paces. Suddenly from the figure comes the most hideous of screams then the figure moves forward.

The Abenaki see enough, the unknown Spirit Ones killed five of their own and then they struck fear into the heart of their most courageous warrior Sastook. Now they come here to this place to challenge more of them and to kill. Not waiting for Tenkiller, they bolt striking due north away from the Evil Ones, hoping they will not follow them to their village. Fear overcomes the Abenaki warriors as they abandon their sleeping robes, food, even their weapons in their headlong rush to get away from the eerie sounds coming at them.

Tenkiller and Sastook stare at the weaving figure of what looks like a man and then watch their warriors race away from the fire in fear. Cold dread and fear race through both warriors as the voice of the Spirit rises again screaming in anguish across the space that separates them.

Looking at each other, the two Abenaki sprint after their warriors in fear. The superstitious Indian nature to believe in the Spirit People is just too strong, anything they cannot explain, they fear.

Blue Elk laughs lightly as he and Lance watch the Abenaki race away in headlong flight. Walking to where the elk skin stretches over a form of limbs that resembles a man, they wait until the warriors disappear from their sight before pulling the hide loose from the poles.

Lance laughs lightly as he tosses the hide to Blue Elk. "That scared them clear back to Canada."

"If I did not know what you did, I would be running too."

"Why is your race so afraid of spooks?"

Blue Elk shrugs. "It is just our belief, since childhood our Medicine Men teaches us to be afraid of the unknown."

"Kinda like our Preachers, yelling and screaming at us from the pulpit on Sunday."

"I did not see the woman you seek." Blue Elk waves his hands. "She was not with the Abenaki."

Lance nods, "Nor I and I didn't see any of the French."

Carefully they approach the abandoned camp and study the trampled down snow for tracks. Under the shelter, Blue Elk finds Tracy's smaller footprints but with the heavy snow covering the ground cannot find where her tracks lead.

"The French and the girl stayed here under the shelter during the night but now they are gone.

Lance studies her track carefully. "Maybe they are with the Abenaki."

Blue Elk shakes his head as he searches among the tracks of the fleeing warriors. "I do not think so; we did not see her run away with the others."

"Tell me, Blue Elk." Lance looks at the Mohawk. "What do you think St Georges did?"

"I believe the French fled south during the night. St Georges is a smart leader, he knows Tenkiller will take the woman north with him when he goes back to his village and the Frenchman still needs her to trap you."

Lance studies the Mohawk. "There are no tracks leading south."

Blue Elk shrugs, "I am guessing but I think this is what he did."

"You're sure she is not with the Abenaki?"

"I am sure; the Frenchman has taken her south with him."

Lance looks off towards the south and then up at Blue Elk. "If we guess wrong, she will be lost to us forever."

"I know this, my friend." Blue Elk paces back and forth studying the ground. "There is no sign of her with the Abenaki. We saw them run from this place. Unless they carry her and in their fright, they would not do such a thing. No, she is with the French, fleeing south."

"If they left before midnight, the snow was heavy enough to cover any tracks the French left or which direction they took." Lance is desperate to catch up with St Georges.

"We will go to the south." Blue Elk looks over at Lance. "Don't worry, my friend, we will find her track. You are of the Spirit world, remember?"

"Very funny," Lance is not amused with Blue Elks effort at being funny. "Split the elk hide, it will cover both of us from the snow and cold."

Blue Elk looks nervously at the hide. "No, it is yours."

"Blue Elk, don't tell me you're scared of a little old piece of hide."

"Blue Elk not scared but maybe elk hide belong to the Evil Ones."

"For Pete's sake, Blue Elk." Lance scoffs, "there is no such thing as an evil one or evil spirits."

"Maybe not for the white man but the red man have many."

"Blue Elk knows the Abenaki, Sastook, was wearing this hide when he followed me here."

The Mohawk shakes his head. "I don't see this, I see hide laying on ground beside Sastook when he yells."

Lance shakes his head in disgust, "Hogwash!"

Chapter 19

St Georges and his three men along with Tracy Trent slip unheeded from the shelter as soon as the fire dies out. The Abenaki post no guards around them, with the Spirits lurking near the camp; no warrior would stray far from the safety of the fire and their friends.

The Frenchman set a horrific pace to the south wanting to distance himself from the Abenaki's hunting grounds before the morning sun shows itself. He knows if Tenkiller wants the girl he will follow but at least the French will be clear of their territory. If trouble erupts, no one can blame the French for defending themselves.

The wind finally subsides and the snow stops falling on the forest during the night and their flight south. The girl is completely exhausted and now needs help to walk. Taking turns, the French support her between them, allowing the tired Tracy to stagger slowly onward.

St Georges knows he blundered by first running into the Abenaki then by trying to use them to capture the white hunter but he had no choice. He had to come up with some excuse after blundering into their hunting party. Now not only is the young, white hunter following but possibly the Abenaki are too. He knows there are no broken promises between the French and Tenkiller, the deal was for the Abenaki to deliver the white to him for the girl. They failed to do this but Tenkiller is arrogant and proud, he would consider St Georges actions as a failure to keep his promises.

At first, the Frenchman leads the small party to the south for several miles then he turns east towards the safety of the Shawnee Villages. He knows even the great Tenkiller will not dare follow them into Shawnee Lands. With so few, safety remains many miles away, as they still must travel through a wild rough forest that holds many dangers.

The sun is up bright as Tenkiller finally got his emotions and fears of the unknown in grasp and stops his warriors in their headlong flight towards their villages. In the eerie darkness with the snow and wind moaning through the trees, the mighty Chief of the Abenaki shows fear and follows his warriors running from what they believe is the Spirit Walkers of the night.

How they offended the Evil Ones, he does not know but now with the storm subsiding and the sun shining brightly, he is now in control of his fears. There is no shame for his actions; the Abenaki teach them from childhood to dread the unknown and the unseen ones.

The warriors stand about their Chief studying their back trail with a queer quietness. No longer are they the subdued and scared warriors that fled from the fire, they too regain their courage. With the daylight, the Evil Ones will go back to their world, at least long enough for the Abenaki to escape from these lands.

Tenkiller looks about at his warriors then over at Sastook. "We must go back for our dead ones and our weapons."

"To do this will bring the Evil Ones against us again," Sastook protests.

"You will do as I say, Sastook." The tall Chief looks around the circle of glum faces. "The sun is high, go quickly and bring them to the village before the Spirits again walk the land."

"What of Tenkiller, what will he do?" Sastook looks over at the Chief.

"I will take five warriors and go for the woman."

"You have many women, my chief." Sastook argues. "This one is trouble for our people, she is the reason the Evil Ones come against the people. She is why Black Panther no longer walks the land."

"The French gave her to me if we capture the white long hunter."

"My Chief, we didn't capture the white hunter."

"He is not a man, the French lie; they didn't tell us he is a spirit."

"The French are our allies." Sastook looks across at the other warriors. "You will have to kill them to take the woman."

Tenkiller glares at the shorter man. "The woman is mine; I will kill whoever gets in my way. We go."

Lance and Blue Elk slog their way through the heavier drifts then brake into a trot where the trail is clean by the heavy winds. The valley they cross is huge. The French can take many paths to escape to the Shawnee lands that lay to the east. Blue Elk knows the Frenchman is smart; he will change directions many times trying to lose any pursuers. First, they must find their trail and then they can race ahead and overtake the French.

Blue Elk tries everything he knows to find the French party, now he looks around in exasperation at the far-reaching forest. He followed St Georges in war so he knows how shrewd and capable of a leader the Frenchman is. However, as smart as the man is, how can he hide a trail of at least four men and a woman in the fresh snow?

"We missed the trail, it is behind us somewhere."

Lance studies the snow-covered trail they are on now. Nothing passed this way, not even the track of a snowshoe rabbit, nothing. It is almost as if the heavy winds blew all the forest animals away before it.

"The French didn't come east to the Shawnee lands; they outsmarted us and the Abenaki."

Blue Elk looks stunned for only a second. "We come east, you are right, the Frenchman heads due south, then he will turn east when he thinks he has lost whoever follows him."

"He now has a bigger lead on us." Lance cusses under his breath. "We must hurry but which way?"

"We go there." Blue Elk points south. "If he does as we think, he will leave a trail that we will cross soon."

"Then you believe if we head south we will cut across his trail going east." Lance understands what the Mohawk is saying.

"Come, we go." Blue Elk turns south away from the eastern sun and hits a faster trot. "We will find his trail."

Blue Elk guessed right. St Georges first led his men south and now he turns due east. He fooled his pursuers but now he has more trouble. He knows whoever follows will figure out what he did. He must hurry, he has to stay ahead of any who follow and the tired woman hampers him. The Frenchman has traveled with raiding warriors from all tribes before they were great runners on the trail and he knows the white, long hunters are great runners. He knows it will take all his wiles and thinking to keep ahead of the pursuit.

Tenkiller leads his men south, when one day later he luckily intersects the trail of the French as they travel to the east. Swinging onto the track, the Abenaki pick up their pace as they follow hard on St Georges trail. The snow diminishes, leaving the French trail plainly visible as it leads south. Suddenly at the fork of a small river, the tracks turn due east back towards the Shawnee Hunting Grounds. Tenkiller knows he needs to overtake the French quick before they meet up with any Shawnee hunting party that happens to be this far afield.

Blue Elk is several paces in front of Lance when he stops dead in his tracks and surveys the small game trail. Kneeling he traces the moccasin tracks with his finger then looks at Lance.

"The trail is plain, the French head east towards Shawnee Lands."

Lance studies the trail. "There are many tracks through here, Blue Elk."

The Mohawk agrees, "The Abenaki follow the French, they are between us and St Georges."

"Abenaki!" Lance stares hard at the trail, "I thought they went back to their villages!"

"Perhaps they killed the evil one." Blue Elk jokes. "It is the Abenaki who follow St Georges."

"Great, now what do we do?"

"The tracks are mixed up; I cannot tell how many warriors follow the French." Blue Elk explains.

Lance switches his rifle to his other hand. "It doesn't matter how many there are, I'm going after the girl."

"The trick you played on the Abenaki will not work again."

"I hope not, come we must catch up before the Abenaki do." Lance motions Blue Elk forward.

Two days and many miles from the abandoned Abenaki camp, the sun breaks through the snow clouds, bright and warm. St Georges is nervous. He studies their back trail for several minutes before ordering Trail Runner to retrace their route to see if they are being followed. The pace the Frenchman set completely exhausts Tracy who is now unable to walk on her own. Now one of the French must carry her on their back.

Trail Runner crosses only one small valley and is standing atop the next hill surveying the massive forest below him when he spots the warriors. There is no doubt; the tall warrior in the lead is Tenkiller. The Abenaki are coming fast; Trail Runner quickly retreats bounding in long leaps across the flat valley back to where he last saw St Georges.

The French let the girl rest but come to their feet quickly as the Shawnee Tracker races back towards them. St Georges knows that by the way the warrior is running trouble is not far behind him.

"Tenkiller follows me." The Shawnee points his bow back to the north. "He is there, not far."

The Frenchman swears, as he must either abandon the girl or fight. His men have long rifles and are excellent shots but if he fires on the Abenaki, he will no longer have them for an ally.

"How many come this way?"

"Maybe this many," Trail Runner holds up his fingers.

"Six." St Georges rubs his chin and looks down where the girl lay. "We can kill them easily."

"If you kill one such as Tenkiller, the Abenaki will make war on the French."

"Well, we sure can't outrun them."

Chapter 20

St Georges stands indecisive looking out across the valley, when suddenly a shot rings out and then another. The Frenchman knows the Abenaki have no rifles so it must be either a lone hunter after game or the white, long hunter attacking Tenkiller and his men. Quickly he and his men get the girl and they push on to the south, eager to get away from the mountains. St Georges knows if it is indeed a fight going on across the valley, whoever survives will be on his trail when it is over.

Blue Elk leads Lance on a fierce chase, racing across the forest floor following the Abenaki and French trail to the east. The Mohawk knows this small valley, coming to a deep gorge, he turns off to the right. The rough terrain necessitates his slowing their pace as he climbs over rock formations and crosses deep sloughs. This shortcut, if he guesses right, will intersect the trail less than a mile ahead and bring them in close behind the Abenaki.

As Blue Elk tops the last small knoll, he ducks back down motioning Lance to do the same. He guessed right, their trail is straight ahead. He can see the Abenaki advancing through the heavy timber less than a quarter mile from where the two lay hiding. Lance sights across a protruding slab of rock, pointing the weapon at a spot less than thirty yards from where the trail angled past their position. At this range he cannot miss but it will be a long shot for the Mohawk with the bow.

"There are six of the varmints, Blue Elk." Lance checks his priming pan. "I can get one, maybe two before they can reach us. Can you hit one through this maze of timber?"

"If you kill Tenkiller, the rest of the Abenaki will run away."

"I do not want them to run away." Lance grips the rifle until his hands turned white. "I want them dead, that way we won't have to fight them again."

Blue Elk agrees. "Tell me, Lance Hawkins, do you enjoy tasting the blood of the Indian, do you enjoy killing?"

"They enjoyed killing my folks." Lance answers the Mohawk, watching as the Abenaki trots along the trail, coming nearer and nearer. "You dang right I enjoy killing them."

"Would you enjoy killing me?"

Lance looks over at the Mohawk aghast at the question. "You are my friend, I would not kill you."

Blue Elk nods. "Sometimes I wonder."

Tenkiller and his warriors trot soundlessly along the sodden, leaf-covered trail that runs right below where the two men wait. They are intent on catching up to the French and getting the girl back, Tenkiller never suspects that death is looking down its barrel at him.

Lance holds the rifle sights right on the big warrior's chest as he pulls the trigger. Only yards from the trail, he quickly reloads and looks for another warrior. Sighting in on the Abenaki again, he is in shock to see Tenkiller with three of his warriors charging towards them up the knoll. Blue Elk is able to kill one.

"How did I miss him?" Lance growls over at Blue Elk.

"Another warrior stepped in front of him as your rifle spoke."

The rifle belches smoke and hot lead again taking out another of Tenkiller's warriors. "There's one I didn't miss." Lance has no time to reload so he lays the rifle aside and draws his knife and war axe as the remaining Abenaki charge through the foliage and throw themselves at them. Two warriors come at Lance as Tenkiller squares off in front of Blue Elk. There is no playacting for Lance this time; he will kill the warriors before him as quickly as possible. His longer arms allow him the advantage to reach out and strike at the Abenaki without coming into range of their weapons. Slipping outside, the first warrior thrusts, he trips the man then splits the shaved skull of the man as he tries to rise.

The second warrior slashes madly as he retreats, trying to avoid the thrusts of the white. Glancing quickly over to where Blue Elk and Tenkiller are rolling around on the ground, Lance steps sideways again and sinks his knife deep into the warrior's vitals.

Looking quickly to where Blue Elk and Tenkiller fight, Lance rushes forward pulling the Abenaki off Blue Elk. The war axe rings out with a sickening thud as it splits the Chief's head, reminding Lance of a melon being split open.

"Thank you, Lance Hawkins." Blue Elk regains his feet looking down at the Abenaki. "He was a mighty warrior, very strong."

"Are you hurt?"

Blue Elk shrugs. "No, thanks to you, my friend, just a few small cuts."

"The French are ahead, let's get on their trail."

"This day you have saved my life, for this I will follow the Frenchman wherever he takes the girl, however long it takes." Blue Elk touches his chest. "I will bring you to the girl."

Lance nods as he looks at the Mohawk almost as if he never saw him before. "Thank you, Blue Elk."

St Georges knows somewhere behind him a fight breaks out or a lone hunter fired twice at a target. Quickly getting his men and the girl to their feet, he starts them off to the east again. There is little time to lose so they cannot wait on the girl to rest now. The lives of his men depend on him throwing his pursuers, whoever they are, from his trail.

With the forest trails wet and soggy, there is no way he can hide their tracks. St Georges studies his men as he follows them to the east. He cannot understand why he fears this young white as he does. He is with three men that are older, well-experienced, armed and excellent shots, while the young white only has one rifle, which means one shot. If the Abenaki win the fight, he and his men still have the advantage. The warriors only have bows, arrows, and primitive weapons. He cusses himself for doubting his abilities, something he never did before. He never had a hunter on his back trail that was unshakable as this white is. St Georges knows the man's tenacity causes him to lose his usual unfailing nerve. Still, the odds are in his favor. How can he lose?

Stopping their headlong flight, St Georges retreats down the trail to try to hear anything from the battle. Nothing, no further gunshots, yells, screams, nothing. Complete silence reigns over the forest giving the

Frenchman a cold shiver as he searches the valley floor for some sign.

Cussing himself for a coward, St Georges knows he has all the advantages on his side. Finding nothing on the trail, he trots back to where his men rest.

"Did you see anything, Sir?"

"There is nothing, no sounds from the forest, no one following our trail."

"What will we do now? The girl is finished." The Sergeant looks uneasily to where Tracy sat slumping against a tree. "She can go no further without rest."

"We will find a good place to ambush anyone following us; there the rest of us will wait for our pursuers while you, Sergeant, will lead the girl to the east."

"She cannot travel fast."

"I know that, which is why we must kill the ones following." St Georges looks over at the girl. "We will catch up once we kill whoever is following us."

Sergeant Boyer looks at the girl. "You are willing to risk your life to keep her?"

St Georges frowns, "I don't care about her; I want the long hunter if he still lives."

Tracy raises her head tiredly and shakes it with contempt. "You Frenchman are not man enough to kill Lance Hawkins. Ever."

"So that is his name." St Georges smiles, "Perhaps my dear, you are right. First we must see if he follows us or the Abenaki."

"He will kill you." Tracy smiles, knowing Lance could be close behind and the thought puts a new shot of energy into her tired body.

Looking down at the Abenaki Chief, Lance rips the polished medallion from his neck and hands it to the Mohawk. "I cannot take this." Blue Elk holds the leather thong that holds the medallion. "You killed Tenkiller."

"You would have, given time, but I wanted to hurry on." Lance looks at the medal. "You were the brave one this day, my friend."

Nodding, Blue Elk places the amulet around his neck. "Thank you, my friend, now let's catch the Frenchman. He can't be far, then we can both go home."

"He's mine my friend, all mine. No matter how it ends, he's mine."

Blue Elk nods. "Agreed, he is yours."

Each man takes different sides of the trail as they trot south. Blue Elk follows the trail, his eyes scouring the ground, while Lance lags behind watching the forest for any sign of an ambush. They both know the French are hampered with the tired girl. They cannot stay ahead of the fast traveling trackers for long.

"Watch closely, the tracks grow fresher." Blue Elk halts momentarily to warn Lance. "They are near, their tracks still seep water."

Blue Elk finds the place where the French let the girl rest while St Georges retraced their trail. "The squaw sat here, they let her rest for she is very tired."

Lance looks at the flat rock and in his mind he can imagine Tracy sitting there. "The Frenchman went back down the trail to see if he could see us."

"If that is so, he fears he is being followed and somewhere ahead he is waiting."

Lance agrees, "Good."

St Georges picks a perfect ambush site to lie in wait for whoever is following whether it is Abenaki or the white, long hunter. A maze of down timber scattered by huge winds lay strung across the valley with few trails leading through it. The French position themselves along a carefully laid trail hiding behind large uprooted trees within easy rifle range.

Sergeant Boyer leads Tracy by the hand, pulling her as fast as she can walk along a small game trail. Ahead, he finds a flat rock ledge that will hide their tracks for a while. Boyer is a big man and monstrous strong. He slings his long rifle across his back as he picks the girl up in his arms as if she is a rag doll and carries her bodily across the rocky ground.

St Georges ordered him to lead the girl east and that is what he is doing. Maybe not on the east trail the Frenchman pointed out to him. No, they now are following the high ridge to the south. Sitting the girl on the ground, Boyer looks down the rough slope that they just traversed.

"Why have you brought me here?" Tracy looks at the Sergeant nervously. "This ridge trails off to the southwest."

Boyer looks down at the girl and smiles. "I'm taking you home, my lady, you've been through enough."

"If you do this St Georges will kill you someday."

"He will try." Boyer looks further up the mountain. "First he has to catch me."

"Do you think Lance Hawkins follows us?"

"First, he probably had to fight the Abenaki." Boyer looks at the girl, "Now he has St Georges waiting to kill him."

"I know, I heard the gunshots."

Boyer looks at the girl curiously, "You care for this man very much, I think."

"We have been friends a long time." Tracy shrugs. "He is the only one trying to rescue me."

"As I am doing now, mon amie."

Tracy nods. "Hopefully, as you are doing now. How can I trust you?"

"I promise I will bring you back to an English settlement, to your home. To get there we must travel silently and undetected through this dangerous ground."

"Are you familiar with these lands, Sergeant?" Tracy asks.

"My name is Pierre Boyette but here in this land the English pronounce it Boyer."

Tracy nods. "Okay, Mister Boyer, are you familiar with these lands?"

"I would prefer Pierre and no, I have only traveled the forest we are now passing through one time. It was after we captured you."

"Great, can you find your way out of here?"

"The forest is forest, it is all alike. We just have to follow the sun." Boyer smiles lightly. "If we head south and west, somewhere ahead, we're bound to hit the road that leads to Frasier."

Blue Elk holds his hand up and motions Lance forward. "The tracks are too easy to follow, even with the wet ground."

"Is Blue Elk afraid of a trap?"

"We will see. You stay far behind and watch for a hiding enemy."

The Mohawk eases stealthily forward, keeping to the side of the trail close to the heavy underbrush. The dark eyes miss nothing as he surveys the heavy timber and dense brush as he passes. Nothing moves, no squirrels barking, nor a bird of any kind makes noise or flies about the forest. Only the dripping of melting snow makes noise along the trail.

The dark eyes of Blue Elk narrow as he spots the fallen jumble of timber less than a half mile. The short hairs on his neck stand on end as he recognizes the same thing St Georges did, a perfect place to hide and ambush anyone following. The trail switches back to the east again after following a southerly direction for several miles. Blue Elk doubts they were sighted as he ducks out of sight as soon as he notices the swath of fallen trees.

Motioning Lance forward, he silences him with a wave of his hand as he crouches beside the trail and then nods towards the down trees.

"Looks like a big blow made it; maybe a cyclone went through here." Lance whispers as he kneels beside Blue Elk. "Really tore the timber up."

"Big winds come here," Blue Elk agrees. "Good place for Frenchman and his men to wait somewhere ahead."

"Blue Elk is right; it would be a dandy of a spot to wait on us."

"What is this dandy?"

Lance smiles remembering he is not with Lucas today. "It means good."

"Why you no say good?" The Mohawk shakes his head. "You confuse this warrior."

"Okay, it's a good place to attack us."

"They are French, they have good rifles." Blue Elk studies the fallen timber. "We must be very careful."

"We have good weapons too." Lance holds up his rifle.

Blue Elk looks closely at Lance. He can read the hunter's mind like a deer's trail. There is no fear in the young, long hunter's eyes, only the desire to close with the ones ahead and kill. Perhaps the deep hate in this one makes him so terrible in battle. The Mohawk saw this in warriors of the Mohawk people after the soldiers of the whites raid a village and kill their families. He knows some of the warriors never recovered, their hate for the whites is just too strong. The Mohawk said they were touched in their mind.

Blue Elk saw many warriors that carry the hate but none hate as this young white does. He watched the long hunter kill without compulsion or regret on several occasions. The dark stains that cover his deerskin shirt are not from animals.

"We will separate and make our way slowly through this place."

"Then what?" Lance studies the fallen timber. "I say we go straight in."

"No, if the French are waiting ahead, we must be silent and creep forward like the cat."

"Then our hunt for the Frenchman is over?" Lance stares at the down jumble of twisted timber. "I know he is there, it is a perfect trap to catch us in."

"Not if they kill us with their long rifles before we see them." Blue Elk shakes his head. "If this happens their hunt for you will be over."

"They will not kill us."

"If they do the girl is lost forever."

Lance nods, "Alright, what is Blue Elk's plan?"

"You will listen now, white man, do not let your hate for the French get us killed before we rescue the girl."

"Her name's Tracy Trent."

"Tracy Trent, it is a good name." Blue Elk studies the trail. "You will go to that side and I will take this side."

"That's your plan?" Lance shakes his head. "That's all?"

"It is enough." Blue Elk nods. "Go slow, be quiet and listen for the call of the dove."

St Georges has his two remaining men lined up along the trail spaced yards apart, well hidden in the dense fallen logs that blew down in great mass. Earlier, after ordering Sergeant Boyer east with the girl, he sits waiting beside the fallen timbers wondering how far the Sergeant could travel with Tracy Trent, exhausted as she was. He should have left the girl behind with Tenkiller; at least he would have some revenge on this Lance Hawkins, now she is just a weight around his neck.

Looking to where his two men wait concealed under the heavy brush, he slaps at a buzzing fly then repositions himself. St Georges tires of waiting and it starts to bore him. He wants to leave this place but he is not so sure someone is following. He questions his own plan, by now he could be a long way towards the Shawnee Villages. He wonders how long he should wait before giving up and moving on.

The day drags on slowly as the cold and damp ground they rest on begins to creep into their bodies. Both of St Georges remaining men look over to where he is hiding and they are hoping he will give up on the nonsense and call them in. Both men fidget as they are hungry, cold, and disgusted. They are ready to quit this silliness and move on.

St Georges is finally ready to give up, it is apparent he was wrong. The shots were probably a lone hunter like he first thought. Turning abruptly, he starts to call in his men just as the turkey-fledged arrow strikes the dead log he is leaning on.

Whirling with the rifle, St Georges fires quickly from his hip as a body lunges towards him. Unable to move out of the way the Frenchman finds himself pinned beneath the deadweight of a body. Kicking and pushing at the body, he stands clear and looks down at the dead Mohawk warrior.

Brush crackles across the trail where his men are waiting. Trying to see through the heavy foliage, St Georges reloads his rifle. He moves sideways trying to get a better view as two bodies stand up clasped in deadly combat. As suddenly as they appear, the two men fall back into the underbrush, out of his sight, then comes the low moan of the death rattle.

The Frenchman gets a quick glance of a man clad in a bloody leather hunting shirt as he tosses one of his men over his head. Then a scream comes from another man as he launches himself forward. He gets enough of a glance to see the ghastly look of death on the tall man's face and it makes him shudder. St Georges has no doubt, he knows right before him locked in mortal combat is the one the girl calls Lance Hawkins. The man he wants dead but the face, a face of pure hate, twisted so badly with hate it sends shivers of uncontrollable fear through his frozen heart. His body will not move forward as the crashing brush and the noise of struggle suddenly ends.

St Georges cannot help himself; the face of this crazy hunter is too evil. Bolting away from the face, he runs terrified pushing and shoving his way through the heavy brush, barely feeling the thorns that tear at his skin and leather clothing. Uncontrollable fear seizes his heart. His legs race as he runs blindly away from the terror behind him that is screaming and slashing at his two men.

Sometimes fear and adrenalin running through a man's body can make him do incredible things. For miles St Georges runs to the east unmindful of anything but escaping the monster he saw behind him. Finally, collapsing along the banks of a small stream, he looks down into a clear pool of water and shudders at the face looking back at him.

He shakes his head then looks back over his shoulder in fear. How can this happen? How can one lone man turn him into such a despicable human being, a coward? Never did he think of himself as a coward but now, he knows the truth. He runs for miles fleeing from another man, not a spirit, not an evil spirit but a living, breathing man. His fright is such that he cannot even control his own legs, letting them run unconstrained, seemingly with a mind of their own.

Blue Elk guessed right, the French are ahead waiting to ambush them as they come down the trail. Sending Lance to the right side, he takes the left and slips silently behind St Georges. Only the last minute movement of the Frenchman causes Blue Elk to miss such a close target. With no time to nock another arrow, the Mohawk launches himself over the fallen logs right at St Georges. Only the height of the fallen trees makes the distance to the Frenchman further, allowing St Georges time to whirl and fire at the warrior.

Lance hears the shot and then Blue Elk's scream but he is too busy, fighting with the other two Frenchmen to come to the Mohawks aide. His knife finds the center of the first man's back and quietly sinks in, down to the hilt. Then he closes in on the other unsuspecting Frenchman.

Hate and revenge race through Lance's veins, he finally can come to grips with the men responsible for the death of his beloved mother. The look on the young, long hunter's face is what St Georges sees as Lance attacks the second Frenchman. The savage curl of the lips drawing back over the teeth is what provokes St Georges fear and causes him to flee in terror away from the crazy fighter.

His war axe dripping with blood, Lance wipes it clean on the dead Frenchman then retrieves his knife and rifle before turning to where he last saw Blue Elk. Fear for his friend grips his stomach as he watches St Georges run blindly away crashing through and over the down timber. Pushing aside the broken and torn up branches, he finds Blue Elk lying against a down tree. Kneeling, he looks into the dark eyes then down at the red stain that covers the warrior's chest.

"You are hurt, my friend."

Blue Elk nods painfully. "Did you kill St Georges?"

"No." Lance shakes his head. "He ran to the east."

"He ran away?"

"As fast as his legs would carry him, I reckon."

"My father told me once a long time ago, this one was a coward against real warriors." Blue Elk smiles weakly. "He makes war only on the weaker ones, not real men."

Lance removes his shirt and places it under Blue Elk's head making him as comfortable as possible.

"I am dead, my friend; soon I will join my ancestors." The warrior speaks weakly. "Go, catch the Frenchman and kill him for me and the girl."

"There is time; first I will heal your wounds." Lance looks at the nasty chest wound knowing he is lying.

Blue Elk smiles and tries to speak as bubbles form on his lips. "Tell my father Ravenhair, I died a warrior's death. Do this for me, Lance Hawkins. Kill the Frenchman then give up the war trail, my friend, and return to your home and people."

Lance starts to reply as the dark face relaxes and turns sideways from him. "I will tell him, my friend, and I will kill the Frenchman for you."

Lance stares off in the direction St Georges took in his headlong flight. He wants to go after the Frenchman but his respect for the dead warrior holds him back, first he has to bury Blue Elk. Finding a heavy, sharp ended limb, he digs into the soft earth near where the young warrior died. Later he will bring Ravenhair back to this place to pay his respects and to bring his son's body back to the Mohawk Village if he wants to.

Two hours later after wrapping the warrior in the elk hide, he finishes covering the grave and then slips his leather hunting shirt back over his head. Looking at the amulet in his hand, he lays it at the head of the mound of dirt along with Blue Elk's bow and quiver of arrows.

"I won't forget you, my true friend." Lance looks up at the tall trees and cloudy sky trying to gauge how long he has left until dark. Scouting around, he finally picks up the tracks of Tracy and another white man. He learns much in his short days with Blue Elk, his skills at reading and following a trail is honed in even more with the young Mohawk's teachings.

The tracks lead off at first to the east then turn south, he knows the small track is Tracy's, the other belongs to a large heavy built white man. The tracks show the toes turn out, not as an Indian walks and they push deep in the soft soil indicating the weight of a heavy man. Studying the tracks, he is curious; St Georges races off to the southeast, while the other tracks head due south.

He watches St Georges flee the valley in an uncontrolled flight in an attempt to escape the one behind him. Looking off to where he last saw the Frenchman, Lance is tempted to go after the man but first he must find Tracy and bring her back safely to the settlement. He can only shake his head in disgust; St Georges escapes him once more. Turning to the south, he shrugs, the Frenchman seems to have nine lives like a cat. Today the killer of his folks evades him again, it cannot be helped. He has to rescue Tracy, she is more important but there is always tomorrow.

The mountains and valleys as immense as they are will never be big enough to hide the cowardly Frenchman. Lance knows a brave man never seeks revenge to hide his cowardice but a coward is different, he will try again. They have to; cowards are weak men who cannot bear the thought of anyone finding out about them.

Chapter 21

Sergeant Boyer holds Tracy's hand gently as he leads her across one valley then up a mountain and across another large flatland covered in huge trees. Plunging through waist deep and ice-cold mountain streams is something he is accustomed to serving in the French Rangers. However, the girl is tiring and wearing out. She needs to dry out and put some warm food in her before she succumbs to the cold.

Any sickness could turn into pneumonia and could make the girl deathly ill. Looking at his back trail, he wonders who will come behind them, St Georges or Lance Hawkins.

Tracy follows his gaze, knowing what Boyer was wondering. "When he comes, I will speak for you and try to convince him to leave you in peace."

"Yes, mon amie but the Abenaki says this one is an evil spirit now, crazy in his mind."

"You don't believe that." Tracy shivers slightly then looks at the trail herself. "You're not a heathen."

Boyer nods. "He is but a lad but he kills so many experienced and older warriors and now maybe even St Georges."

"He killed only the ones responsible for killing our folks, Pierre."

"I was there too." He looks down at her. "I killed no one but I was there and the one that follows knows this. He will not let me live, even for you. I haven't seen this Lance Hawkins but Sastook says his eyes are blood red as the moon when he is mad. His face is hideous to behold and his teeth come to a point like a wolf's."

"Surely you don't believe this." Tracy looks into the man's eyes for answers, she already knows his answer. "He is just a boy."

"Yes mon amie, I believe this. He is like the ones of old, a demon that lives off the blood of his enemies. He will kill me, I am sure of it."

"We'll see." Tracy trembles even more, now he even has her thinking Lance is some kind of depraved monster on the loose in these mountains. "I will do my best for you, Pierre."

"You must have a fire before you catch your death." Boyer starts gathering wood.

"The smoke will bring whoever is out there straight here."

Pierre shrugs. "No matter, I feel I am a dead man now anyway and you cannot become sick so far from the settlement."

Tracy follows the big Frenchman as he leads her to an outcropping of rock and starts to kick together a fire. She shakes uncontrollably as the small blaze starts to gather strength in the twilight.

Removing his large hunting shirt, Boyer hands it across to her. "Remove your wet clothes and put this on while I try to find us something to eat."

Nodding, she looks at the huge chest covered in curly brown hair and the muscled up arms, wondering how such a huge man could be afraid of a youngster like Lance.

Almost as if he is reading her mind, Boyer looks deeply into her eyes. "No one can fight the devil himself."

"You lived with the Indians too long, Pierre." Tracy explains, "He is not a devil or a demon."

"Perhaps you are right. Dry your clothes, Tracy Trent, get warm while I try to find us something to eat before it gets dark."

"Thank you, Pierre Boyer."

"For what, mon amie?"

"For caring, for taking care of me." Tracy smiles. "For being so kind and gentle."

Night falls and the cold starts to seep into Lance's tired muscles forcing him to find shelter in a small cave so familiar to the mountains. Building a fire, he looks down at his ragged clothes. For over a month he has been on the trail, the new clothes McDowell gave him at Frasier are already filthy rags. The deer hide moccasins are wearing thin even though he tries to patch them. His homespun pants and leather hunting shirt are in tatters, he looks like one of the hermits that use to live near their old farm back in Virginia.

Returning to the warm fire after setting two rabbit snares, Lance reaches his hands out to the flames. His hollow eyes stare hauntingly into the fire thinking of all the fighting, trailing, and killing. What did he gain? The Frenchman, St Georges, is still alive. Tracy is still a captive somewhere ahead and Blue Elk his trusted friend lay dead in the cold ground.

Poking at the small sticks that burn and spit sparks as they glow, Lance can only shake his head tiredly. He knows that he gained nothing but he also knows given the opportunity to do it all over he would do the same. His mother's face wavers before him in the flames, smiling kindly the way she always did at him. With his resolve returning, the hate he now carries returns with a vengeance. Never will he rest until St Georges and all the Frenchmen responsible are dead. It can never bring his mother back but he will avenge her death if it is the last thing he ever does.

Waking with a start in the middle of the night, Lance feeds the small fire then slips from the cave to check his snares. One fat snowshoe rabbit dangles from the second snare. Quickly skinning the plump rabbit, Lance washes him in a cold brook then places him on a green limb to sizzle over the fire. His mouth waters eagerly as he watches the meat start to turn brown and drip grease into the flames. Sitting near the cave entrance eating, he studies the half-moon and tries to figure out how far ahead Tracy and the other Frenchmen are.

He remembers when he first entered this valley, there was a small knoll and now it lies before him once again. If he is right, Frasier's Settlement should be less than two days south of the cave he took refuge in the night before. He tracks Tracy and the Frenchman but he cannot understand why the man is heading straight for the English settlement at Frasier, unless the man is lost. Surely, he knows Frasier will be a hostile place for one such as he.

Lance doubts Tracy will know where she is, even he is not dead certain Frasier is as close as he thinks. He knows Tracy is close, tomorrow he will catch up with the Frenchman. Once Tracy is free, he will take her to Frasier and then get back on St Georges trail. He touches the hickory handle of his father's knife lightly. Tomorrow he will send another Frenchman into the next world, another payment for his mother.

Boyer nudges Tracy awake and hurries her into her dry clothing then places a huge oak leaf with two roasted brook trout in her hand. "I am sorry Tracy; I could only catch these small fish for you to eat."

"You are as hungry as I am." Tracy takes a fish and extends the other one to him. "Take one."

"I am a man." Boyer thumps his chest making the girl laugh lightly. "You eat them; I must take care of you."

Looking around at the tall trees and the hill that slopes off to the south, Tracy hands Boyer back his shirt. "Thank you Pierre, you are a gentleman."

Donning the leather shirt Boyer is embarrassed. "Come, we must go, it will be light soon."

"Do you think we're still being followed?"

Boyer shrugs. "I am a soldier, not a woodsman or a hunter. I was ordered to go with St Georges. I do not know the forest like the long hunters of the English or St Georges. I do believe the devil is out there waiting for daylight so he can track us."

"If he was truly the devil, he wouldn't have to wait until daylight." Suddenly it dawns on her making Tracy look fearfully out into the dark. "Maybe it is Tenkiller and his Abenaki warriors or even St Georges."

"We must hurry along Tracy and find the English Settlement before whoever it is catches us." Boyer follows her gaze. "To me, they are all devils as life means nothing to them."

"That is strange talk for a soldier, one who kills for a living." Tracy tosses down the oak leaf and starts to her feet. "But I am ready."

"Yes, I am a soldier and for you I would kill, mon amie." Placing his big hands on her arm, he helps her from the ground as he looks deeply into her eyes. "I could not bear for any of them to put their hands on you again."

Standing in front of the Frenchman, she touches his face lightly, studying it like she never saw him before. "Thank you Pierre, you have turned out to be a friend, maybe a very special friend."

Lance follows at a dog trot on the track that shows plainly, stamped into the wet ground. He pays little attention to the dense woods that he is passing through or the possibility of an ambush. Intent on catching the Frenchman ahead he hurries on knowing he is quickly closing the gap. This close to the settlements and with all of his enemies dead, he has little fear of running into any hostile warriors. He knows St Georges probably still flees towards the land of the Shawnee, leaving only the Frenchman and Tracy unaccounted.

Lance tracks them to a small cave, the place where she lain shows plainly and the deeper impression of the man is nearby. Lance's face went dark with jealousy and hatred as he studies the soft ground beside the burned out fire. Slipping quickly back outside he looks off to the south.

Frasier can only be a few miles distance, curiously the tracks still point due south straight towards the stockade. If the Frenchman continues on this path, he will cross the Wilderness Road that leads straight to the stockade.

Kneeling beside a narrow stream, Lance reaches down and cups his hands for a drink of the clear cold water. The small tracks that show plainly are where she crossed the stream. It is Tracy's tracks, the footprints he followed for so long. The trail still leads to the south, straight for the English Stockade. Lance does not know why but now there is no doubt, the Frenchman is heading for Frasier's Settlement with the girl.

Straightening, he turns slightly to the west. If the Frenchman is heading for the road, Lance plans to race ahead and intersect them when they turn towards the stockade. He still cannot figure out the Frenchman but there is no way he is going to let him reach Frasier and sanctuary if that indeed is what he is planning. This one was with St Georges ever since he started tracking them; he is one of the ones responsible for the death of his family.

Boyer looks around carefully as they step onto the rough and rutted Wilderness Road that leads to Frasier. "We're here Tracy, this is the road. The English stockade should be only a mile or so west of where we're standing, you're safe now."

Smiling with relief, she follows him eagerly as the big man turns west. The rough road was hacked and hewed out of the wilderness when the settlers first made their way to settle and it is now what they call Frasier's Settlement. The small stream that flows off towards the larger Delaware River is called Frasier's Creek. Big enough for a canoe to navigate but it is not deep enough to carry the larger boats that carry supplies to the settlements. Out of necessity when the settlers founded the settlement, the wilderness road was cleared. Rough as it is, with stumps and large rocks that the large wagons have to navigate around, it still permits the ox wagons to bring trade goods and whatever is needed down the wilderness trace and on to the settlements.

The trains were heavily armed to protect them from the possible hostile attack that might be lurking in the brush. The trains are few, which gives the rough road time to grow its short grass.

Boyer stops suddenly as the road turns back due south. Now the road narrows as the rough brush presses in tightly against it. Only yards ahead, standing straddle legged in the middle of the road, the roughest looking stature of a man they ever saw stands blocking their way. The Frenchman is in shock as he looks at the tall thin man or beast that stands across the road looking at them with the coldest, deep set eyes he ever saw.

Stepping around him, Tracy looks at the boy she knows. "Lance, is it really you?"

Not a word came from the scarecrow, only silence as it stands with the rifle across the crook of his arm and his feet spread wide. Tracy draws in her breath as she looks into the wild crazy eyes.

"Lance, it's me Tracy. Don't you recognize me?"

His red eyes are even larger and scarier by the haggard thinness of his face. He looks down at her feet then back up at her eyes. "I know you Tracy; now get away from the Frenchy."

Stepping in front of Boyer, she protects his body with hers. "He brought me safely here."

"Move out of the way, Tracy Trent." Grabbing Boyer's rifle Tracy cocks it and points the weapon at his middle. "I won't let you kill him, Lance. I'll shoot you if I have to. Ain't you killed enough?"

Laying the long rifle softly on the ground without taking his eyes from Boyer, he pulls the hickory handled skinning knife. "I ain't killed me nearly enough of these French."

"Please, don't make me, please Lance."

"He killed your folks, Tracy." Lance stares in disbelief at the muzzle. "Mutilated them, him and St Georges are all that's left of the murderers."

Shaking her head in denial, she points the rifle. The man thing before her is not her lifetime friend Lance Hawkins. She does not know what he has become. "No, not Pierre, he didn't kill anybody at our farms."

"I seen him at your Pa's farm with St Georges." Lance looks over at the big man. "No one could be mistaken about this bear."

"He's a French soldier, Lance. He was ordered to go with St Georges but I'm telling you, he didn't kill anyone."

Lance starts forward. "He was there, now he's gonna die, get out of the way and let him fight like a man, if he can face a man without his cutthroat heathens backing him."

The rifle rises. "No, Lance no, don't make me kill you."

"Move, mon amie, I have to fight him." Boyer takes the rifle and moves her aside. "A man has his pride, Tracy."

"No Pierre, neither of you has to die."

"Do you worry about him or me, Tracy?" Boyer steps forward pulling his own hunting knife as he faces Lance.

The Frenchman is not taller than Lance but he is heavier through the chest and arms. Lunging forward he feels the breath knocked out of him as he lands hard on his back. His dark brown eyes stare death in the face as the razor sharp blade rises for the final strike.

"No! The scream stops the death thrust of the blade then she throws her body between the knife and the stunned Pierre. "Please Lance, if you ever thought anything of me, let him live."

Grabbing her dark hair, Lance jerks her backwards trying to get a thrust at Boyer as she fights against his powerful grip. "Move Tracy!"

"No!" She hangs onto Boyer's shoulder as hard as she can. "No, I'll hate you forever for this." Relaxing Lance stares hard at the look she gives him then releases his grip and stands up. "It's that way with you, is it?"

"He saved me, Lance and I love him for it."

"Take him then." Lance shakes his head. "Look at this Frenchman over breakfast ever morning and think of your folks."

"I won't have to do that, Lance Hawkins." Tracy hovers between the two men as he retreats several steps in confusion and rejection. "He wasn't responsible for their deaths."

"Thank her Frenchman; every day of your life, you thank her."

Backing further away from the two people, Lance picks up his rifle and quickly disappears into the brush that lines the north side of the road.

Tracy helps Boyer to his feet then looks to where Lance disappeared before their eyes. "You were right, Pierre."

"What do you mean?"

"He's no longer the Lance Hawkins I knew." She shudders as she leans on his shoulder. "He's crazy or something."

"No mon amie, he let me live because you asked." Pierre smiles down at her. "If he was crazy, he wouldn't have let your friendship stop him. He's still your friend; do not think badly of him."

"But he's changed."

"Yes, he saw his folks killed and he has been through hell for one so young. Please, listen to me. Do not think too harshly of the lad." Boyer smiles down at her. "I am a strong man, Tracy. The strongest I've ever known but he threw me to the ground like I was a child."

"He's crazy, that's what makes him so strong."

Boyer nods as he tries to dust himself off. "I have never felt such power. I see now how he killed so many, so easily."

"All except St Georges." Tracy tries to find the figure of Lance in the timber. "He said all except you and St Georges."

"One day it will happen." Boyer nods. "This one will never give up and quit."

Tracy agrees as she looks once more at the forest. She wonders would he ever come back for revenge on Pierre Boyer. "Let's go home, Pierre."

Chapter 22

Disappearing inside the cover of the dense brush, Lance turns and looks back at the man and woman knowing they can no longer see him from where they are in the road. He studies her face looking at her beautiful features for the last time. Since they were young, he always thought of her as his. He followed her through the mountains for months, suffering cold and hunger to rescue her. Now he knows Tracy is lost forever to him.

He almost killed the Frenchman in his rage and now he is glad she was able to prevent the knife from falling. Yes, he lost her but if he killed the Frenchman, she would hate him forever. With her safe and well cared for he can now turn his complete attention on St Georges.

First, he will go to Bacons for new clothes, powder, ball, and a few supplies. He does not know where St Georges trail will lead him. Maybe he will not return from this journey and he wants to see Lucas one more time.

The gates of Bacons stand wide open as Lance stands in front of the stockade. They post no guard making him shake his head in disgust; the settlement never learns anything. It is unlikely but the Shawnee could be hiding in the near forest waiting to attack. Several minutes pass as he stands in plain sight and watches but still no one discovers him.

Finally giving up, he strolls proudly through the stockade gates where a woman throwing dishwater from her porch yells out in fright when she discovers the tall, dirty figure staring at her.

"It's me Mrs. Ferguson, Lance Hawkins."

The heavyset woman almost faints from shock but recovers quickly when the scarecrow of a man speaks. "Lance, is it really you? Land sakes lad, you look a sight."

"I'm sorry to have frightened you." Lance looks around at the sleepy settlement. "Where is everybody, why are there no guards posted?"

"The men are over at the big house having one of their meetings." The heavyset woman rolls her eyes. "You know how their meetings go."

"My brother, Lucas is he there too?"

She shakes her head. "No, you couldn't know, he returned to your Father's farm with your sisters."

Lance looks at her in shock thinking Iona and May Lynn were still safely at Frasier. "They're here, how?"

"You look terrible. Come in, have something to eat, and then I'll tell you all about what happened."

Lance sits at the table and downs biscuits and sorghum molasses with oatmeal mush. It was months since he ate anything without hair on it or anything he did not have to kill.

Mrs. Ferguson walks back in from outside and lays new buckskins on the table with moccasins and a heavy leather coat. "I took these from Mister Wilson's store but you can settle up with him later."

"But, I can't just take them without asking." Lance stammers as he fingers the soft deer hide clothes.

"Sssh, you saved this settlement and Frasier and rescued the girls. I will pay for them myself if Mister Wilson objects."

Nodding he looks over her and smiles. "Thank you, I guess I am a mite ripe."

"Tell me Lance, did you find Tracy Trent?"

"I found her, she's safe at Frasier, they'll be along soon I expect."

Mrs. Ferguson looks curiously over at the haggard face then smiles. "I've fixed you a bath in the kitchen. When you're finished eating, you get into that water young man and then into your new clothes. Don't expect your face will need scraping yet."

"No Ma'am, I reckon not but I'll take the bath and clothes and I'm a thanking you."

For the first time in months, Lance feels like a new man as he steps out onto the porch of Mrs. Ferguson's cabin with new clothes on and a full stomach. Startled when loud clapping and cheering breaks out around him, he steps back slightly towards the doorway.

The innkeeper and store owner, Samuel Wilson steps up in front of the tall youth, extending his hand.

"Mrs. Ferguson says you didn't want to accept the clothes Lance but they're yours and anything else we have here at Bacons that you might need."

"Thank you, Mister Wilson. I'll need powder, shot, and a few supplies." Lance looks past the store-man at the young woman at his side. "Hello Miss Piffle."

The broad smile of the young girl covers her entire face making it radiate. "Oh Lance, you're back."

"I'm back." He smiles.

Wilson smiles down at his beaming daughter. "You will be staying this time. Mrs. Ferguson says you rescued Tracy Trent and she's at Frasier."

"She is there."

"Will she be coming back here soon?"

"I don't know." Lance shrugs. "She'll probably get married soon. Perhaps her and her new husband will come back to her farm."

"Married, but I thought you and..." Piffle cut her words off then smiles coyly at him.

"I'll be seeing my brother then I'll be going out again." Lance looks over at the girl who freezes at the words.

"Why lad, why risk your life?" Wilson asks. "You've done enough."

"It isn't finished yet Mister Wilson. The Frenchman who led the raid, St Georges is still alive."

"Alright Lance, I won't try to persuade you to stay here as it wouldn't do any good but you know you're welcome." Wilson looks down at his beaming daughter. "I believe I can speak for all of us."

The crowd of well wishers disperses slowly as every man present shakes hands with Lance then ambles off to their work. Only Wilson and his daughter Piffle stand beside the hunter.

"You do what you must, Lance. I'll be here waiting when you return. That is if you want me?" Piffle touches his hand lightly. "No matter how long you need."

Lance looks into the big blue eyes and sadly replies. "Do not wait Piffle, I'm not fit for any decent woman."

Piffle frowns slightly. "You, Lance Hawkins are good enough for any woman, too good for some. You're the only man I've ever wanted, ever. I will be waiting right here for you. Don't you ever say that to me again."

Blushing dark red at her words, Lance turns towards the store man. "I will pay you for these supplies Mister Wilson, when I can."

"Alright son but you don't have to."

"Mister Wilson, when I came in this morning there were no guards posted." Lance looks over at the shorter man. "One day the Shawnee will be back so you need guards posted at all times."

"I'll see to it personally." Wilson sticks out his hand. "You hurry back to us; we need strong men like you here."

"Piffle." Lance looks down at the upturned face embarrassed.

"Yes, Lance."

Clearing his throat, Lance shuffles his feet. "Piffle, don't waste your life waiting on me. I don't know if I'll ever return."

"I've loved you since the first time we met so you let me make up my own mind about that Lance Hawkins." Piffle takes his hand. "Now, let's get your supplies. The sooner you get going, the sooner you'll return to me."

Lance stands in the shade of the forest looking out at the peaceful farm he knew and loved so well. Lucas must be stronger as he has been busy. The house and outbuildings are repaired and the fields are plowed and laid for the spring planting. Several times, he watches as Iona and May Lynn come outside to bring in firewood or kindling.

Lucas walks slowly from the small barn carrying an axe. The old familiar long rifle of Ham Hawkins rests easily in his right hand. Lance notices the slight limp that Lucas walks with. Lance smiles, as he knows Lucas is lucky to be alive.

His heart beats lighter as he looks at the small farm and his siblings. He wants to walk into the yard and embrace each of them but he knows the girls will become upset when they find out he is going out again.

He wants to stay but something drives him from inside, the Frenchman must die. Lance cannot rest until St Georges pays for the killings he did and the ones he will do in the future if left alive. He knows there will always be another Frenchman to replace him but before he finishes, at least St Georges will die.

Slipping closer as Lucas walks to the woodpile, Lance signals their childhood call of the angry blue jay, followed by the bark of a grey squirrel. Lucas busy at splitting wood never looks up as the call rings out. Again the call sounds over the barnyard, this time causing Lucas to drop the axe and pick up his rifle. Lance calls out one last time then watches as Lucas makes his way cautiously towards the near woods.

"You're looking well, brother." Lance steps from his hiding place and embraces the surprised Lucas as he enters the forest.

"Lance!" The older brother cannot believe his eyes. "It's you, little brother."

"It's me alright, how are you?"

"I'm well, a few aches and pains is all." Lucas embraces Lance a second time as tears well and start to roll down his face. "We've been worried sick."

"How are the girls?" Lance asks.

"They're well but they miss you," Lucas replies.

"I will see them when I return." Lance turns towards the cabin. "Tell them I am well and will return soon."

"What about the Frenchman?"

"I've got to see him dead Lucas, dead."

Shaking his head, Lucas follows Lance's gaze towards the cabin. "I wish it didn't have to be so but perhaps when he is dead you will find peace again."

Lance agrees and reaches out his hand. "I will never find peace again, brother."

"I feel responsible." Lucas shakes his head. "If only we came home that night."

"That's over with and forgotten." Lance looks about the farm. "The old place looks good."

Lucas thinks back. "I remember telling you to kill them all. I made you swear and I was wrong."

"No, you weren't Lucas." Lance replies. "They're all dead, except St Georges now."

"It was a hard and dangerous task I set you to." Lucas sobs quietly. "I had no right."

"It doesn't matter brother. I'm fine." Lance pulls him close and hugs Lucas. "I will return."

The forest is quiet and peaceful as Lance slips silently along the small trail that leads to the north and east towards Shawnee Lands. The weather is perfect for a forest runner, the sun returns temporarily, warming the valley floors with its brightness.

Lance saw many hunting parties of different tribes in the last few weeks, but he knows now he is in the hunting grounds of the fierce Shawnee. Now, he will have to be cautious. He misses Blue Elk; he grew to depend on the Mohawk Warrior who became his friend.

Years ago, he traveled this land when his father brought his family west into the land of the Allegheny. Those were happy days for him, traipsing with Lucas through the vast and mighty mountains but today Lance will not let his mind focus on them, as he needs to concentrate on everything around him. A lone warrior out hunting could spot him and send a death-seeking arrow without warning.

Lance is not sure where the villages of the Shawnee lie but somewhere ahead he will cross a larger trail that will tell of their location.

The sun is high overhead shining down brightly through the tall branches of the large oak and hickory trees that grow abundantly throughout the mountains and valleys. Lance stands silently watching the antics of two large grey squirrels as they scamper along tree limbs jumping from one tree to another. Three weeks pass since his departure from the log cabin he calls home. Now he finds himself in this remote wilderness looking for one lone white man, seemingly an almost impossible task. Finding the Frenchman will be difficult, only with a bit of luck or perhaps a touch of destiny will he find St Georges in this vast wilderness before someone discovers him. The squirrels bound after each other from tree to tree oblivious to anything around them at the moment.

Suddenly, both squirrels stop scampering along the limb they were on and lay flat trying to conceal their presence. Lance's eyes narrow as he instinctively crouches dead in his tracks, ready to run if necessary. Several times in the past weeks, warriors from different tribes chase him through the woods but each time he easily outdistances his pursuers.

He always enjoys the chase and on several occasions, he shouts out his cry of triumph as the warriors following him give up in exhaustion. Lance doubts there is a warrior of any nation that can match him in speed or stamina. Today if it becomes necessary to flee again, he is sure it will be no different.

The valley he is crossing is large, mostly flat but densely populated with immense trees and heavy underbrush. Lance studies his retreat route in case it becomes necessary to run and then he focuses his attention in the direction the squirrels are watching.

He knows someone is coming and getting closer as the squirrels flatten themselves even more. Within seconds, a column of warriors show themselves momentarily then disappear again behind the brush. Lance is well hidden as the warriors grow closer and the brush parts again.

The warrior in front with the Mohawk scalp lock looks familiar as Lance strains his eyes to see the warriors clearer. They are indeed from the Mohawk Nation, he saw the same type hairstyles and dress many times in the last months.

Suddenly the leading warrior comes into clear view causing recognition to flash across Lance's face as he studies the familiar warrior.

"Ravenhair!" Lance cannot believe his eyes, the father of his friend Blue Elk is less than fifty paces in front of him.

Declining to show himself for fear they would attack before Ravenhair has a chance to recognize him, Lance waits until the warriors disappear down the narrow trail then follows slowly behind them. He wants to talk with the Mohawk knowing they are an ally of the Shawnee and might know the whereabouts of St Georges. He will follow until they make camp and then he will try to contact Ravenhair, alone if possible. With the death of Blue Elk, he is not sure the Chief will still be on friendly terms with any white man.

The sun rests as dark comes once again on the land. Ravenhair and ten Mohawk Warriors sit talking in a circle about the fire and their voices carry across the small clearing to where Lance stands listening. Nothing of importance carried to him on the air, only the small talk of long ago hunts and the bravado of proud warriors talking of the war trails they followed.

The night is as dark as the bottom of a well, as the lone white steps forward into the light of the campfire. Seeing him, the warriors leap to their feet and crouch in fear. All heard the tales of a tall white man, maybe an evil spirit but a killer that roams the forest killing any warriors he encounters.

Ravenhair studies the tall figure's silhouette in the glare of the fire then stands slowly extending the sign of peace towards Lance.

"My friend, the young long hunter is welcome at my fire." Ravenhair steps forward and extends his hand. "Hawkins, my son's friend and my friend is welcome here."

Lance accepts the hand then steps closer to Ravenhair. "I am sorry Ravenhair, your son Blue Elk is dead."

"I know this, we followed your trail for many days." Ravenhair nods sadly. "We found where you fought the Abenaki and found the body of Tenkiller. We also found where you buried my son with his bow and the medallion of Tenkiller beside his place in the ground."

"I am sorry. He was a true friend to me." Lance replies slowly. "Blue Elk was a great and brave warrior."

"A good son to me, one to be proud of." Ravenhair inhales deeply. "The medicine woman Satia told Otter he would never return to us."

Lance looks over to where Otter waits for them to finish talking. "It is good to see the Otter again. How is your leg?"

"It is completely healed, thanks to you and the white girls."

Lance replies, "I will always be in your debt and you will always be welcome at my fire."

"My son, we found where you and Blue Elk fought with the Abenaki but the signs did not tell me all I need to know. Tell me, how did he die?"

Lance looks at the Mohawk Warriors. "He died in battle, a great and courageous warrior. The long rifle of St Georges killed him. It was Blue Elk who killed Tenkiller of the Abenaki as they attacked us. He fought the great Abenaki Chief with only his knife and defeated him. Only a coward with a rifle such as St Georges could have killed Blue Elk."

"St Georges, the Frenchman, is a coward," Ravenhair agrees.

Lance replies. "He would not face your son, the courageous Blue Elk hand to hand. As I said, the Frenchman killed him with the long rifle while Blue Elk was unarmed."

"I have long known the Frenchman for a coward." Ravenhair nods sadly.

"I have come for him. He is the last I will look for." Lance shrugs. "But he must die by my hand."

"Then my son, what will you do?"

"I do not know, now I have lost everything." Lance thinks of Tracy. "My own people fear me as if I am a devil of some kind."

"The tall, dark haired woman you came for, what happened to her?" Otter questions.

"She is to be the woman of another."

Surprise covers Otter's face. "After all you have sacrificed for her?"

"She thinks I am crazy, an evil one who only wants to kill."

Ravenhair studies the sadness in the voice. "Sometimes it is best to let go of one like this."

"What do the Mohawk do in Shawnee Lands?"

Ravenhair motions Lance to the fire where they all sit back down. The other warriors stare nervously at the white man before them. They heard so much of his exploits, of his being an evil one. The Shawnee warriors still speak of him looking over their shoulders fearing his name will make him appear.

"We came for a council with the Shawnee, a council of war to go against the white settlements."

"Led by St Georges."

"No more, the Shawnee lost many warriors, now they think the Frenchman brings the evil spirits down on their tribe."

"And St Georges?"

"He is dead!"

"By whose hand?"

"By mine!" Ravenhair throws the dark hair of the white man onto the ground at Lance's feet. "For the death of my son, Blue Elk."

"How did you know?"

"We track where you fought, we found Blue Elk's body and he was killed with a long rifle." Ravenhair nods sadly. "We see where you follow girl and another white man and then we come to this place and find St Georges alone with no other Frenchmen."

"You could read all of this on the ground?" Lance is curious.

Otter laughs lightly. "The Frenchman is all alone, his men all dead, and the Shawnee no longer trusting him."

"And?"

"Our Chief Ravenhair challenged St Georges to fight." Otter looks over at the Mohawk Chief. "He even offered to take him to fight you."

"Enough, the Frenchman is no longer." Ravenhair stops Otter from saying more. "St Georges is dead."

"Then it is finished." Lance stares into the flames, he felt empty. "Over."

Ravenhair agrees. "It is finished except for the healing, my son. I Ravenhair, Chief of the Mohawk, wish that you come with us and live with the Mohawk and myself as my son until you have forgotten your sadness. Then perhaps you will wish to return to your own people and the light haired one."

Lance looks up in surprise. "How did you know of a light haired girl?"

"Satia, she sees her in the smoke." Ravenhair smiles, "Our Medicine Woman is never wrong."

"I wish this too, Lonamourchee." Otter smiles across the fire.

"I could never replace your son, Blue Elk." Lance looks at Ravenhair.

"Blue Elk died a great warrior's death with honor and I, Ravenhair am proud." The big warrior nods sadly. "We will speak no more of this."

"He was a good son." Lance agrees.

"You will be my new son. We will hunt the deer together and live happily, Lonamourchee." Ravenhair smiles at Lance.

"What is that name?" Lance does not understand the word.

"It is what the people of the north woods call you now, Lance Hawkins." Ravenhair smiles, "Lonamourchee, Long Hunter and protector of the whites, and the adopted son of Ravenhair."

"What does it mean?"

"Lonamourchee, it means Killer of Enemies and the Avenger." Otter smiles broadly. "A name I wish I carried."

Lance looks into the bright blaze where the face of his mother smiles back at him. Lance smiles as he looks around at the gathered warriors. Perhaps he finally found peace with himself. Suddenly, the face of Piffle Wilson appears beside his mother; yes, he knows he finally found his peace.

The End